VEGA JANE

AND THE

REBELS' REVOLT

DAVID BALDACCI

Illustrated by Tomislav Tomić

MACMILLAN CHILDREN'S BOOKS

First published as *The Width of the World* in the US 2017 by Scholastic Press
First published as *The Width of the World* in the UK 2017 by Macmillan Children's Books

This revised edition published as *Vega Jane and the Rebels' Revolt*
by Macmillan Children's Books 2021
an imprint of Pan Macmillan
The Smithson, 6 Briset Street, London EC1M 5NR
EU representative: Macmillan Publishers Ireland Ltd, 1st Floor,
The Liffey Trust Centre, 117–126 Sheriff Street Upper
Dublin 1, D01 YC43
Associated companies throughout the world
www.panmacmillan.com

ISBN 978-1-5290-3796-8

1 3 5 7 9 8 6 4 2

A CIP catalogue record for this book is available from the British Library.

Printed and bound by CPI Group (UK) Ltd, Croydon CR0 4YY

To Sandy Violette and Caspian Dennis,
for being so awesome from day one

A PLACE CALLED TRUE

We landed invisible, on the cobbles, and were nearly killed.

Petra Sonnet cried out, Delph Delphia grunted in surprise, my canine, Harry Two, yipped and I, Vega Jane, jerked back on the magical tether holding us all together, as a deafening contraption charged past us.

It was boxy and made of metal and had doors with windows on either side. It also had what looked like four wagon wheels, but the infernal thing was moving of its own accord with no sleps pulling it.

It was puffing and wheezing, with what sounded like metal clanking on metal, and in a few moments, it turned the corner and vanished from our view.

Delph looked at me, his face pale. 'What was that?'

I shook my head because I had no idea what it was. Rattled, I scratched Harry Two's remaining ear.

We all had scars from our journey across the Quag.

Delph's arm had been burned and blackened.

Harry Two had lost an ear.

Petra had injured her hand.

And I had the mark of the three hooks on the back of my hand. It had magically burned on my skin by some unknown means.

I was about to return us to visibility by spinning my ring round when a pair of males appeared, both of them cloaked.

We froze, each holding our breath.

'You sure it was from here?' the taller of them asked the other.

The male nodded.

My mind was whirling. These were the blokes we had seen earlier, after escaping the Quag. How could they have followed us?

I glanced at Delph and Petra. They looked as terrified as I felt.

I pointed to the right and we shuffled off round the corner.

We set our tucks down and I whispered, 'They followed us. How?'

Petra shook her head. But Delph said, 'You reckon they can detect magic? Because you done that to get us here.' He pointed to the magical tethers that kept us all invisible.

I looked down at my wand like it had just bitten me. *Could that be true?*

Delph said, 'Look.' He was pointing to the right. Down the cobbles at the very end of the street was a tall building made of stone and brick and timbers. I stared up at its highest point.

'Steeples,' I said in wonder.

'It's got a bell too,' said Delph. 'Me dad said Steeples had a bell once, before it broke.'

2

'Steeples?' said Petra, looking confused.

'The place back in Wormwood where Wugmorts would go to listen to Ezekiel the Sermonizer telling us to be good while scaring us half to death with tales of how badly our lives would turn out regardless of what we did,' I explained.

At night Steeples had always been empty. This building might be the same.

We shouldered our tucks and crept along the cobbles until we came to the double wooden doors of the entrance.

There was a sign next to it.

'*Saint Necro's*,' I read. I glanced at Delph. 'What do you reckon that means?'

'Dunno, do I?' he replied. 'Never heard-a no Saint Necro. Alls I know is Steeples.'

I tried the doors but they were locked. I pointed my wand at the heavy wrought-iron lock and was about to whisper '*Ingressio*' when Delph grabbed my arm.

'Magic,' he said warningly.

I nodded and slowly lowered my wand.

Then Petra noticed a window on the side. 'It's not locked.'

Delph boosted her up first and she slid through. I followed. Delph lifted Harry Two through the opening and into my arms, and then he brought up the rear.

We were inside a vast chamber that was far larger than Steeples, though it had similar brightly coloured windows, rows of seats and a raised area up front where sermons were no doubt given. I wondered whether the sermonizer who spoke here was as depressing as Ezekiel. Petra said in a hushed tone, 'Where do we go now?'

I pointed to a set of stone stairs. 'Let's see what's up that way.'

'Why not down?' said Petra, pointing to another set of stairs that apparently led to a lower floor.

'No,' I said. 'Up is better.'

She gave me a sceptical look, but I didn't wait for her approval. I walked over to the stairs with Harry Two beside me. Delph and Petra hurried after us.

That's when we heard the footsteps at the entrance.

We ducked down between two sets of pews as I heard someone say, 'Ingressio.'

The doors flew open.

I lifted my head a bit so I could see over the backs of the pews. It was the same two cloaked figures.

But this was impossible. I hadn't used magic before they got here. How could they be—

I looked down at the mark on my hand. Was it that?

As the footsteps drew closer, I heard one of the males say, 'Are you sure?'

I peered over the edge again in time to see the other bloke hold up his wand. 'See for yourself,' he said.

The wand was glowing. He spun round to face where we were hiding.

'There!' he snapped. He pointed his wand and said, 'Infernus!'

'Embattlemento!' I instantly cried out.

His blast of fire ricocheted off my shield spell and he had to duck to avoid being incinerated.

The second bloke rushed forward, casting spell after spell our way, each more powerful than the last.

Petra cast a shield spell as well, and his magic rebounded off it and smashed into the pews, destroying them.

Spells were now being cast so quickly I could barely follow them.

Glass shattered. Wooden pews disintegrated, and a small statue exploded when hit by a glancing blow from a rebounding spell. I had never been in such a battle as fast and fierce as this one. Though we were still invisible, we were in terrible danger of being killed simply by being in this confined space.

I was hurling spells so quickly I could barely remember thinking of the incantation before sending it off. When I glanced at Petra, I saw both terror and fury in her eyes. Somehow, this filled me with resolve.

I slid on my belly, squeezed under a pew, came up behind the bloke and said, *'Impacto.'* He was blasted off his feet and flung against a wall.

But the bloke rebounded off it, turned and fired multiple spells in my general direction. I ducked, then threw myself over a pew. I turned in time to see Delph get slammed against another pew.

I heard Petra cry out as she was hurled over another pew, crashing on the floor.

I whirled round on the same bloke and fired every spell I could think of, but he was deflecting them left and right. My arm was growing weary, and Petra had not recovered enough to help me. When a spell hit so close to my head that it made me dizzy, I ducked under a pew for a moment to catch my breath and clear my senses.

When I looked back up I almost cheered as I saw Delph

slam into the male, lift him up, turn him upside down and pile drive him into the floor. I had seen Delph use that same move in the Duelum back in Wormwood. The bloke went limp.

The next instant a light shot right past my face, hit the wall behind me and knocked a hole in it. The spell knocked me head over heels and broke the magical tether keeping the others invisible.

'Got you!' roared the other bloke who had shot at me as he pointed his wand right at Delph's exposed chest.

Before I could regain my feet and aim my wand, a voice called out, '*Subservio.*'

Petra's spell hit the bloke square on. He instantly went rigid and his wand hand dropped. He simply stood there, looking blankly ahead.

We rose on shaky legs and approached him.

'Thanks, Pet, you saved me,' said Delph weakly.

'That was quick thinking, Petra,' I said.

She let out a long breath. 'I'm . . . I'm just glad it worked.'

Delph pointed at the wand still held in the bloke's hand.

I stared down at it, stunned.

Etched on his brightly glowing wand was the mark of the three hooks! The same mark that had been burned on to my hand. The mark on the wand was pulsing as though it was alive.

Delph said, '*That's* how they found us. Your mark, it must give off a signal.'

I nodded. But what was I to do? I couldn't very well cut off my hand.

'Vega Jane, your glove!' said Delph.

'My what?' I said distractedly.

'Your glove. It has powerful magic. See if it can block the signal.'

I plunged my hand into my cloak pocket and pulled out the glove Alice Adronis had given me in order to handle the Elemental, which was now also my wand.

I hastily pulled on the glove, covering the mark.

I looked at the fellow's wand and breathed a sigh of relief. The mark of the three hooks was gone from it and the wand was no longer glowing.

'That was brilliant!' said Petra to Delph.

I saw him smile.

'It was very smart of you, Delph.' I turned, pointed my wand at the unconscious bloke, and removed any memory he might have had of this. I did the same with his mate. Next, Petra and I repaired the damage to the building.

Finally, I turned the ring back round, attached the magical tethers, and we became invisible once more. It was only then that I released the blokes who had attacked us from the spell.

They both looked around.

One said, 'What the blazes are we doing here?'

The other fellow shook his head. 'Last thing I remember I was in me bed. And that's where I'm going back to,' he added.

He turned and left. His mate gave the place one more searching look and joined him, shutting the doors behind him.

I let out a long breath. 'Now let's go and find a proper place to hide.'

The long winding staircase carried us upward. It would, I was sure, lead all the way to the bell tower. But I stopped short of that. There was a door to the right. I tried it. Locked. I pulled out my wand, and a moment later the door opened.

I had grown accustomed to being able to do things like this, but I never wanted to take it for granted. I had come to completely adore being a sorceress!

Inside the room were old leather trunks. There was also a window, just as I'd hoped.

I closed the door behind us and locked it. I pointed to the window. 'When the light comes, we can watch the goings-on down there. Get the lay of the land. In the meantime, we should get some sleep. We'll take turns keeping watch.'

I offered to take the first watch, and the others settled down on the floor, with their tucks as their pillows. We had retrieved some blankets that were stacked neatly in a corner, for the floor was hard and the room was cool.

I took up watch by the window for a bit with Harry Two lying next to me. I didn't see any movement down below. In the distance I thought I heard a long, high whistle of sorts, but I couldn't be too sure of that, for the sound carried strangely up here.

I finally turned to some of the trunks and, trying to remain as quiet as possible so I wouldn't wake the others, I started searching them, hoping they would give us some idea as to the place we were now in.

The first trunk was filled with clothes. Trousers, coats, shirts, shoes and frocks. Even some hats. They were of a style, cut and material I had never seen. I pulled them out.

If we were going to fit into this place, whatever it was, we had to dress like the others who were here.

I put these aside and opened the next trunk. When I saw what was in there I felt like I had happened upon a treasure trove.

Books! I pulled a number of them out, sat on my haunches and, using the conjured light from my wand, began to look through them.

The first few books were filled with what seemed to be sermons that someone like Ezekiel would deliver. However, the next book was far more interesting and potentially useful.

It was entitled *A Book of True*.

True, I quickly came to learn, was the name of the place we were in. There were words in the book that I had never seen before: *years, horse, man, woman, church* and *motor* being among them. Fortunately, there were accompanying pictures. Thus I learned that man and woman were like our male and female, and both were referred to as people, not Wugmorts.

My education continued. A *horse* was our slep. A canine was a *dog*. Sessions translated to *years*, which were divided up into twelve *months*, and the twelve months were divided up into something called *days*. Slivers were *minutes*. Sixty of those minutes represented something called an *hour*. The *church* was the place we were currently in. And a *motor* was the contraption we had seen rumbling along.

Oh, and there was something called the *morning*, which apparently was when the sun was coming up, and the rest of the light was called the *day*. And the Noc was called the *moon*.

I leaned back against the coolness of the stone and repeated these words over and over. I didn't know that learning a new language would be required here, but why not? Everything about this journey had been totally unpredictable. Just because we had escaped the Quag, that simple rule needn't change.

If we wanted to fit in here, we couldn't very well go around this place calling horses 'sleps' and the moon 'the Noc'.

As I continued to read, I learned that True had experienced several *centuries* (each century is one hundred sessions!) of peace, following some difficult periods of war and uncertainty. There were pictures of Wugs – or *people* – engaged in fun activities with their youngs, who were called *children*. I looked at the illustrations of the smiling children and wondered how that fit with what I had been told about the ruthlessness and savagery of the Maladons, the magical race that Astrea Prine had told us had beaten her kind in a great war. Presumably the Maladons now ruled this place.

Unless . . . perhaps these people had fought and overthrown the Maladons? If so, they must be magical. How else could they have beaten the powerful sorcery the Maladons supposedly possessed? After all, they had thrashed my kind, who were powerfully magical in their own right.

And most telling of all, I believed we had run into a pair of Maladons twice already. So they *were* here. It was truly puzzling.

I continued to read and learn as much as I could.

I gazed at the picture of the motor and marvelled how it

could move without sleps, or horses, pulling it. Had it been created by magic?

Before I knew it, the sun was coming up outside. I had forgotten to awaken Delph or Petra to take over my watch. But I was not tired in the least. My head was filled with all this new information; my mind was swirling with questions and possibilities. But mostly questions, I had to admit.

I moved back over to the window and looked out. With the sun coming up, I could see things quite clearly now. True was larger than it had appeared last night. I could see spires of many buildings in the distance. Wugmorts – I caught myself – *people* were emerging from buildings. I waved my wand and muttered, '*Crystilado magnifica.*' Instantly, I was seeing all of this as though it were inches from my face.

Fortunately, the people looked like us at least; otherwise it would be awfully hard for us to fit in. And their clothes looked like the ones I had pilfered from the trunk. Again, a good thing. But we might stand out anyway. We were three strangers with a canine. How would we explain our presence here?

A clattering sound caught my attention, and in my magnified line of sight came another motor speeding down the cobbles. It was followed by a second, which looked different – it was bigger, with different levels, and had more people riding in it. They rode in one lower and one upper level. At one corner the bigger motor stopped and some people got off and others got on. On the side was a sign that read TRUE TRANSPORT. This must be how they moved from one place to another, I thought.

'Blimey!'

I whirled round to find Delph and Petra staring over my shoulder.

'You didn't wake us to take a watch,' said Petra disapprovingly.

'I thought I'd just let you sleep,' I replied.

Delph said, 'Vega Jane, you can't do this alone. I know I can't do magic, but I didn't fight my way across the Quag to be useless!'

Delph never talked to me that way and his words cut into me like a hurled blade. I composed myself and said, 'You're right, Delph. But I've learned quite a lot actually.'

I took some time showing them the clothes and the books and telling them of the new words I had learned, like *people* and *dogs* and *morning* and *horses* and *motors*. They took it all in, though I could tell they were even more overwhelmed by it than I had been.

Then I heard Delph's belly rumbling.

It was then that I realized I was starving. I looked in my tuck to find that my larder was basically empty. Delph and Petra did the same, with similar results.

Harry Two looked hungry, but then he always did.

'Here.' I handed them the clothes I had found. We swiftly dressed and put our old clothes and boots along with the spare new items in our tucks. I slipped the book on True into my coat pocket.

Petra said, 'But what now? We can't go outside, can we?'

'I've seen lots and lots of Wu—' I stopped. 'I mean I've seen lots of *people* coming and going. And almost never did I see one of them hail another. I think this place is far larger than we initially thought. If there are lots of blokes around, then maybe, in our new clothes, we can blend in with them.'

'But what about Harry Two?' asked Delph.

'You saw the pictures of canines — I mean *dogs* — in the book. I've seen four people walking ca—' I stopped again, frustrated by having to learn a new language so quickly. '*DOGS!*'

Delph said, probably equally frustrated, 'Can we speak Wugish for now?'

I nodded. 'Yes, but we can't when we're dealing with blokes from here. We have to start thinking in their language, Delph. Since only those from Wormwood are Wugs, we have to call the blokes here *people*.'

'That makes sense,' he replied.

'Maybe best we say nothing at all, till we hear some of them blokes talk,' suggested Petra.

'That's a good idea,' I replied, giving her a smile. I wanted to like and trust Petra, I really did. And if she turned out to be a Maladon, I hoped I could kill her before she killed me.

Delph nodded. 'All right, then. But how will we get food? We got nothing to pay with.'

'We'll cross that bridge when we get to it,' I said gamely.

I returned us to visibility and we headed downstairs.

I had just opened the front doors when a voice cried out.

'Oi! What in blazes are you lot doing here?'

I didn't even look for the source.

As we had so often done in the Quag, we ran for it.

2
THE ABSENCE OF EVIL

We sprinted as hard as we could, turning corner after corner until we stopped, hunched over, breathless.

'W-what-wh-who was that?' Delph finally got out.

I shook my head. 'D-dunno. But he saw us for s-sure.'

Petra drew in one long replenishing breath and said, 'He was some bloke in a long black cloak with a white collar round his neck. Older, grey hair. He had some papers in his hand. Maybe he works there. Doubt he was there last night or else he would have heard all the fighting.'

I looked at her admiringly. She'd had the good sense to look at who had yelled at us. I had just run.

'We'd best budge along,' said Delph nervously.

I followed his gaze to see folks on the cobbles staring at us as they walked by. Some were on two-wheeled things that were propelled along – at least it seemed – by their feet. Strapped to the front of the contraption, where the rider placed their hands, was a wire basket to carry things. I had seen a picture of this in the book too. It was called a *bicycle*.

We darted across the cobbles only to almost be hit by a motor. The male behind the wheel raised a fist at us, and a great honking sound, like an enraged goose, blasted out.

My heart beating painfully fast, I turned left and we trooped single file to another corner, where I turned right. And stopped.

Wugs – I mean *people* – were queued up outside a shop. I knew why. The most wonderful smells were coming from within. My belly rumbled.

'Blimey,' said Delph, staring up at the sign over the shop. *'Caspian's Creations.'* He looked at me. 'What you reckon that is?'

I said, 'I reckon it's a place to eat. Look.'

There was a window in the front of the shop and we could see people seated round neatly spaced wooden tables. They had plates and cups and saucers in front of them and were chomping away using shiny metal knives and forks and spoons.

'Reminds me of the Starving Tove back in Wormwood,' said Delph.

'Reminds me'a nothing,' declared Petra. 'I've never seen anything like it.'

Her tone and look were of absolute wonder. It made me think, not for the first time, that as bad as I had had it in Wormwood, it was but nothing compared to what Petra had endured living in the Quag.

Delph and Harry Two's face and snout, respectively, were pressed against the glass as they peered longingly inside. Behind a wooden counter there were males and females in aprons filling – I supposed – orders of customers.

15

Behind them I could see other folks dressed in white shirts and aprons, labouring over stoves and pots and pans. Piled high in wire baskets on the counter were loaves of bread and stacks of pastries and chocolates. On racks next to them were cakes and pies and . . . the most delectable puddings. My head was spinning.

I could see paper and coin exchanging hands between those behind the counter and the customers. With sinking spirits, I saw that it looked very different from Wormwood coin.

Delph had evidently seen what I had because he said, 'You reckon we can find something to do to earn some proper coin so we can buy food?'

I heard a noise and looked round.

A large motor had pulled to a stop in front of the shop. The metal grille had a name etched on it: ZEPHYER.

There was a bloke in front behind the wheel, and there was a bloke way in the back. He was dressed in very fine clothes indeed. He wore a tall black hat. His nose was red and bulbous.

He yelled at the fellow in front, who jumped out and came swiftly round to the back.

The window came down and the bloke with the high hat could be heard clearly.

'Go on, Wainwright. I don't have time to eat a proper breakfast and that's your fault. Get my usual, immediately. I can eat along the way.'

The male called Wainwright, who was dressed in knee-high brown boots, a jacket with lots of shiny buttons and a hard-sided cap with goggles wrapped round it, said pleadingly, 'But, sir, there is a very long queue.'

'That is not my problem, is it? Here, take the money.'

I watched as he opened a brown leather pouch he'd taken from his coat pocket. He withdrew a piece of paper and a few coins. This must be *money*. From here I could see that he had more paper and more coins in the large pouch.

These were the moments in my life where clear choices could be made. Do it or don't do it. Often, the decision was difficult. This time, it was easy.

The bloke obviously had far too much money. I was just going to relieve him of a bit, and he'd be none the wiser.

I looked round and slowly withdrew my wand, hiding it inside my coat sleeve.

'Delph,' I said, out of the side of my mouth, 'I need another one of your little distractions.'

'What?' He glanced from me to the bloke in the motor. 'Oh, right.'

He looked around for a moment and then cried out, in his deep, carrying voice, 'Oi, look at that!'

Everyone within earshot glanced sharply that way, including the two blokes at the long motor.

'*Rejoinda* some of the, uh, money stuff in that bloke's pouch,' I muttered under my breath.

Some paper and coins shot from the pouch, zipped past the chin of the fellow in uniform, who was looking across the cobbles like everyone else, and landed neatly in my other hand.

I slipped the paper and coin into my pocket and we joined the queue.

'That's stealing, ain't it, Vega Jane?' admonished Delph.

Petra said, 'So what? It's how me and Lack survived in the Quag all that time.'

'We're not in the Quag now, are we?' countered Delph sternly.

'Do you want to eat or not?' I said.

Well, *that* shut him up good and proper.

We finally made it inside the shop and stepped up to the counter.

A female in a long white apron with a matching cap faced us. Her skin was paler than mine and her eyes were large and round. Her long black hair was pulled back into a knot at the nape of her neck.

'What would you like, dearie?'

'Um, what do you have?' I said timidly.

She pointed to a board on the wall that listed lots of things. 'All that there, plus what you see on the counter.'

Petra said boldly, 'What do *you* like the best?'

The female smiled, looked at her and said in a low voice, 'Well, I must admit, number four is my absolute favourite.'

'Sounds good,' I said. 'For the three of us.'

She looked down and saw Harry Two. 'Dogs outside, please. He's a cute one, though. What do you call him?'

'Um, Harry.' I figured telling her his real name would only prompt questions I didn't want to answer.

'Why, the poor thing's gone and lost most of an ear,' she noted, clucking sympathetically.

'I know. He, uh, got into a fight with another cani— dog.'

From the corner of my eye I saw Delph tug down the sleeve that covered his blackened arm and Petra slipping

18

her injured hand into her pocket.

I quickly led Harry Two outside and told him to wait by the window. Then I went back inside and paid for our food. The female gave me back some other paper and a few coins and I put them away in my coat pocket.

'That's an odd glove, dearie. And just the one too,' she observed.

My throat constricted a bit. 'My mum gave it to me. I lost the other. But I keep it on for her.'

'Well, ain't that nice of you. I've got three daughters of me own, you know.'

I smiled weakly and hurried off.

A group of blokes left their table and we took it. When our food came, I took a portion out to Harry Two.

When I rejoined Delph and Petra, my gaze caught and held on her.

She was staring down at her meal like it was the most beautiful sight she had ever laid eyes on: scrambled eggs and bacon and fat sausages and warm buttered bread and hot tea and porridge topped off with a pile of kippers.

She caught me looking and her face reddened. I reached out and took her hand.

'I know what it's like to be hungry. But I was never hungry like you and Lack were. So I say eat up and enjoy a very fine meal.'

She smiled. For the next ten slivers all we did was eat, swallow and drink.

Delph mumbled between mouthfuls, 'Looks like the food ain't so different here.'

Petra glanced at him. 'Maybe for you. I've never had

such a feast in all my life.'

I saw that she was fumbling with the fork, knife and spoon. I cut up a sausage slowly, so that she could copy me.

When our bellies were full, we rose and made our way out. Harry Two had long since finished his meal and was relieving himself against a corner of a building.

'What now?' asked Petra. 'We should have a look around.'

'We find a place to stay,' I said firmly. They'd both slept all night but I hadn't.

We began walking.

'Where do you reckon the Maladons are, Vega Jane?' Delph asked.

'Are we sure there *are* Maladons here?' asked Petra.

'Who in the blazes do you think those two blokes were last night?' I snapped. I was worried. I'd thought the Maladons would be easy to spot because they would be hideous in figure and murderous of temper. The blokes last night just looked like everyone else in True. That was a scary thought – not knowing who the Maladons were until they pulled their wands.

Delph looked at all the bustling activity.

'It don't look like what I thought it would,' he remarked.

Delph was exactly right about that. We had been told that the Maladons were evil.

So why did everyone look happy and . . . free?

We walked around True for a while. Every corner revealed something new and different to see. The large double-decked motors I had seen from the church window carried folks where they wanted to go. They paid coin, or *money* rather, for the ride.

We watched folks walk in and out of buildings. Many carried packages and bags, and some had youngs in tow or in their arms. Some pushed around baskets on wheels that had very young youngs inside of them swathed in blankets.

I inwardly sighed. *Not youngs. Children.* I couldn't help but think of my family. My parents, my brother, John, and I would often take walks together. I remembered my father's strong grip, my mother's loving smile and my brother's curiosity about all things. Tears prickled my eyes. I noticed Petra watching me curiously.

'Let's budge along,' I said.

There were blokes on some corners holding stacks of papers and calling out, 'Warehouse fire blamed on lax hygiene.' Then other blokes would take one of the papers in exchange for some money. I had no idea what any of it meant.

Some hurried along and others moved more slowly. There were males in shiny uniforms with lots of brass buttons standing in the middle of the cobbles, directing the motors where to go and whether to stop and start.

There were males wearing aprons selling food and drink to passers-by. Children rushing around and exhausting their mothers and fathers. Folks chatting as Wugs did back in Wormwood.

But the thing I *wasn't* seeing disturbed me most of all.

Where was the MAGIC?

Aside from the pair last night, I had seen nary a wand nor a spell cast. There were no evil creatures to battle.

But those blokes from last night *could* do magic. They had very nearly killed us. I was convinced they were Maladons.

How else would they have been able to track the mark on my hand? So how did that murderous presence, which we had expected, match up with the serene world we were seeing now?

I scratched my head. The whole thing was sixes and sevens as far as I was concerned.

'Uh, Vega Jane,' muttered Delph, 'I think a bloke is following us.'

I forced myself to keep looking ahead.

'Why do you think that?' I asked nervously.

Petra answered, 'Because he's been behind us since we left the place where we ate. Don't you use your eyes?'

I shot her an angry glance, but I was upset with myself. If Delph and Petra had noticed this, why hadn't I?

I crossed to the other side of the cobbles, quickly enough that Delph and Petra had to hustle to catch up. I turned to look back at them, but really I looked at the fellow behind us.

It wasn't hard to spot him. He was short and plump and he was hustling across the street, his gaze locked on us. He wore a matching jacket and trousers with a white shirt, a long strand of red material round his collar and an oddly shaped hat that I had seen other males here wearing.

'What do we do now?' asked Petra as we hurried along.

I looked ahead. There was little alley coming up. 'Down here.'

As soon as we turned into the alley, I pulled out my wand, conjured the lasso, attached it to the others and then turned my ring backwards. Invisible, we moved back against the brick wall of the alley and waited.

We didn't have to wait long.

The bloke came hurtling into the narrow space and then stopped dead, looking up and down the alley.

He ran down the alley until he reached the end. He looked left and right, then he hustled back to where we all stood watching him.

He took something out of his pocket, lit it with a match and blew smoke out of his nostrils as he tapped his shiny shoe against the cobbles and rubbed his chin.

My fingers loosely gripped my wand. Round my waist, Destin, a chain that, among other things, allowed me to fly, hugged me a bit tighter.

Petra had her wand at the ready too. She looked intent and not even slightly afraid.

I turned back to our pursuer. If this bloke *was* a Maladon, he didn't look remotely dangerous. Even pathetic Cletus Loon from Wormwood could take the little twerp if need be.

He finished his smoke, crushed it underfoot with the heel of his shoe and, giving the alley one more penetrating look, turned and left. We waited a bit to make sure he was gone good and proper, and then I reversed the ring and lifted the spell of the conjured lasso.

'Who you reckon that bloke was?' asked Delph.

'A spy for the Maladons, maybe,' I said. 'Only . . . if he were magical, you'd think he would have used his wand to find us in here.'

'Aye, that's a right good point,' said Delph, looking impressed by my logic.

'But that means that the Maladons may control this

23

place and use some of the folks here to help them. Even if they can't do magic, they're our enemies.'

Delph looked unnerved by this. 'So everybody here might be against us?'

'It's possible, Delph,' I said.

As I continued to gaze around, something struck me. Everyone here looked very different from one another. I know that blokes look different from other blokes. But back in Wormwood, Wugs all looked pretty much the same. Same general facial features, hair colour and pale skin. Morrigone with her blood-red hair was really the sole outlier. Here I was seeing features and skin colour I'd never seen before. Black and brown and skin far paler than mine.

'Well, we're strangers here,' said Petra, interrupting my thoughts. 'That prat who chased us from the church might have told others about us. So if these Maladons are smart, they'll send more blokes after us. We can't stay invisible forever.'

'Aye, that's a right good point too,' said Delph, gazing admiringly at Petra.

'So what do we do now?' Petra asked.

They both looked at me – or all three of them did if you counted Harry Two, which I always did.

I thought quickly. 'We still need to find another place to hide. Until dark.'

'OK, but where?' said Petra.

It was then that we heard a great roaring sound.

'Come on,' I said.

We rushed off over the cobbles in the direction of the racket, finally coming out into an enormous square filled with folk rushing hither and thither.

That's when we saw it. A long metal thing all strung together. It had windows and there were people inside it. At the head was a huge black contraption that made the motors we'd seen look positively puny by comparison.

Smoke belched out of what looked to be a metal chimneystack as it roared along, then slowed and disappeared behind a large building.

I looked at the others and we raced towards the building.

From inside I could hear a voice boom out, 'The 9:10 express train to Greater True, boarding now. The 9:10 express train to Greater True. All authorized persons, please make your way. And ladies and gentlemen, and the kiddies too, mind the divide between the train and the station platform.'

Delph said, 'Express train?'

'Seems to be a way that people get about,' I said slowly.

Petra said, 'Greater True? What's that?'

I said, 'Greater means bigger. So, like True, but bigger?'

But something the voice had said was bothering me.

Who were these authorized persons?

I stared up at the brick building that this express train had apparently pulled into. The sign on it read TRUE TRAIN STATION.

My gaze ran over the large facade.

'I think we've just found our hiding place,' I said.

'What, with all these blokes?' said Petra sceptically.

'That's kind of the point,' I shot back. 'Let's go.'

3
ABANDONED

The train station was a cavernous place, even bigger inside than it had looked from the outside. It was filled with people carrying bags, rushing about. There weren't this many Wugs in all of Wormwood.

On one wall was a large sign. On it were the names of I supposed places, and next to them were numbers. People would stop and stare up at it, glance at timekeepers wrapped round their wrists and then scurry on.

'It's a schedule,' opined Delph. 'Tells the people where the trains are going and when. We had something like that back at the Mill.'

I nodded. It was still so shocking that a place like this could exist right next to the Quag. And that Wormwood could be on the other side of that Quag, a village stuck well back in another time as compared to here, which had motors and trains and just . . . stuff that I had to admit was far nicer.

As I looked around, I could see a sign blinking over an entrance leading to a long sleek train that had pulled into the station.

GREATER TRUE.

I saw males — *men* — standing in front of the glass doors that led to the train. A line of folks had queued up in front of the doors. They were all very well dressed and clean, like the angry bloke in the big motor. They held out their tickets and then something else to the two men. I drew my wand, hiding it up my sleeve, and muttered, *'Crystilado magnifica.'*

I could see clearly now what the 'something else' was. It was a small notebook, with their picture and name inside. They were all holding up their hands to the fellows at the entrance. There was something on their palms, but I couldn't see what it was.

I noticed that one bloke had left his notebook behind on a bench. I ventured over and picked it up. It was filled with writing and some pictures too, of a kind I had never seen.

'Blokes here do seem so happy, don't they?' said Petra, with mild disgust in her voice.

She was watching a woman on her knees scrub the stone floor with a large sponge and a bucket of soapy water. The woman was smiling and humming away as though she had all the coin in the world, without the back-breaking job she was performing.

I looked around. Petra was right. I noted the pleasant expressions on just about everyone I saw. It had been the same back at the cafe — except for the angry bloke in the long motor and the bloke who had chased us from the church. Just about everyone else looked very content.

'Come on,' I said. 'We can't stand around here.'

I spotted a set of stairs and we hustled over to them and started climbing. We kept going, passing blokes along the way until we stopped passing anyone and were all by ourselves. We turned right and left and then up another set of steps. We passed down a corridor with a series of doors lining it. I used my wand to see behind the doors. They were rooms filled with odds and ends. But then one appeared that was not.

I opened the door and we stepped through.

It was empty, but set against one wall was the backside of the sign we had seen holding the schedule for the trains. There were slits in it. Through them I could see the interior of the train station we had just left. I leaped back when the sign started to vibrate.

'What the——!' I exclaimed.

'New train times,' Delph said.

'Right,' I said.

It was all unnerving. I had anticipated seeing death and destruction and the Maladons ruling over all of it. But there was none of that here. There was peace and prosperity and apparent freedom.

I was so disappointed. And then I immediately felt guilty. Who wouldn't prefer peace to war?

We had left Wormwood to find the truth. The truth of our past, and then the truth of our future. Now, I began to wonder what that was. Did the Maladons even exist any more? It had been eight centuries since the war, after all. A lot could have happened in that time.

I looked up at Delph and could tell from his expression that he was thinking the exact same thing.

'Maybe the Maladons got beat,' he said. 'Beat by the blokes what live in this place.'

I shook my head. 'They'd have needed magic. Other than the two that followed us, we haven't seen anyone perform any. And there's something else.' I held up my gloved hand. 'Their wands could detect the mark of the three hooks. That's our symbol: peace, hope, freedom — everything the Maladons hated. So the two we fought in Saint Necro's *had* to be Maladons, otherwise how would they know to track the three hooks?'

Petra and Delph looked as bewildered as I felt.

My mind was so tired I couldn't really think any more. The sign began to whir again and in those spinning pieces of metal I saw my own mind whirling wildly out of control. What if I was wrong? What if the Maladons didn't control this place?

What if Astrea Prine and her lot had made a colossal mistake that had doomed all Wugmorts to the bleakest existence possible?

I looked down at my wand. *Magic might be* useless *to me if there is no battle to fight. If there is no war to win. If there is no grand enemy to vanquish.* My brother, John, was back in Wormwood, enduring the tutelage of Morrigone that had already transformed him into something unrecognizable to me. Had I left him for no good reason?

A sudden thought hit me.

My parents! And my grandfather!

Were they here, in True?

I glanced up and found Delph staring at me.

'Don't make much sense, does it?' he said.

29

'What doesn't?'

'Well, your grandfather Virgil's this Excalibur, right?'

'Right.'

'An Excalibur?' interjected Petra curiously.

'Right powerful sorcerer from birth,' explained Delph. 'He left Wormwood in a ball of flames a long time ago when me and Vega were just wee things.'

'What's your point, Delph?' I said sharply.

'So maybe he came here. And maybe he saw the same thing we did.'

'You mean a peaceful place where everyone is so very happy and well fed?' I said snidely.

'Right. But then he summoned your parents, like Astrea said he done. Why would he'a done that if something weren't outta sorts? I mean Virgil was always one smart bloke. Don't think he woulda done that for no reason, eh?'

I mulled this over. What Delph said *did* make sense.

But then my mind veered to another possibility. One that perhaps even Delph had not considered.

My grandfather had not summoned *me*. He had left me behind. My parents had never tried to contact me.

Which could only mean one thing. That they were just fine with me spending the rest of my life in Wormwood – without them.

'What are you thinking, Vega Jane?' asked Delph, who was watching me closely.

I felt tears rising to my eyes, but I looked away. I didn't want Delph to see me like that. And I definitely didn't want to display any such weakness in front of Petra.

I composed myself and said, 'I'm thinking that we're

30

going to have to figure this out on our own. Because I don't think there's anybody here that can or will want to help us.'

I looked at each of them in turn before settling my gaze back on the floor.

'We're alone.'

4
THE LATE TRAIN

Delph and Petra fell asleep on the floor with their heads on their tucks. Harry Two had his head on my lap and was snoring softly. As usual I could not sleep. Whether here, in the Quag, or back in Wormwood, sleep had never come easily for me. My mind was whirling too fast.

I looked enviously over at Delph and Petra, close together, perhaps too close. This was going to come to a head at some point, I knew. I just didn't know what the result would be.

Restless, I turned to look out through the back of the sign. It must be very late. In fact, the train station was quite empty now, with nary a bloke toting a bag in sight. I couldn't see the front of the sign, so I didn't know if any more trains were coming in.

I had slumped down and closed my eyes when I heard it. A low, faraway whistle. Then another. Then, a rumbling. It was growing closer.

I opened my eyes and looked around.

'It's like last night, eh?'

I turned to stare at Delph, who was awake and looking at me.

He said, 'When we were coming to True, we heard it. It was about this time of night, I reckon. The whistle. And the rumble.'

He was right. We *had* heard these sounds when flying towards True last night.

'It's late for a train, isn't it?' I said.

Petra woke and sat up.

The rumblings became louder and louder. Our gazes were fixed through the slits in the sign on that part of the station. We could see through glass doors the location where the trains would come into the station.

Though it was now dark, I knew we would have no trouble seeing the train come into view because they had little lights on inside. I had seen that on other trains.

The rumbling became very loud, and I tensed, but the train never appeared. Instead, the rumbling sound faded.

'What happened to the train?' said Delph. 'Where did it go?'

'There's only one way to find out.' I got up and headed to the door. The others followed me.

We reached the main floor of the station and peered around.

In a low voice Delph said, 'Vega Jane, maybe being invisible would come in handy now.'

I nodded and ensnared everyone with my magical tether, then turned my ring the wrong way around. We instantly vanished from sight. As we moved along, I kept gazing around and listening. I thought I could hear something, but it wasn't clear where it was coming from.

We passed through the glass doors and stopped at the edge of the train platform, where shiny metal rails ran in parallel between stout wood. This was what the train ran on, and it was clever indeed. It might have been something my brother, John, would have invented, given the opportunity.

'Where could the train have gone?' said Petra. 'I mean, doesn't it have to run on those metal things?'

Delph said, 'It had to be close or else we wouldn't have heard it from where we did.'

'Maybe there's another place for the train to stop.' I looked down. '*Under* the station?'

They both looked at me quizzically. 'Why would it do that?' asked Petra.

I felt my skin start to tingle all of a sudden. I didn't know why. I had always relied on my instincts. Maybe they were sending me a message.

'Why would a train be coming in this late at all?' I asked.

Delph said, 'To keep it secret-like from everybody, cos most folks are sleeping now.'

'Exactly.'

Petra looked around and pointed. 'Those stairs head down.'

We went over to the staircase. It was so dark we could see nothing. I said my incantation, pointed my wand and the area was magically magnified.

'Big doors,' said Delph. 'With a bunch'a signs that say *DO NOT ENTER*.'

'I bet they're locked,' added Petra.

I had no doubt they were. I led the way downward and

when we reached the doors, I pointed my wand and said, 'Ingressio.'

I heard locks click, and one of the doors moved an inch or so. I pushed it open just far enough for me to peer through.

There was a short corridor and yet another set of doors. We passed through these, and then the stairs headed steeply downward.

Soon, it felt like we were about a mile underground.

We stepped through the last set of doors and looked around.

It was dark and musty and huge. Easily as big as what was up top.

Delph said in a hushed voice, 'Do you hear that?'

It was a rumbling sound, but not like the noise before. It was lower.

We went over to a door set in the wall and put our ears to it. We could hear something.

I pointed my wand and said, 'Crystilado magnifica.'

Revealed on the other side of the door was a long hall. It was full of people: men, women and children. They had all clearly just got off the train, and were marching along in silence, carrying small tucks.

Next to them the darkened train was sitting on the tracks, the engine belching smoke.

'Wait here,' I said. 'I'm going to see what's going on. Petra, keep your wand ready.'

I released the tether once they were safely hidden. Invisible, I used my wand to open the door just enough to allow me to slip through. Luckily, no one was watching the door. When the last of them had passed by, I fell in behind the group.

At certain points along the way were more cloaked blokes holding wands. Maladons – they had to be. When the line wasn't moving fast enough, they roughly pushed people along. As I watched, a small girl with dark skin was knocked down by one of them. When a woman I supposed was her mother went to help her, she was also struck, and she fell next to her daughter.

The others marched on, not once looking back at their fallen comrades. As the column disappeared down the long hallway, the mother and daughter were jerked up by two men, taken over to a far wall and lined up against it.

'Tis a heavy price to be paid for dawdling, vermin,' one of the men hissed. He raised his wand.

Without even thinking, I raised my wand and said, 'Impacto.'

The spell shot out from the tip of my wand and blasted both men off their feet. They sailed through the air and landed hard against the floor of the platform, their wands flying from them.

I rushed forward to help the girl and her mother, but they stood there without moving. I realized they must be under the *Subservio* spell. I released them from it and they looked around in confusion.

'Are you OK?' I said.

I had forgotten that I was still invisible. The mother screamed, clutched her child and they ran off in the other direction, away from the column.

'Wait!' I said. But then I heard feet running towards me.

I leaped out of the way as a group of cloaked Maladons with raised wands rushed past me. I heard the sounds of spells being cast and people screaming.

I turned and ran in the other direction, towards where the column of downtrodden had headed. I reached a door through which they must have passed, eased it open and slipped through.

On the other side of the door was a long, dark hall. I heard noises coming from the other end. People were talking in raised voices. Obviously everyone was on alert now.

'*Crystilado magnifica*,' I said, pointing my wand ahead. What I saw made me freeze.

The room was enormous, cavernous really; easily the largest room I had ever seen.

In the middle of it was a huge crowd of people, including those who had got off the train. In front of them, on a large white wall, were blurred images, moving back and forth.

Everyone in the room was staring at it, transfixed.

I could hear a sound. Like the images on the wall, I couldn't make out actual words; it was simply murmuring, something less than a whisper and a bit more than silence.

The mass of people were now rocking from side to side in unison. Then each reached out and gripped their neighbour's hand.

I looked back at the wall. And as I looked at it and as I listened to the murmurings, I could feel something happening to me. I began to sway back and forth. My mind felt loose, hazy. It wasn't frightening. In fact, it felt right; it felt safe. I wanted it to happen. Memories that I had started to fall away from me. I felt good. My eyes began to close.

'Vega Jane! Are you here somewhere?'

My eyes snapped open and I looked wildly around.

'Delph?' I whispered. 'I'm over here, by the wall.'

From the darkened shadows stepped Delph, Petra and Harry Two.

I revealed myself to them by turning my ring back around. 'How did you get down here?'

'Some angry blokes with wands come through, and we decided where we were hiding wasn't all that safe. They went through a door and we slipped in behind them before it closed. Finally worked our way down here.'

'What'd you find out?' Petra asked.

'All those people from the train – I think the guards are doing something to their minds. If you hadn't called out, I think I would have lost *my* mind.'

I was thinking about the *Omniall* spell I had used back in the Quag to banish the mind of a creature called a wendigo. Was that what was happening here – a banishment of all those people's minds?

'Then what happens to 'em, do you think?' said Delph.

'Maybe that's why it's so peaceful here,' I said slowly, the puzzle blocks tumbling into place in my head. 'Why blokes get along and all. Why even people scrubbing stones are smiling like they have the life of leisure.'

We began to head back the way we had come until we could see the train once more.

'Shhh,' said Petra.

A group of cloaked figures with wands was approaching.

Quickly, I made us invisible again and we darted into the shadows.

I peered out at the figures. They *had* to be Maladons. They were dressed like the blokes at Saint Necro's.

In as low a voice as I could manage, I said, 'They know someone who shouldn't be is down here.'

The Maladons were walking side by side, spanning the entire passage and waving their wands in front of them. Light was coming out of the end of each.

I ducked back down and eyed the open train carriage door directly behind us. It was our only possible escape. 'This way, quick!' I hissed.

We moved backwards and on to the train carriage and leaped inside. Thankfully, it was empty.

I risked a quick look out the window and saw the Maladons heading our way.

'It's like they know where we are,' I hissed.

We hurried to the rear of the train and shrank back against the wall.

The Maladons entered the train and looked around. They walked slowly up the carriage, then turned to go. Only one hesitated. To my surprise, he took a long sniff, breathing in the air. He frowned.

Invisibility did not shield our *smell*. Perhaps the accursed bloke was sniffing out my canine.

I raised my wand and whispered, '*Confusio.*'

The spell hit him and he blinked. He turned and followed his mates off the train.

With a lurch and a long rasping noise, the train pulled out of the station.

I let out a long breath of relief. Then I thought of those people in that room having their minds emptied and filled up with nothing but tosh.

It was like my life in Wormwood – filled only with lies.

'Vega Jane,' said Delph, 'who do you suppose is driving this here train?'

'Dunno, do I?'

'And where do you suppose we're heading?' asked Petra.

'Same answer,' I said irritably.

5

MR ENDEMEN

When we were clear of the station, the train gathered speed and we were soon roaring through the dark countryside.

Covered by the invisibility shield, we searched the rest of the train, but every carriage was empty. We were the only ones on the entire train. Where were all the other passengers?

One of the carriages was different from the others. There were no windows, and, ominously, there were chains attached to each seat.

We went back to our carriage and settled in our seats, looking at each other anxiously. Delph said, 'I wonder who they put in chains? The ones they were messing with?'

I shook my head. 'Not them. I think they stay in True. You don't need to chain people who can't think for themselves.'

Petra said, 'But there's no one on the train.'

Delph looked up ahead and said, 'Some bloke's got to be steering this thing, don't he?'

I took out my wand, pointed it towards the front of the

train and said, '*Crystilado magnifica.*'

There were two males sitting in comfortable seats, chatting. They were wearing blue uniforms with caps, like the blokes I had seen directing the motors on the cobbles. In front of them, set into a large wooden board, was a vast array of shiny buttons and levers. Facing them was a large window showing what was in front of the train as it sped along. One of them lit a pipe.

I relinquished the magnification spell.

Delph seemed relieved. 'Well, at least someone is steering.'

'I wonder where we're going, though?' said Petra. 'Are they picking up more folks?'

'To bring them back here in the middle of the night and do things to their minds?' added Delph nervously.

I looked out the window and wondered how long till our destination, and what we would do when we got there. I touched my temple. The effects of whatever was happening in that room back in the bowels of the train station were gone, for the most part. But something lingered in my mind. Something so pleasing and wonderful and perfect, that it instinctively horrified me more than anything I had seen or fought in the Quag.

I looked back from where we had just come.

A place called True.

Ironic, I thought, since I now doubted there was even a smidgen of *truth* in the whole place. Simply more lies, like back in Wormwood.

Lies.

Ironic too that my kind – who were supposed to be the

good ones – and the evil Maladons used similar methods to keep people in line.

I rubbed my temple again. Images hovered at the edges of my mind, images associated with that wonderful, blurry feeling. I wanted to try and remember more.

A hand was reaching down from what looked to be the sky. In it was something truly bedazzling. I tried to focus. In the palm of the hand was . . . me! I was smiling and felt as light as air. I had never felt so perfect and happy and beautiful. The possibilities were truly limitless. I could accomplish anything. And what I wanted to accomplish was . . .

Here the images darkened a bit, but that didn't detract from my happiness in the slightest. I had a very brief vision of myself baking bread. Then I was on my hands and knees washing the cobbles. The next instant I was sweeping the floor. I felt happy. Whatever my desires turned out to be, I would be perfectly satisfied.

I opened my eyes. They weren't *my* desires.

They were the desires that someone else was telling me were my own.

What was being taken from those people was simply their lives. And the only thing the poor blokes had to do was keep on living the life that someone *else* had chosen for them.

The train roared on.

Delph took the first watch.

For once I slept soundly. The gentle swaying of the train carriage was hypnotic. I awoke refreshed, my mind once more eager to take on what lay ahead of us.

43

As Delph sat back in his seat and dozed off, I glanced out the window and noted the passing countryside. I glimpsed clusters of small homes, cows and sheep dozing or grazing, the bulge of a knoll, a stand of trees, open fields.

I looked down at Harry Two. He had never fallen asleep. Now his hackles were up and his fangs were bared.

'Delph, Petra!' I exclaimed.

They immediately awoke.

'What is it?' whispered Delph nervously.

'The train is slowing down.'

It was indeed now rapidly decreasing its speed.

I looked out the window, but there was only darkened countryside. There couldn't be a station hereabouts, could there?

Then I froze.

Things were whirling across the sky, so fast I could barely see them. They were like shooting stars, only far closer to the ground. I knew what they were.

They were coming for us.

'Get up,' I said. 'We have to get out of here.'

The flying shapes were now paralleling the path of the train. One pulled up close to our window.

It was a male dressed in a suit and a waistcoat. A brown bowler hat, like the one Duf Delphia used to wear, somehow managed to remain on his head despite the speed at which he was travelling.

A wand was clutched in his hand.

He peered inside the train carriage, his gaze sweeping all points of it. They had realized that we had somehow got on to the empty train. And they had caught up with us.

'Vega,' said Petra. 'Look!'

On the other side of the train were two more figures. They had their wands out too.

I grabbed the others and pushed them flat to the floor. A moment later the windows on the train exploded inward, showering us with glass, as spell after spell blasted across the width of the carriage.

We crawled on our bellies towards the rear of the carriage. Shattered glass cut my face. I heard Delph moan as a piece of wooden seat smacked him in the leg.

I thought about putting up a shield spell, but I knew that would certainly give us away as things magically rebounded off it.

A man shot through the open window and landed on the floor. He held his wand up, moving it back and forth, as though he was using it to ferret us out. I pointed my wand directly at his chest, backing the others away into the small vestibule.

Suddenly the carriage door was ripped open and another man hovered there. He was, like his companion, dressed neatly in a suit and bowler hat. He alighted on the floor.

Petra had her wand out and it was pointed at his chest. I held up a finger, signalling her to wait.

Just then, the train slammed to a halt, throwing us against the inside of the vestibule.

We picked ourselves up and jumped from the train, hitting the ground and rolling for a few feet. Fortunately our magical tether held. We peered through the long grass.

The train sat motionless while blurred figures soared around it. All the windows in all of the carriages had been blown out in the search for us.

The two blokes in the blue uniforms who had been steering the train were hauled out and dragged in front of the carriage by two men in suits and hats.

The taller of the two twirled his wand in his hand as he surveyed the drivers, who looked terrified. This was the bloke I had seen flying next to the carriage. When he took off his bowler hat I could see that he had straight dark hair, combed neatly around his head. His nose was long with not an imperfection on it. His mouth was but a slash of lips, cruel and remorseless. His eyes were so dark it was like looking at twin morta barrels.

He ran a hand through his hair and replaced his hat. When he spoke, his voice was calm. 'You saw no one?'

'No one, Mr Endemen, sir,' said one of the train drivers, his voice quivering.

Endemen replied, 'Yet they *were* seen.'

What did he mean — that we were seen? We were invisible.

Endemen continued smoothly. 'A tall young man with long dark hair, a pretty young woman with long blonde hair and a dog with one ear partially missing.'

My heart sank.

'And there was another. A girl. Even taller than the blonde. Darker hair. She's gangly and dirty.'

My knees went weak. How had anyone seen me?

'We . . . we saw no one, sir,' stammered the same man.

Endemen scrutinized him. 'And, as per your duties, you did a *thorough* search of the train before you left the station? We've had stowaways before, as you well know.'

The men in uniform were silent. Though I couldn't see

46

their faces fully, I could only imagine the terror that was going through them.

Endemen snapped his fingers.

Instantly, six more blokes wearing suits and bowler hats appeared out of thin air and encircled the pair, wands out.

'W-we did search,' said one of the men. 'Only we hadn't any reason to believe that—'

The driver would never finish what he was saying.

'Rigamorte,' said Endemen. The blast of black light hit the man full in the chest. He toppled forward and fell still.

I drew in a quick breath of air.

His companion dropped to his knees, his hands clasped together.

'Please, sir, Mr Endemen, we meant no harm. We was only—'

'Rigamorte.'

A moment later he joined his colleague on the ground.

Endemen looked down at the pair as though they were no more than bothersome insects.

He slid his wand back into his inner coat pocket and looked around. We ducked down into the grass.

'Dispose of these, Creel,' Endemen said to the shorter man standing next to him. 'Provide the standard evil Campions explanation to their families, appropriate compensation for their loss, any help we can convey, et cetera.'

'Yes, Mr Endemen.'

I felt my head whirling. *The evil Campions?*

Creel pointed his wand downward at the bodies and mumbled something I didn't catch. The two corpses were instantly bound in heavy blankets, with rope cinched tightly around them. Creel rose into the air and used his wand to direct the covered bodies to do the same. Then he was off in a flash of light.

Endemen looked at the others, who were all dressed as he was: pinstriped suit, waistcoat, tie, brown bowler hat, shiny shoes. And deadly wands.

He said, 'We will spread out and search this area, from the air to the ground. Keep the spell work to a minimum. Signal if you see anything. Wait for me before you kill. I want to ask some questions. Right, let's get to it.'

We silently lifted into the air and flew away as fast as I could manage. Petra was on the end, her wand pointed behind her at the group of evil sorcerers, who could fly fast and kill even faster. I knew if they spotted us, the fight would be a short one. We were no match at all for them.

The image of the two frightened men tumbling to the dirt was burned into my mind. I doubted I would ever forget it.

Then, just as the train faded from view, my wand swung downwards. And so did we.

Try as I might, there was nothing I could do.

We were plummeting from the sky.

6
A GUIDING WAND

Just as it looked like we would slam into the ground, my wand pointed slightly upward and we landed hard, but safely. I looked up in time to see a half dozen forms heading our way. It was Endemen and his cohorts.

My wand jerked towards the left and I felt myself being pulled to my feet by the power within it.

With my wand pointing the way, we raced towards the thick woods.

We reached the treeline and plunged into the welcome cover of the trunks and canopies. We ran until we could run no more. Then we stood, bent over, gasping for air. Even Harry Two was panting heavily.

Slowly, we all straightened.

I looked at Delph. He stared back at me. His features wore the same expression as mine:

Terror.

Petra broke the silence and said breathlessly, 'Well, I think we truly found the Maladons.'

'What now, Vega Jane?' said Delph.

I made us visible and said, 'We need to find a place to hide out.'

Just then, my wand jerked so violently to the left that I was nearly pulled off my feet. I had no way to stop it.

I was yanked through more thick forest, over a knoll, down to a narrow stream and, once I forded it, the wand pulled me back into the thicket of trees.

The others were running behind me, doing their best to keep up while my wand forced me along.

I raced through still more trees, dodging thick trunks and bending low to avoid branches and tearing through bushes, which left me scratched and bloody. But still my wand pulled me on. I was exhausted and growing more and more scared with each lunge of my legs and heave of my chest.

And then I cleared one last stand of trees and stopped dead.

Because my wand was no longer pulling me along.

It was simply pointing straight ahead.

I was standing in front of an old, enormous rambling house. It was a higgledy-piggledy mix of lichen-coated stone, aged brick and blackened wood. Its roof was made of mossy slate shingles of the kind that I had seen back in Wormwood. The windows were old and mullioned and the front door was stout oak with rusted iron bands across it. Half a dozen chimneys sprouted from its roof, but not a single one belched smoke. The place looked abandoned. The grounds around it were all grown over, neglected and full of weeds. A meandering stone path led from the edge of the grounds up to the front door.

With a rush, Delph, Petra and Harry Two hurtled into the clearing beside me.

'What the Hel, Vega Jane,' gasped Delph.

Petra looked at me suspiciously. 'What was all that about? Taking off like that without a word.'

Harry Two was staring at the house I'd just discovered. It seemed like his eyes were actually sparkling at the sight of it.

'It was my wand. It . . . it had a mind of its own.' I pointed at the house. 'It was leading me here.'

Delph straightened, saw the place and gaped.

Petra gasped. 'What is that thing?'

'I don't know,' I said. 'But I reckon we should go see what's inside. It's clearly been abandoned.'

'But what if those blokes happen upon it?' pointed out Petra. 'It's enormous. You can't exactly miss it.'

She had a point there.

The next moment though, we heard voices and footsteps.

'Quick,' I snapped. I raced up the meandering stone path and to the front door.

The others sprinted behind me.

I saw with a quick glance that there was a brass plate bolted to the wall next to the door. On the plate was a word.

EMPYREAN.

'Vega Jane,' said Delph. 'Let's become invisible again before we go in.'

'Good idea.' I turned the ring round and attached the magical tethers. We vanished from sight.

The portal opened at my push and I breathed a sigh

of relief. We all slipped through the door and I closed it quietly behind us.

We crept over to one of the windows and peered out.

Petra saw them first.

'There,' she said in a low voice.

From the left a man emerged from the woods. I caught a breath, for it was Endemen.

He was followed by two of his men. They all three had their wands out. Dressed in their immaculate suits with their bowler hats perched on their heads, they looked completely out of place in the woods.

They were *hunting* us.

And they would kill us if they found us.

Although we were invisible, we ducked down lower in the window as Endemen's gaze passed over us.

Endemen and his men were now within ten feet of the house.

I turned to Petra. 'If you have to, use the *Impacto* spell on the other two. But leave Endemen to me.'

She nodded, her eyes full of fear.

I had tried to sound confident, but I wasn't. I had the sinking feeling that whatever spell I used against him, Endemen would easily parry it before finishing me and then the others off.

The men started towards the house. Delph took Lackland's old, rusted sword out of his tuck and was holding it ready.

Even as I found his gaze, I knew what he was thinking.

A sword against a wand was not really a fair fight.

Harry Two nudged my arm and glanced at the window.

He wanted me to look back outside.

Endemen and his blokes were talking in low tones.

'They must have gone another way,' said one of the men to Endemen.

Endemen was frowning, his gaze sweeping around. Occasionally his gaze hit the house squarely, but he looked right through it.

The wonderful truth hit me.

I said, 'He can't see the house.'

'Aye, he can't,' agreed Delph.

'Is it because of your invisibility spell?' asked Petra in a low voice.

I shook my head. 'I can't think how it would be able to hide a place this big.'

'Look, they're heading off,' exclaimed Delph.

We watched as the men walked back to the woods. As Endemen reached the treeline, he turned around for a moment and looked thoughtfully in our direction.

As though attached at the hip, the four of us immediately ducked down below the windowsill.

When we looked back out a few seconds later, he was gone.

We collectively breathed a sigh of relief.

I turned to look over my shoulder at the interior of the house.

'Who lived here, I wonder?' asked Delph.

'Dunno. But I'm awfully glad it *is* here.'

'What do we do now?' Petra wanted to know.

I squared my shoulders.

'Find out what this place is, of course,' I said firmly.

7

EMPYREAN

Virtually every building I'd ventured into since leaving Wormwood had held elements of incredible danger. This place might not be any different.

'Be alert,' I said to the others as we moved forward.

The first obvious thing was the size of the place. Though from the outside it didn't appear nearly that large, it seemed to me that both Stacks *and* Steeples would fit comfortably inside this place.

A suit of armour stood guard in the large entrance hallway. It was spotless, though it had several large dents in it. In a holder by its side was a long, deadly-looking sword.

Every room we entered seemed larger than the last. The walls were wood, or stone, or tile, or even metal. The furnishings were large and comfortable. There was weaponry on the walls, battleaxes and lances and swords and knives and other things I didn't recognize, but which looked deadly enough.

The place was lighted by things we couldn't see. It seemed to me that captured in the ceiling were little swirls of illumination, almost like the cucos we had seen back in the Quag.

There were fireplaces aplenty, and bathrooms like the one I had seen at Morrigone's ages ago.

We entered a book-lined library with a large desk and comfortable chairs. Next, there was a kitchen so enormous it was hard to see the other end. It had a huge blackened metal stove and a fireplace with a large pot hanging from an iron hook. There was a long wooden table for eating and a cupboard full of plates, cloth napkins, cups and utensils, all neatly stacked.

I poked my head into another cupboard that was full of food of all types, again all neatly organized and obviously fresh. Though the style was old, from the worm-eaten beams on the ceiling to the venerable and colourful rugs on the knotty walnut floors, it all looked well kept.

And yet it was abandoned. Strange.

What fascinated me the most were the portraits on the walls. They all had the names of the subject on a little brass plate attached to the frame. I recognized some of them.

Bastion Cadmus's painting hung over the enormous fireplace in a room that was the largest we had seen thus far. He was a tall, strongly built, fierce-looking fellow with a short black beard, startling green eyes and thick brows that nearly touched in the centre of his forehead. I could understand why our lot had made him their leader. His masterful, tough, confident appearance seemed to fit the type.

So was this his old home? If so, that gave me some hope. He was a good bloke.

Astrea Prine's portrait occupied a prominent place in the library between two sets of bookcases. She looked like she had when we'd stayed at her cottage in the Quag. Young, intense, a bit foreboding really. A portrait of my ancestor Jasper Jane hung in a dark corner of a short hallway. Maybe because he liked to dabble in *dark* sorcery. But he had helped me in the Quag, or at least his soul had. Although the Fifth Circle of the Quag, which he had designed, had very nearly killed us all!

Then there were many other portraits of people I had never heard of, but who apparently held some important place in the magical world.

I found Delph in one corner of a room off the main hall staring up at one painting. I went over. The image was of a male astride a winged slep, or *horse* I guess these blokes would call it. On his shoulder was a large, menacing-looking hawk.

'Who is it, Delph?'

He pointed to the nameplate at the bottom of the painting.

'*Samuel Delphia*,' I read aloud. 'Delph, he's an ancestor of yours!'

Delph nodded. 'It looks like he gets along with beasts. Same as Dad. Bet they woulda got on right well.'

I put my hand on his shoulder. 'I bet they would have.'

He rubbed his eyes and wiped at his nose. 'I miss him, y'know, me dad. Hope he's OK.'

'I miss him too, Delph. But remember, he wanted you to leave Wormwood.'

'I know, Vega Jane. I know.'

56

Then his expression changed.

'Hang on, though. There was that bloke Barnabas Delphia back at Wolvercote Cemetery. And now Samuel. They were both magical – but *I'm* not. No mark on my hand or nothing.'

I studied his face. Delph wanted to be magical, more than anything. But it wasn't in my power to make him so.

'I know I never would have got this far without you, wand or not.'

He smiled at me and then looked around. 'You think this is a friendly place, eh, Vega Jane? I mean, it seems to only have our kind in the paintings. No Maladons, right?'

'Right,' I said cautiously. 'But remember how things started with Astrea Prine. And she's our kind.'

At my words, Delph instantly gripped his sword more tightly. Petra and I kept our wands at the ready.

I *wanted* to believe that this was a friendly place, but I had been fooled before.

Finally, I led us back to the kitchen and we set about making a meal, although I kept us invisible. We needed to keep our guard up.

I got the stove hot and put cured ham and sausages and a great slab of beef that was perfectly fresh into a big skillet. Petra started cutting up vegetables she'd found in containers in the pantry. Delph got the kettle in the fireplace filled with water from a pump in the sink and started a fire under it. He announced that he would be making soup.

There was a chamber off the kitchen behind a thick door. It was freezing inside and for good reason. In addition to the meat I had already got out, there was milk and cheeses and other perishables, including dough for bread. I took as much as I could carry.

Very soon the aromas of all the cooking food commingled into a mass of flavourful scents that made my mouth water. Poor Harry Two was actually panting in anticipation. But still, I felt uneasy.

Petra seemed to feel the same. She whispered, 'Vega, all this food here is good and fresh.'

I nodded.

'Someone lives here,' I whispered back. 'They might be here right now.'

'Why don't they show themselves?'

'Well, *we* haven't shown ourselves yet.'

'Right, but they must know someone is here. We're moving things around.'

'They might be scared. Things floating through the air and all.'

'They might,' she said, clearly not believing this.

Petra and I had laid out the plates, bowls, cups, utensils and napkins on the long wooden table.

I put food down for Harry Two, and when everything was ready we commenced eating, and didn't stop until our bellies were near to bursting. I had never had enough food to eat growing up and I savoured every mouthful, every bite and every swallow of the deliciously cool milk. After all, I had no idea what the next day would hold for us.

We finished our meal and walked up to the second floor of the house, reached by a broad, balustraded stairway that reminded me of the one at Stacks.

I looked at the others. 'Maybe we should all stay together

58

and invisible for the night.'

'No way,' Petra snapped. 'That'll make us an easy target. We searched this floor. There's no one up here and there are three bedrooms in a row. We can each take one and we'll be close enough to cry out if something happens.' She paused. 'Or Delph can stay with me and Harry Two with you.'

'Why not Delph with me and Harry Two with you?' I retorted.

'Because your canine will be pining all night for you.'

I glanced at Delph, whose face had turned red. 'Let's just each take a room,' I said tersely. 'Delph's room can be in the middle and I can put a shield spell on his door so *nobody* can disturb him.'

Petra gave a faint smile. 'Fine,' she said.

'And the term is *dog*, not canine,' I pointed out.

I released the tethers, and we said our goodnights and trudged off.

I turned my ring around so I became visible. If anything were going to attack us, I didn't want them to only go after Delph and Petra.

My bedchamber was large and well furnished. I hung up my few pieces of clothing in an ornately carved wardrobe, undressed and climbed into bed.

The house had inexplicably grown dark as soon as we finished our meal, so we had found and lit some candles, which we had carried upstairs.

Harry Two jumped up on to the bed and settled down at the foot of it.

I blew out my candle and lay my head back against the pillow.

That's when I saw it.

Or rather *her*. A woman was staring down at me from the ceiling.

I very nearly screamed.

Then I realized it was simply a painting of a young woman. She had long, flowing blonde hair and large blue eyes. Her cheeks were pink and healthy, but the expression on her face was the saddest I had ever seen.

I felt my own mouth curving downward and my forehead knot into a frown as I stared at her.

I wondered who she was. Why her portrait was on the ceiling and not framed on the wall like the others.

And why I could see her at all, given that it was pitch dark.

I sat up and lit my candle.

That was when I received my second shock.

She'd disappeared. The ceiling was now merely blank plaster.

I thrust off my bedcovers and stood on the bed and then on my tiptoes to get a better look. I held my candle as high as I could.

There was nothing to see.

I sat back down and blew out the candle.

And waited.

Sure enough, she appeared. Only now her hair waved slightly, as though in a breeze.

I grabbed my wand off the nightstand and held it ready.

But she made no sudden movements. Her eyes now blinked and her mouth moved slightly. I had the distinct impression that she was watching me.

'Who are you?'

The words floated down to me, soft, lovely sounding, but inked in them was despair and loss.

I-I'm Vega Jane.

I gasped when the woman, body and all, floated down from the ceiling to sit next to me.

Harry Two turned to stare at her. But he made no sound. This gave me courage; usually he sensed danger before I did.

'Vega Jane?' she said.

The large eyes took me in, from head to foot.

I nodded. 'Who are you?'

'I am called Uma.'

Uma? Uma? I had seen that name somewhere; I just couldn't remember where.

'Is this your home?' I asked.

I realized, though, that I could see pretty much right through her. Her clothes were not of this time. She was clearly from the past.

'No. But I came here often. I like it here.'

'Are you . . . ?'

She nodded. 'I *am* dead. And have been for a very long time.'

I realized where I'd seen the name before. On a gravestone at Wolvercote Cemetery, right before we'd entered the First Circle of the Quag.

'You're Uma Cadmus? Your father was Bastion Cadmus!'

She nodded.

'Are you a ghost?'

She shook her head. 'Not a ghost, no.'

'I'm not seeing your soul then, am I? I saw my ancestor Jasper Jane's soul once.'

'No, I am not a soul.'

Well, I had exhausted all my possible choices. 'What are you, then?'

'Regret.'

'Regret? What does that mean? We all have regrets.'

'Indeed we do. But some are far greater than others. If they are powerful enough, they can consume you completely. That is my fate. For eternity.'

With that ominous answer, she vanished. I lay back in bed after giving Harry Two a reassuring pat.

So this wasn't her home, even though there was a large painting of her father downstairs. This place must have belonged to someone else. And regret? I wondered what she regretted so much.

I pulled the bedcovers up closer around me, as though the bit of fabric would protect me from all evil.

That's when I heard the scream.

8

THIS HOUSE OF MINE

I sprinted into the hallway, Harry Two barking at my heels. I released the shield spell on Delph's bedroom door and it flew open, revealing an anxious-looking Delph in his nightshirt.

'It's Petra!' I exclaimed.

We ran to her door, my wand out and ready. Delph reached the door first and tried to open it. He bounced off.

Petra screamed again.

Delph charged the door once more, slamming his full weight against it.

He was flung back off like he weighed nothing.

I pointed my wand and said, 'Ingressio.'

My spell rebounded, but I saw the door buckle a bit.

'Impacto,' I cried out, and the door exploded into fragments.

We rushed inside to see Petra hanging upside down from the ceiling, a maelstrom of light, flashing figures and fire all around her struggling body. Objects were striking her from all angles, and each collision caused another cut to her skin.

I was so stunned by what I saw that for a moment I didn't know what to do, but Petra's cry focused me once more.

'Vega! Help me!'

I raised my wand and cast a shield spell around her.

The lightning-fast objects bounced off it and whizzed around the room.

Delph, Harry Two and I had to duck.

I raised my wand once more. *'Paralycto.'*

The explosion of whizzing things froze in mid-air.

We slowly rose. I pointed my wand at Petra at the same time as I said to Delph, 'Get ready.'

I shouted, *'Unlassado.'*

A light shot out from the point of my wand and hit the ceiling next to Petra's feet.

She was freed and plummeted down, into Delph's arms.

I watched as she wrapped her arms around Delph's thick neck and buried her weeping face in his massive chest.

''Tis OK,' he murmured to her. ''Tis all right now, Pet.'

Delph looked past me over her head, and I saw his eyes widen in terror.

I whirled around, my wand at the ready.

The breath caught in my throat.

In the doorway stood the suit of armour that had been in the entrance hallway. Even as I watched, a gloved hand rose and opened the metal visor.

I staggered back because there was no face behind the visor, only darkness.

A voice boomed out as the gloved hand pointed straight at Petra.

'*She* is a Maladon! *She* must die the death of a thousand wounds.'

I kept my wand raised.

'I'm . . . I'm not a Maladon,' Petra said weakly.

'Liar,' roared the armour. 'We know. We always know when one is in our midst. And we are never wrong. We waited until she was alone, lest she try to hurt the two of you.' Now the helmeted head turned in my direction. 'You are obviously a sorceress and not a Maladon. Thus, you must kill her. She is your sworn enemy.'

'No,' I said. 'She's not my enemy. She's my friend.'

'*Kill her!*' the suit of armour screamed.

'No!' I yelled back.

'Then you leave me no choice.'

It drew out its long sword and raised it up high.

I darted to stand between the armour and Petra.

'To kill her, you have to kill me. And I'm, well, I'm a handful, I am,' I finished awkwardly.

The armour stared at me. If a faceless thing can stare, that is.

'You turn against your own people?' said the armour.

'I turn against no one. Um, what is your name?' I asked, trying to calm things down.

'Lord Unctuous of Pillsbury,' he announced in a dignified voice.

'OK, Lord, um – is it Lord Unctuous, or Lord Pillsbury, or all of it?'

The armour took a moment to consider this. 'Lord Pillsbury will suffice,' he said.

'OK, Lord Pillsbury. Petra here has helped me fight and defeat a number of Maladons already. We just managed to escape a bloke calling himself Mr Endemen, right outside the house.'

When I said the name *Endemen*, I saw Lord Pillsbury's metal body flinch.

He said gruffly, 'Endemen? Endemen, did you say?'

'Yes, I do say. Who is he?'

'A Maladon,' barked Pillsbury. 'A horrible, mad, evil, ruthless, disgusting—'

'Right,' I said, interrupting. 'Well, that one I'd figured out on my own.'

'He is very dangerous,' Lord Pillsbury said more soberly.

'I saw him kill two blokes and smile about it.'

Lord Pillsbury shivered in his armoured hide. 'Most distasteful.'

'But he couldn't see this place, could he?' I said.

'Obviously not. Else he would be inside now, attempting to murder us all. The enchantments around this structure are designed to make it totally invisible to Maladons.'

I pointed at Petra. 'But *she* can see this place. She's inside it. So logically speaking she can't be a Maladon.'

Pillsbury's visor swivelled around to Petra. He looked her up and down. A moment later he swivelled back to me.

'I think you might have a point,' he conceded.

'I think I might,' I said smoothly.

Lord Pillsbury lowered his sword. ''Tis a bit delicate, though. Our anti-Maladon warning enchantments are normally quite accurate.'

'Your best one being that this place is hidden from them?' I said.

His visor nodded. 'Quite right. Well, absolutely no

sense in allies fighting among themselves.'

I relaxed and lowered my wand. Something he'd said made me curious.

'Lord Pillsbury, you said you had never been wrong about Maladons being in your midst. But if they can't see this place, how could a true Maladon ever come to be here?'

'Ah, well, that was *before*, wasn't it?'

'Before what?'

'Before the war. Before they started calling themselves the *Maladons*,' he said derisively.

I still didn't completely understand, but I was curious about something else. 'And you're . . . what, exactly?'

'I'm part of the rear guard, left behind to do our best to prevent the Maladons from finding any of our kind. To do whatever we can to wreak havoc on the blasted creatures. We've been quite successful with the first part.'

'And the wreaking-havoc-on-the-Maladons part?' I enquired.

'No luck at all, I'm afraid. But it's early days yet,' he added confidently.

'Early days!' Delph blurted out. 'It's been about eight hundred years, mate.' He frowned and nodded to Petra, who was still in his big arms, much to my annoyance. 'She's bleeding, by the way, Vega Jane.'

'Holy Steeples,' I cried out. I ran past Lord Pillsbury, dashed down the hall, grabbed the Adder Stone from my cloak, ran back and waved it over Petra, thinking good thoughts. Her cuts and gashes instantly vanished, along with the blood.

I looked at Delph. 'I think you can let her down now,

Delph,' I said, trying to sound as casual as possible, though I wanted to rip her out of his arms.

'Right.'

He nearly dropped poor Petra on the floor.

I turned back to Lord Pillsbury, who was staring at me closely.

'Did . . . did this young gentleman call you Vega *Jane?*'

'Well, that is my name.'

'Do you mean to say that you're a *Jane?*'

'Yes. And this is Delph Delphia and Petra Sonnet and my dog, Harry Two. We were in the town of True, do you know it?'

His helmeted head swivelled back and forth. 'No. But then again, we never leave this place.'

'Which might be why you haven't managed to wreak havoc on the Maladons,' I replied gently.

'Once more, I believe you have a point, milady.'

'How many more of you are there?'

'About four dozen, if you count the outside staff and the lads in the cellar.'

'Are you all suits of armour?'

'Oh, no. I'm the only one of those. The major-domo, as it were. The rest are a mishmash of lamps, the odd bit of furniture, various household instruments, that sort of thing. Some of the portraits, though they don't get around much, being hung on a wall and all. They do add a bit of style, I've always thought. And five marble statues, three rakes, two wheelbarrows and a scythe that take care of the grounds. All good blokes.'

Petra said, 'Well, the grounds are in pretty bad shape.

68

Maybe you should spend more time tending them rather than trying to kill your guests!'

'Petra,' admonished Delph. 'They didn't know.'

'They didn't ask either. They just stormed in here and commenced attacking me!'

Lord Pillsbury nodded his visor. 'I do apologize for our, well, our unseemly behaviour. Regarding your observation about the grounds, there's been no real reason to keep them up, having no one staying here who can enjoy them.'

'How did you all come to be?' I asked.

'Our masters bewitched us long ago. Long before the war. We served them faithfully.' He added sombrely, 'Right up until the end.'

'When I mentioned the Endemen bloke, you seemed to know who he is.'

'We've seen him lurking outside and heard his men refer to him by name. He knows something is here; he just doesn't know what . . .' He paused. 'And we've also seen him kill. People. And he kills animals for pleasure.'

That foul man. I automatically put out a hand and scratched Harry Two's one remaining ear.

'What would you do if he finally overcame the enchantment and was able to see this place?'

'We would of course fight to the death. Those were our instructions. We would gladly give our lives – well, whatever it is we actually have – to defend this place.'

I looked around. 'What exactly *is* this place?'

'Why, if you're truly a Jane, you should know.'

'Know what?'

'Empyrean is your ancestral home, Mistress Vega.'

9

A HEART REVEALED

'My . . . ancestral h-home?' I spluttered.

Lord Pillsbury nodded. 'Absolutely. Empyrean belongs to you. The last Jane in residence was Mistress Alice Adronis – Alice Jane, before she married Gunther Adronis and he came to live here with her. You might have seen his portrait. He was quite big-hearted, was Master Gunther.' He added sadly, 'Perhaps too big-hearted.'

'So you knew them?' I asked.

If a suit of armour could show emotion, Lord Pillsbury did then.

'I had the honour of *serving* them, yes.'

'What were they like?' I asked. I well remembered the dying Alice Adronis. She had seemed noble and brave and all those good things. But I also knew that Alice was one of the fiercest warriors we had, killing Maladons left and right.

'They were very kind, Mistress Vega. Very kind indeed. They wanted no part of a war. But they fought because they had to.'

It was as though the metal bloke had read my mind.

'That's good to know, Lord Pillsbury.'

'Please, call me Pillsbury; the "lord" part is just for show. It would bring all of us staff much joy to be able to once more serve the House of Jane. The outside staff is champing at the bit to get the grounds up to snuff, I can tell you that. Now they have proper reason.'

I glanced at Delph and Petra. They were standing there open-mouthed.

I turned back to Pillsbury. 'Well, all right, Lor— um, I mean, Pillsbury. If you're sure.'

He clicked his metallic heels. 'Quite sure, milady. Now, as it is rather late, I would suggest that you all return to your bedchambers. That will give us time to spruce up the place. We were not expecting company, you see. Would you like to convey your breakfast orders now? Mrs Jolly is a fine cook.'

'Mrs Jolly?' I said. 'We made ourselves dinner, but we didn't see anyone in the kitchen.'

'Well, the fact is, Mistress Vega, we couldn't see you! Gave us quite a turn when doors started opening and pans, knives and plates started floating through the air. Mrs Jolly was quite naturally hiding in the broom closet half frightened out of her twigs.'

'Out of her twigs?' I said. 'What exactly *is* Mrs Jolly?'

'A broom, hence the broom cupboard. But she does a steak and kidney pudding that is – well, if I required food, I'm sure I would enjoy it very much. Now, your breakfast orders?'

Delph spoke up at once. 'I'll have, well, pretty much everything.'

Pillsbury swept a long quill from the inside of his visor and wrote this down on the metal palm of his hand. 'The full breakfast, outstanding.' He looked up at Delph. 'Yes,' he said appraisingly. 'I would imagine it takes quite a lot of wood to keep your chimney hot, young sir.'

His visor came to rest on Petra. She scowled back at him.

'You tried to kill me.'

Pillsbury said in an apologetic voice, 'Yes, miss, I did. Ever so sorry that we got off on the wrong foot. Now, what can we arrange for your breakfast?'

She suddenly looked uncertain. 'I'm not sure.'

I said, 'Perhaps you might be able to suggest something for Petra?'

Petra shot me a grateful look while Pillsbury said delightedly, 'Oh, absolutely, milady. Some eggs, perhaps? Mrs Jolly does a wonderful omelette with bacon and tomato with just a touch of the freshest basil. A few croissants, some porridge – and the sausages really are worth trying.'

'That . . . that sounds wonderful,' said Petra.

'Smashing,' said Pillsbury, turning to me. 'And you, Mistress Vega?'

'I'll have what Petra's having,' I replied.

Pillsbury wrote all this on his palm. 'Excellent. Well.' He looked at the pulverized door. 'Mistress Vega, perhaps you might be able to rectify this?'

'What? Oh, right, I'll fix it.'

I pointed my wand at the shards of wood, recalled the proper incantation Astrea had taught me and said, 'Assemblage.'

The pieces of wood flew back together into a door that hung itself neatly back on the hinges.

'May I say, very nicely done, Mistress Vega,' said Pillsbury.

'You don't have to call me that, you know.'

'As a Jane, you are now the mistress of this house. We are here to serve you.'

'How do you know I really am a Jane?' I said curiously. 'I just said I was. I could be lying.'

He pointed at my wand. 'That is Mistress Alice's wand. I will never forget it. It was also her—'

'Elemental,' I said, cutting in.

'Precisely so. Only a true Jane could wield magic with it.'

I glanced at the re-formed door. 'So that was a test, then?'

'I do apologize. But one can never be too careful in such troubled times, milady. Now I'm off. I hope you sleep well. If at any time you need anything, you only need to say my name and I shall appear.'

And with that, he turned and lumbered out of the room.

We all looked at one another.

Delph gasped, 'Pretty unbelievable.'

Petra was looking around in awe. 'Of all the luck.'

Delph yawned. 'I'm off to bed. See you at breakfast.' He ambled off.

Petra sat on the bed, looking defiantly at me. There was a strained silence.

'I'm not one of those Maladons,' she said at last. 'I don't care what their blasted enchanted whatsit says.'

'No, I don't believe you are.'

'Yes, you do!' she shot back. 'I see the way you and Delph look at me. Even Harry Two there watches me closely, like I'll attack you given the chance.'

'Don't be silly.'

'Silly! One of your *servants* just tried to kill me!'

'And I stopped them. Why would I have done that if I thought you were a Maladon?'

'I've got Maladon blood in me, haven't I? That's what they were sensing.'

'So what? You can *see* this place, can't you? Even if you have a bit of Maladon blood in you, it's obviously been outweighed by, well, the good stuff.'

I sat on the bed next to her. I knew what it was like to feel different. I'd felt that way back in Wormwood when I discovered I had powers that no one else there did. I also wanted to know things about my past. I wanted to know what was beyond the Quag. Other than Delph, no one in Wormwood was interested in any of that. It made me feel like an outsider, like I didn't belong.

'Petra, you have no way of controlling who your ancestors were, or what they did. Same as me.'

'But at least your ancestors were good. Mine were evil. Just like that Endemen bloke.' She looked away so I wouldn't see the tears in her eyes.

I put a hand on her shoulder. 'You're not evil, Petra. Without you we wouldn't have made it here. You were brave and strong and you fought *against* the evil. Not for it.'

'But what if . . . what if I change?'

Her eyes were fixed on mine. I knew what she wanted

74

me to say: that she could never become evil. That she could never truly become a Maladon. But I couldn't say that. I could only tell her the truth.

'I trust you, Petra. I've trusted you with my life before. And I will trust you with my life again.'

'You really mean that?'

'I really mean that,' I answered.

Our eyes met for a long moment. Then she touched my hand with hers and said, 'I trust you too, Vega. You've saved my life, more times than I can count.'

'We have to be there for each other. We're both magical. Delph isn't. We can't let anything happen to him.'

'I'd die before I let him come to any harm,' she said immediately.

This both pleased and bothered me.

'Get some sleep,' I said.

She nodded and slid under the covers.

As I reached the door, I turned back to see her watching me.

I closed the door behind me and walked slowly back to my room with Harry Two beside me.

I shut and locked my door and climbed under the covers.

I took out my wand and stared at it. It had led me here – to Empyrean. The home of Alice Adronis.

Alice and her husband, Gunther. Uma Cadmus. Her father, Bastion. All the others in those portraits. They were my past. Some were my family. And, so it seemed, my future too.

10
UMA AND JASON

A polite rap on the door woke me. I rubbed my eyes and sat up in bed.

'Hello?' I said groggily.

''Tis Pillsbury with your breakfast, Mistress Vega.'

'Oh, OK. Come in, then.'

Harry Two popped up when the door opened, and there was Pillsbury, his metal gleaming so brightly that I suspected he might have polished himself up during the night. He was carrying a short-legged wooden table, upon which sat several dishes covered with pewter lids.

Pillsbury placed the little table over my lap.

He uncovered the dish lids, revealing a wonderful array of food, all smelling delicious.

I looked up at him and said in a near moan, 'This is fantastic, Pillsbury.'

'Mrs Jolly will be so pleased.' He uncovered one more bowl, which had a divider. One half was filled with food and the other with water.

'I took the liberty of preparing Harry Two's meal as well.'

He set this on the floor, and Harry Two jumped down, gave a bark of thanks and dug in.

Pillsbury unrolled my cloth napkin and handed it to me, and then poured out a steaming cup of tea.

'I hope everything will be to your liking, Mistress Vega.'

'I'm sure it will. I'll come to the kitchen and tell Mrs Jolly myself.'

'She would be extremely pleased and honoured if you did,' he said. 'When you're done, you need only say "Pillsbury" and I will return to collect the dishes.'

As he turned to leave I said, 'Uh, Pillsbury?'

He immediately pivoted. 'Yes, milady?'

'I had a visitor in my room last night. Her name was Uma.'

'Oh, dear. I had no idea. I thought she might have left us. It has been a very long time since I've seen her.'

'I know she's Bastion Cadmus's daughter. I saw her grave in the Quag at Wolvercote Cemetery.'

He gave a sharp intake of breath. 'You . . . you saw her grave?'

'Yes, I did. The tombstone said . . .' I paused, thinking back.

Pillsbury said sombrely, *The Strength of Love, the Fallacy of Youth*. We knew the Cadmuses well. They visited often when Mistress Alice was alive. Such happy times. It was so very sad what happened.'

'What *did* happen?'

He said imploringly, 'Please, miss, your food will grow cold.'

I looked down at the tray. Curiosity wrestled with

hunger, and hunger won.

'OK, but when I'm done, will you tell me?'

'You need only utter my name,' he said a bit grimly.

He left, and I instantly started to eat. The food was wonderful. I thought I could hear myself purring.

Twenty minutes later I was done. I pondered what to do next. I moved the tray aside and opened the door next to my bed. This was a bathroom, like at Morrigone's back in Wormwood.

I did my business, cleaned up, changed into fresh clothes, left my room and knocked on Delph's door.

'Delph? Are you decent?'

The door opened, and Delph stood there, fully dressed in some of the clothes we had nicked from Saint Necro's back in True. A white shirt with a collar, a waistcoat, a tweed jacket and trousers, and sturdy shoes. He had cleaned up and washed his hair, which was long, thick and smelt wonderful.

'Have you finished eating?' I said.

I saw that Pillsbury had brought in an entire rolling table to accommodate Delph's breakfast. I could also see that every plate and bowl was clean.

'Yep,' he said. 'That Mrs Jolly knows her way round the kitchen, she does.'

'Come to my room. I want to ask Pillsbury about something that might be important.'

'OK. What about Petra?'

I glanced down the hall at Petra's door. 'After last night, let's just let her have a lie-in,' I said.

Back in my room, I said the name 'Pillsbury'.

He instantly appeared at the door, as though he could perform the *Pass-pusay* incantation.

'Yes, Mistress Vega? All done, are we?'

'Yes, Pillsbury, and it was absolutely amazing. Now, I want you to tell Delph and me about Uma Cadmus.'

Pillsbury shuffled forward. 'Yes, miss, of course.' He hesitated. 'Now, where to begin.'

'Perhaps at the very beginning?' I suggested.

'Yes, yes, of course.' He cleared his throat as Delph and I settled down in two comfortable chairs to listen.

'Bastion Cadmus was the leader of our people, and he and his wife, Victoria, had only one child, Uma. She was everything to them.'

'How sad that she died so young,' I said.

'Yes,' said Pillsbury, not meeting my gaze. 'Very sad indeed. Uma was a lovely girl. Beautiful, and so full of goodness. As she grew up, it naturally became a topic of discussion and speculation as to whom she might marry one day.'

'I'm sure there were many young men who would have been right happy to marry her,' I said.

'Oh, indeed there were. But you have to understand that although this was before the war with the Maladons, there was already unrest. The Maladons' leader, the accursed Necro—'

'Necro?' I exclaimed. 'There's a Saint Necro in the town of True. It's a place where people go to worship.'

'Indeed?' he said curiously. 'Necro's followers *did* worship him, though he was a foul man.'

'You knew him?'

79

'He came here, several times. You see, there were efforts to forestall a war. Talks, discussions, negotiations. The Janes and the Adronises and Bastion Cadmus were at the head of this effort. I well remember the bloke. His face, oh so pale and smooth, and his voice, so silky. But there was pure evil in him. I knew from the moment I laid eyes on him that these efforts to avoid war were doomed. Necro wanted to rule not only the Maladons, but *everyone*.'

'And Uma?'

'Well, Uma *did* find a young man whom she dearly loved. His name was Jason. He was, ah, Necro's son.'

'What?' I nearly shrieked.

'Blimey,' said Delph. 'That was a bit awkward, eh?'

'More than a bit,' conceded Pillsbury. 'They kept their relationship a secret for a long time. But it was eventually discovered.'

'And what happened?' I asked.

'At first our side thought it was a positive development, that it might help with a truce. That perhaps Uma and Jason, who was very unlike his devilish father, might come to power one day and ensure peace. But alas, that was not to be.'

'Why not?'

'Jason died,' Pillsbury said simply.

Delph said, 'How did he die?'

'He was stabbed. His killer was never caught, but there were suspicions – that his father had had him killed. You see, Necro did not want a truce. He wanted war. He said that our side was responsible and swore revenge. It was all part of his plan.'

'But to kill his own son?' I said.

'As I told you, Necro was evil. He would kill anyone if it meant his rise to power would continue.'

'And Uma?' I asked.

'So very sad. She was found shortly after, along the banks of the river. It is thought that she could not bear the news of his death.'

'Holy Steeples!' I exclaimed.

Delph shook his head sadly. "Tain't right,' he said. 'Just ain't right.'

'Then what happened?' I asked breathlessly.

'War,' he said simply.

'And our lot lost,' I finished.

His visor nodded up and down. 'Yes, quite so. Our lot lost.'

As he finished speaking, I had only one thought:

We could not lose again.

11

A PAINTING COMES CALLING

Pillsbury had suggested we might like to see Jasper Jane's workshop and we'd readily agreed – the sad story of Uma and Jason had left us in a sombre mood. Seeing my ancestor's chambers was unnerving. They reminded me a great deal of Thorne's laboratory back in the Quag.

The chambers sat in the very highest turret at Empyrean. There were tables and benches overflowing with odd devices, huge old books, and reams of parchments covered in spidery handwriting. Shelves and cabinets against the walls were crammed with bottles containing different-coloured liquids and jars with bits of things I didn't recognize. Big bottles with tubing connecting them stood on one long table in the centre of the room. Little canisters I recognized as the flame boxes we used at Stacks were under some of the bottles. Animal hides and heads of unfamiliar creatures were nailed to the walls or seated on tall pedestals.

Harry Two let out a protesting howl when he saw the myriad animal heads. Delph just stared in silence.

Pillsbury said proudly, 'Master Jasper had quite the active mind. Was always researching something or other. Would be up here all hours, days on end. I'd have to bring him his meals in here. And the smells.' His metal body shivered. 'They were memorable; I'll leave it at that.'

I stared around, feeling oddly nervous. This room had belonged to a member of my family, a family I had never even known existed.

Pillsbury, perhaps sensing my unease, said, 'May I leave you to it, Mistress Vega? I have a few things to attend to.'

'Oh, right, yes, go ahead, Pillsbury. We'll be fine.'

He gave me a comically deep bow – I actually thought he might get stuck halfway – and then he was off.

'Blimey, Vega Jane,' said Delph. 'What do we do with all this?'

'There might be some information here that could be useful. We just start looking.'

We had begun to search the chamber when a dishevelled-looking Petra appeared in the doorway.

She said crossly, 'I've been looking all over for you two. I saw Pillsbury on the stairs. He said you were up here. Why didn't you come and get me?'

I said, almost truthfully, 'We thought we'd let you sleep in, Petra, after last night.'

She eyed me suspiciously. 'Right, well, thanks. It *was* nice to have some extra rest.' She looked around. 'What is this place?'

I explained about my ancestor Jasper, and about Uma and Jason.

'That's very sad,' she said at last. 'You think there might

be some answers here?'

I shrugged. 'Who knows?'

We continued to search. We found many things, many obscure, inexplicable things. Some showed that Jasper, as Astrea Prine had already told me, was indeed intrigued by dark sorcery.

I found an old diary in a desk drawer. There was no writing inside it, so I thrust it into my pocket, thinking that I would make use of it with my own notes.

A mirror encased in silver was lying on Jasper's desk and I held it up to my face. My hair was a mess and I smoothed it down.

And then my heart stopped.

Uma was inside the glass.

I nearly dropped it.

Her mouth was moving. I couldn't hear what she was saying, but then she wasn't talking to me. She was talking to the figure who came to stand beside her.

He was, well, he was spiffing gorgeous. Tall and broad shouldered with long dark hair and the most amazingly beautiful blue eyes.

He actually looked a bit like Delph, come to think . . .

When I looked closer, I saw he had his arm around Uma's waist. They looked at each other, so obviously in love, and I knew who he was.

Jason, Necro's son.

The two tragically doomed lovers were right here in front of me.

As I continued to watch, they leaned towards each other and kissed. I felt my cheeks growing red.

Embarrassed that I was intruding on such a private moment, I looked away. When I glanced back, the glass was empty.

They were gone.

'Vega Jane?'

The voice came from right beside me and I jumped, dropping the mirror. It hit the desk and shattered.

I glared at Delph.

'Look what you made me do,' I said crossly.

'I was calling you and you didn't answer. I thought something was wrong. Like you'd –' he glanced down at the shattered mirror – 'had magic done on you or something.'

I picked up the pieces of the mirror. 'Sorry.'

'What's going on?' Petra asked. 'Find anything?'

I held up the pieces of the mirror. 'I just saw Uma and Jason in this mirror kissing.'

Petra looked sceptical. 'In that glass. You're sure?'

I rolled my eyes. 'You think I might have imagined a dead bloke kissing a dead woman who was on my bedroom ceiling last night?'

'Maybe,' she said, with a grin. 'Come on, it must be nearly time to eat.'

We returned to our rooms to wash. Pillsbury informed us that lunch would be served in the conservatory, whatever that was.

When I came out of the washroom, I noticed it.

There was a painting hanging on the wall across from my bed that hadn't been there before. As I drew closer, I could see who it depicted.

Alice Adronis.

Alice *Jane* Adronis, more precisely.

I had wondered why I had not seen a portrait of her until now; it was her home, after all.

I remembered the painting I had seen of her back in Astrea's cottage in the Quag. She had been dressed fetchingly in a dazzling gown with a plunging neckline, her hair piled on top of her head, her features so sharply defined, her expression commanding. She was very beautiful, but I had been more captivated by the sense of strength and barely restrained power in her whole being.

In this portrait, Alice was in full battle gear, chain mail, helmet in one hand, the full-size Elemental in the other. This was Alice Adronis perhaps at her most comfortable, most natural. Most formidable. A warrior, about to enter a battlefield and fight to the death with every bit of strength, courage and cunning she had.

I had seen her do this very thing.

I had also seen her die.

I looked into her eyes, which seemed to hold flames in their centre. I knew that Alice would be unafraid of even Mr Endemen. She would battle him as an equal. She would win.

I said, 'Pillsbury?'

An instant later he was standing at my doorway.

'Yes, Mistress Vega?'

I pointed to the portrait. 'Did you put that in here?'

He came forward and stared at the painting, bewildered. 'No, I didn't. I've no idea how it came to be here. But you should know – the house has its peculiarities. Things come and things go. Things turn up where they *naturally* should be. That's the best way I can explain things. And now I must see to lunch.'

In another instant he was gone.

I slowly turned back to the painting and received another jolt. No. *That was impossible.*

I rubbed my eyes.

When I looked at the portrait once more, it was all as it should be. Alice stared back at me from the depths of the oils and canvas.

But for one moment, one chilling, electrifying, terrifying moment, I'd thought . . .

I'd thought that it was *me* in the portrait.

12
A CHOICE TO BE MADE

The conservatory turned out to be huge with glass walls supported by a metal framework. There was a door leading outside to the rear grounds, which now looked spectacular, with everything in bloom.

I said so to Pillsbury. 'Well, the lads worked all night to get things up to scratch for you,' he said proudly.

'Where are they?' I asked.

He pointed to another part of the garden. Through the window I could see marble statuary toiling away in the grounds. A rake was collecting grass clippings. Further back a scythe was mowing down weeds. Then a wheelbarrow came into view. It was full of twigs and dead leaves and was rolling itself down a flagstone path.

'The outdoor staff,' said Pillsbury proudly. 'All fine lads.'

'Please give them my thanks.'

'I will indeed.'

Another door leading into the conservatory opened and in whirled what appeared to be Mrs Jolly. She was, as Pillsbury had said, a broom – but on the top of the broomstick, which fanned out to a good six inches, was set a pair of eyes, a nose and a mouth, which were not made of wood and seemed very similar in appearance to mine. She broke into a lovely smile that warmed my heart like a cosy fire.

'Hello, luvs,' she said brightly.

'Hello,' we all said back.

'Your cooking is the best I've ever had,' I told her.

She beamed as Delph ravenously eyed the cart she had pushed in. Even with the little lids on, the most wonderful aromas were escaping.

The lids came off and the plates rose into the air and then settled neatly on a table where napkins and cutlery suddenly appeared at three place settings. There was even food and water for Harry Two.

Petra looked dazed. After the life she'd led in the Quag, this must have seemed like the most wonderful world imaginable: a beautiful home, food prepared for us, servants galore and a safe warm bed in which to sleep without the worry of snarling beasts.

It would be very easy to live here forever, I thought.

'Now, tuck in while it's still hot,' Mrs Jolly advised, and whirled out again.

Delph and Petra began to eat hungrily. I found myself hesitating, though.

'What's up?' asked Delph in between bites. 'Not hungry?'

'No, it's not that.' I sighed. 'I was thinking about everybody back in Wormwood. And those living in the Quag. They don't have food like this to eat, except perhaps for Morrigone and Astrea Prine. They're not living in such comfort either. Or safety.'

Delph looked stricken at my words.

Petra, however, shrugged. 'So what? Everyone has a different lot in life. This is yours. That is theirs.'

I looked at her in surprise. She sounded cruel and uncaring.

'We had nothing for the longest time,' said Delph. 'We crossed the Quag, where we were in danger every sliver. I think we might've earned a bit of comfort, eh?'

His words were eminently reasonable, but they made me more upset than Petra's had.

'I don't want to forget where I came from,' I said. 'Even if you don't seem to care.'

He looked hurt and I immediately felt bad. But I couldn't take it back. So I got up and went outside and into the garden.

I found a bench in a secluded spot, out of sight of the house. I just wanted to be alone and to think.

I had to admit, I loved this place. I loved everything about it. I had never owned anything in my whole life. To be told that this magnificent place was mine . . . well, I just could hardly believe it. And yet a big part of me also didn't think that I deserved it. After all, I hadn't built it. I hadn't fought in a war. It wasn't really mine at all.

As I sat there, Harry Two bounded around the corner. He had no doubt sniffed me out. He sat next to me by the bench and I idly stroked his fluffy ear.

Just then, something was moving in my pocket. I yelped and shot to my feet, wondering wildly if it was a snake.

But then it came flying free and came to rest suspended

in the air in front of me.

It was the blank diary that I had found in Jasper Jane's room.

As I watched, spellbound, the pages started to flip open. They were blank.

A voice seemed to rise from the pages, like fog from the ground, and said, 'At midnight, the fourth staircase, the third hall, the last door on the right.'

Then the book fell to the ground.

Harry Two and I looked at it, and then at each other.

I stared at it, making no move to retrieve it.

After a while, I slowly bent down and picked the book up. I flipped through the pages but they were still all empty.

My breath was coming fast and my chest felt tight and constricted.

Midnight? Fourth staircase, third hall, last door on the right.

I looked up at Empyrean. I calculated that this spot would be right near the top of the house, near Jasper's old chamber.

And at midnight that was exactly where I was going to be.

I lay awake, heart pounding, listening for the large grandfather clock down the hall to gong the time.

When it hit the first stroke of midnight, I got up and crept from my room with Harry Two on my heels. I could have had him stay behind, but frankly I wanted some company. I had the diary in my pocket. I had brought it just in case it would be useful somehow.

We went quietly up the massive staircase until we

reached the very top landing. Then we snuck down the third hall and reached the last door on the right.

I stared at the wood of the door, suddenly unsure of what to do. Finally, I reached out and turned the knob. It was locked.

I took out the diary, waiting for the voice to tell me how to proceed, but it was silent.

I thrust it back into my pocket and pulled out my wand.

I pointed it at the door; as soon as I did, it swung open noiselessly.

I crept into the room, Harry Two beside me. His hackles were up and a low growl was emitting from his throat. It was like he was trying to warn whatever was in here that we were not to be trifled with.

As we stepped fully into the room, the door shut behind us, and I heard the sound of the lock turning. I didn't know why I was surprised. Pretty much every creepy room I'd ever gone into had a door that shut and locked behind me.

The room, dim before, now became fully lighted. As my eyes adjusted, I gasped.

The walls were filled with objects that left me weak-kneed.

Bloody clothing hung on one wall. On another was a whole line of weapons that were also bloodstained. One axe had a big chunk of metal taken out of it. A sword blade was broken in half. A dented shield hung next to a chain-mail helmet with a hole in the forehead. A breastplate had four large gashes in it. Everywhere I looked was the evidence of a battle hard fought.

And ultimately, as I now knew, a war lost.

I wandered the space for a very long time, hours it seemed. Around every corner I turned there was something new to see. The room seemed to go on forever.

That was when I saw it, at the far end, dimly lit. A coffin. Its top was open.

As I approached it, two tall bronze torches resting in holders on either side of the coffin burst into flame, allowing me to see that the coffin was made entirely of shiny metal. In Wormwood, we only used simple wooden coffins to bury our dead.

Harry Two and I drew nearer. A body of a man lay inside, surrounded by soft white cushioning.

He was pale, his eyes closed, his skin tight, his hands folded over his chest. At the base of his neck was a long darkened mark.

Someone had slit his neck from one side to the other. He was dressed in fine clothes that reminded me of the garments I had seen in the paintings back at Astrea Prine's cottage in the Quag. He looked familiar, somehow, but I couldn't place him.

Clutched in his hands was a wand, one of the finest wands I had ever seen, though I really hadn't seen that many. It was made not of wood or crystal, but of silver.

I skirted around the edges of the coffin until I came to the shiny brass plate at the foot of it.

HERE LIES GUNTHER ADRONIS, HUSBAND OF ALICE, AT THE PLACE HE LOVED MOST, EMPYREAN.

I looked back down at the body.

Gunther Adronis. Alice's husband. Empyrean had been

their home. She was buried at Wolvercote Cemetery, yet he was here.

I realized that I was trembling all over. This room was so terribly sad. There was death and defeat and despair in it. I had no idea why the diary wanted me to come here.

As if in answer to my unspoken thought, the diary began to tremble in my pocket once more. With shaky hands I took it out and held it up.

The pages swirled, and again the same voice said, '*You must know the price that will have to be paid. You must look upon these walls and upon that body and fully understand what is demanded of you. It is awful, but it is necessary. If you are unwilling to pay this price, then you may stay here, at Empyrean, in comfort and safety, until your last days. But if you are willing to pay the price, aid will be there for you.*'

I looked down again at the body in the coffin and my stomach lurched. Gunther was no longer there. Instead, lying inside the coffin, with necks neatly slashed, were Petra, Delph and I.

I turned and ran pell-mell from the room, down all the stairs and back to my room. I flung myself on my bed and lay there. A moment later Harry Two, panting, jumped up and lay next to me.

He nudged my hand, but I didn't respond.

So many had fought and died in that war – the war that had been lost. Did I want to sacrifice myself to that same fate? And Delph and Petra too?

Harry Two nudged my hand again.

I pushed him off, but he wouldn't stop.

'Harry Two,' I began.

And then I stopped.

It was not Harry Two looking back at me. It was his face, but not his eyes. His eyes were different.

I knew those eyes. They belonged to my grandfather.

And though Harry Two could not speak, a sentence formed in my head:

Be not afraid, Vega, for you are never truly alone.

13

THE PERIL OF PETRA

I rushed from my room, down the hall and, not bothering to even knock, I pushed open Delph's door and called out his name.

He sat up in bed.

'Vega Jane?' he said warily. 'Are you OK?'

I stumbled forward, took a moment to calm myself and then perched on the edge of his bed.

I told Delph about the diary's message, my visiting the room, what I had seen, and the body of Gunther Adronis. And, finally, the image of our three bodies lying there in the coffin.

As I spoke, he sat up straighter and straighter and his eyes grew wider and wider.

When I got to the part about Harry Two's eyes and hearing my grandfather's voice in my head, he gripped my arm.

'Y-your grandfather? Was he inside Harry Two?'

I said, 'Am I going mad, Delph?'

I was suddenly so tired I lay down on the bed and curled

into a small ball.

Delph rubbed my shoulder. "Tis OK now, Vega Jane. You're safe.'

I turned over to face him.

'That's the thing, Delph. We *are* safe here. If we stay here we won't be harmed. But we didn't come all this way for that did we?'

He studied me. I had always known there was far more to Delph than most folks believed. Big, strong, simple Delph. Only he wasn't simple. Not even close. He had proved that time and again.

'That's what you meant at lunch,' he said.

I nodded.

He looked around the room. "Tis a nice place. A very nice place. A bloke could get used to being here, all right. Especially after the Quag.'

'In the Quag, everything can kill you,' I noted.

He nodded and gave me a weak smile. 'But you're right. We didn't come here to live in a place like this. We came here for answers.' He paused. 'But we need to be smart.'

'How?' I said eagerly.

'Well, to start with, we need to go on little scouting trips. Like me and my dad would do when we would go hunting in the forest. You find out where what you're hunting likes to be so you don't keep searching the wrong places; then you go out, learn things and come back to safety to sort through them. Way I see it, we nearly died in True because we had no safe place to return to. This can be like our camp.'

'All right,' I said slowly. 'That makes sense. But I want to

97

go now, when it's dark.'

'What do you mean, *I*? You're not going to go alone, Vega Jane,' he said firmly.

'I am, just at first, Delph, to get the lay of the land.'

He began to protest, but I rose from the bed.

'It's just the way it has to be, Delph. I'll see you when I get back.'

I added, to myself, *I hope.*

I quickly dressed, wearing clothes that we had taken from the trunk in True, and slipping my cloak on, I retrieved my wand from the nightstand, put the Adder Stone in my pocket and took the diary as well. The thing hadn't spoken to me again, but one never knew when it might do so once more.

When I was done with that, I looked at Harry Two, who sat still as a statue on my bed.

'You stay here, Harry Two. I'll be back soon,' I said, giving his solitary ear a rub.

I left the room and hurried down the hall.

I passed by Delph's door. I knew he wasn't sleeping. He would be up until I got back, I was sure.

I next passed by Petra's door and then stopped. I'd just see if she was awake or not, I thought, and let her know what I was doing.

I took out my wand, pointed it at the door and said quietly, *'Crystilado magnifica.'*

A split second later I could see inside her room. She wasn't asleep.

Petra was squatting down on the floor, her wand twirling

in a practised fashion between her fingers.

She pointed it at a chair next to her bed and muttered an incantation.

'*Mutatio hydrus.*'

As I watched in horror, the chair transformed into a writhing mass of deadly vipers.

The next instant she calmly said, '*Rescindo.*'

I realized. That spell had been in a book in Jasper Jane's workroom.

A book of *dark* spells.

Even as I looked, I saw her consult a torn page in her hand.

She had stolen dark spells from my ancestor's room and was now practising them.

I had told Petra that I trusted her. And I had. But now?

Petra rose, put her wand and the page away, got into bed and blew out her candle. I waited long enough to hear her breaths lengthen.

I retreated and continued on down the hall. *I hope I don't run into Pillsbury*, I thought, and as soon as I thought his name, there he was.

'Mistress Vega?' he said, sounding confused. 'Where are you going?'

'Just out for a stroll, Pillsbury. I won't be long.'

Before he could say anything else, I opened the front door and then closed it quietly behind me.

I looked out into the darkness and then turned and eyed the facade of Empyrean. So solid, so peaceful.

Remaining here for life would have been so . . . easy.

I looked down at my ring, turned it round and vanished

instantly. An idea occurred to me then – an idea of where I might go.

I reached down, tapped my right leg twice and muttered, 'Pass-pusay.'

I had one destination in mind.

Greater True.

Nothing happened.

OK, I thought, *let's give this another go.*

'Pass-pusay,' I said, and in my mind this time my destination was not Greater True, but the town of True.

An instant later I was standing in the middle of a street.

I looked around. This was True all right. That's when I realized: maybe the *Pass-pusay* incantation only worked if the place you wanted to go to was one you had already *been* to. *It would have been nice if Astrea Prine had told me that*, I thought irritably.

Now I had to get to Greater True. Under cover of invisibility, I headed to the train station.

An hour after I arrived at the station, the big marquee board announced the boarding of the early morning train with a final destination of Greater True.

With Destin around my waist, I took to the air and waited, hovering there.

A few minutes later, the train pulled out of the station and headed onward.

I followed from the air. The trip included a few other stops at stations along the way. These places were far smaller than either True or Greater True. Two people got off at one stop, and another climbed aboard at a second stop. The countryside in between was dotted with small homesteads and, where the winks of lights were more numerous, perhaps tiny villages that appeared even smaller than Wormwood.

Finally, I could see tall buildings rising up in the distance. I passed the train, reached town and landed. Unfortunately, confused by the lingering darkness, I landed in the middle of a roadway.

The next second I leaped out of the way of a huge motor flashing past.

I pressed myself against the stone wall of a building and took a long look around.

The streets were empty of people, which made sense, it being so early. The buildings were larger and grander than what I had seen in True. Some were made of stone, others of fine brick. They rose higher than anything I had observed in True. As a former Finisher back in Wormwood, I marvelled at the intricate carvings, mouldings and cornice pieces. I knew that it had taken great skill to craft all these things.

I slowly walked to my left, tugging my glove tighter over my hand to make sure the mark there was covered.

The next second I flattened myself against the wall again as I heard footsteps racing towards me.

Around the corner came a small, old fellow dressed in a suit, huffing and puffing.

He was followed by three men in suits and brown bowler hats.

It was not much of a chase. They caught up with the fellow, and one of the Bowler Hats raised his wand and the spell hit the little fellow in the back. He slumped to the pavement, crying out in pain. They advanced, wands raised.

I pulled out my own wand, pointed it at the blokes and said three times rapidly, '*Anesthe.*'

All three instantly crumpled to the pavement.

I waited to see if any other Bowler Hats showed up. But none did.

The old fellow cowered for a few more moments, his hands over his head, then he rose cautiously to his feet.

I said softly, 'Run.'

That did the trick. He took to his heels and was soon out of sight.

My own heart was pounding. Clearly, Greater True was not as peaceful as True – and Endemen's men were here. I would have to find a place to hide until the sun came up.

And hope that I survived.

14

GREATER TRUE

I ended up huddling under a bridge, cold, wet and miserable, but at least sheltered from the torrential rain. I managed to drowse off, but was abruptly awoken by the sound of marching. It was coming from directly above me.

Still invisible, I crept out from under the bridge. It had stopped raining, thankfully, but it was still cloudy and there was no sign of the sun, though I could tell that it was morning.

I scrambled to a spot where I could see the top of the bridge.

A stream of black-helmeted and booted men was striding across the bridge in a double column. As they reached the end where I was, I saw that they weren't men. They were boys.

They all carried what looked to be very sophisticated mortas supported by straps over their shoulders. They all wore scowls. Their arms and legs moved in perfect synchronization.

The one leading them brandished a gleaming sword and

was calling out orders. Another in the front carried a flag. On it I saw a symbol.

It was a five-pointed star, but it had two black dots in the centre of it. As the columns drew closer, I could see that the black dots were actually eyes.

The column marched on.

Shaken, I looked around to get my bearings as Greater True awoke from its slumber. The pavement was slick with the rain, but the windows glistened as shafts of light broke through the shallow storm clouds and reflected upon them. Noises were starting to percolate out of various spots.

The streets were well maintained and immaculately tidy. I couldn't see a bit of rubbish anywhere. Even the air seemed more pure than what I was used to.

As I watched, the wind drove the clouds away and sunlight swept down and embraced me.

Motors were starting up, and several of them began to appear on streets near the bridge.

I could see the people inside the motors. They were all expensively dressed, I thought. A man and woman dressed in handsome clothes came down the cobbles. They were tall and good-looking, with pompous looks on their faces.

Walking behind them was a smaller man dressed in a stiff suit and wearing a shiny hat. His shoes gleamed. As I looked more closely, I recoiled.

His eyes were blank. All white, no pupils. The elegant woman opened her handbag. As she did, something – a small bottle – fell out and plummeted towards the cobbles. The smaller man darted forward just in time to catch whatever had fallen and held it up to her.

She snatched it from him. 'You almost let it shatter, you fool,' she snapped.

Her companion raised his hand and struck the other man across the face so hard his bowler hat flew off his head. The smaller man didn't respond, just retrieved his hat and followed them, rubbing at his swollen cheek.

I was furious at what I'd seen. And my anger overcame my common sense.

'*Engulfiado.*'

The geyser of water hit the man and woman directly in the chest and sent them toppling backwards onto the cobbles. By the time they had staggered to their feet, they were soaked and filthy, their condescending expressions wiped clean.

I couldn't stop myself from smiling.

As more people emerged from the grand buildings, I noted that several were followed by either a man or woman dressed in the same fancy clothing and walking behind them like some sort of pet – and not a well-loved pet either. Their eyes were all white.

I didn't have time to take it in though. A crisis had presented itself. Barely a hundred yards in front of me, Endemen had appeared, three Bowler Hats behind him.

I shrank back, watching as Endemen surveyed the streets, his gaze flitting over where I stood, invisible. Then it landed on the legion of morta-toting boys still marching past.

Endemen strode over to stand next to a man in uniform, who was surveying the columns of marchers.

Endemen said, 'Their training is going well, I fancy?'

'Very well,' said the man. 'It's a nice crop of recruits. Perhaps one of the best yet.'

'Good. Very good indeed.'

'They are our pride and future, after all.'

Pride and future? What exactly did that mean? These boys were no doubt being trained up as warriors. But the thing was, they were using mortas as their weapons. Did that mean they had no magical abilities?

I thought of something else.

I wanted to see what was on the palms of the people who lived here.

Invisible, I skittered forward until I was very near a group watching the boys march along. One of the men raised his hand to shield his eyes from the sun.

Burned on to the palm of his hand was the same symbol I had seen on the flag: the five-pointed star with the pair of hideous eyes.

I drew back, shuddering. All of these people must have that terrible symbol burned into their skin.

I glanced back at Endemen, whose attention had now been caught by the couple I had soaked.

He said quietly to the other Bowler Hats, 'The *Engulfiado* spell, undoubtedly.'

'Clearly,' said one of the Bowler Hats. 'We will explain it to the citizens as a water-main break. But there was no sign of the person performing the spell.'

'Hmmm. What can you tell me about the other matter?'

I was certain I knew what the 'other matter' was; me knocking out three men last night.

The man said, 'We sent a response immediately, but

we were too late to apprehend the culprit. The men were rendered unconscious. We believe it was . . . not by ordinary means.'

'And the quarry?' asked Endemen.

'He was captured two streets over. And dealt with summarily.'

My heart sank. I had saved the man for the length of two streets only.

Endemen went on. 'I do not like what I am seeing. The breakdown of law and order. Of respect. We must come down hard on any who show similar signs of independence. I will recommend that we increase the intensity of the Mesmerizer. And we must have periodic updates on it for our, ah, friends.'

'Of course, Mr Endemen. Right away, sir.'

Mesmerizer?

I thought back to what I had seen in True. Could the Mesmerizer be that *thing* on the wall that had hypnotized people and taken their minds away?

Endemen said, 'And there have been no additional sightings?'

'None, I'm afraid.'

'The matter cannot be allowed to remain in such a state,' Endemen said softly.

'No, sir,' the man replied quickly. 'Of course not.' I noted a hint of fear in his features.

Endemen nodded and strode off, followed by his men.

Curious, I scurried after them, reaching a darkened alley in time to see Endemen take off his hat and look inside it.

There seemed to be a light shining from the interior of the hat.

He put the hat back on. 'I have been summoned,' he said. 'You remain here and keep watch. Keep me informed.'

'Yes, Mr Endemen.'

Endemen rose six feet into the air, and shot off so fast that in a few seconds he was visible only as a distant blur.

And before I could really think about it, I sprang into the air and soared after him.

15

MALADON CASTLE

I hadn't flown this fast in my life. Yet Destin appeared up to the task. My eyes began watering with the speed and I had to put on my goggles.

I managed to keep Endemen in sight as we flew higher and higher. Finally, we reached such an altitude that we plunged into a bank of low-level clouds.

My stomach seemed to lurch into my throat. I couldn't see one hand in front of my face. I was flying blind, and I was terrified that I would plough right into Endemen if he halted for some reason.

Thankfully, cold and drenched with moisture from the clouds, I finally flew free of the mists and took up the chase once more. I could see Endemen ahead. He was wearing no goggles but seemed to have no problem seeing. He was flying in a prone position, his arms at his sides. His bowler hat was still perched neatly on his head, unaffected by our speed and the buffeting winds.

Finally, he started to slow down. I matched his reduction in velocity. I could feel Destin around my waist.

Its chain links were like ice.

As Endemen slowed, he also began to descend.

I looked down and gasped.

Spread out far below us was a rugged mountain shrouded in blackness, though it was fully light out. And on the very topmost part of that mountain was an enormous building.

I pointed downward and continued to follow Endemen as he hurtled towards the dirt.

He landed smoothly with not even a stumble – I had to admit, the lout was a remarkable flyer, far better than me.

I hovered ten feet off the ground, waiting. The building I had seen from above was now revealed to me.

It was a castle with high, blackened stone walls, battlements and turrets. It looked a bit like Stacks in Wormwood, only bigger.

Endemen was marching towards the largest pair of gates I had ever seen. They made the massive doors back at Stacks look puny by comparison.

A flag waved from the topmost battlement. As I gazed upward, I could see the symbol clearly. It was the same image that the black-booted and helmeted lads back in Greater True had carried on their flag: the star with two terrifying eyes at its centre.

When he reached the portal, Endemen took out his wand and waved it from left to right in front of the massive entrance. The mighty gates silently swung inward.

He passed through the opening. And then the doors began to close.

I drew a breath, put my head down and shot through the narrowing gap, clearing it seconds before the wood thudded shut behind me.

I landed softly and peered cautiously around. I could see Endemen. He was just ahead of me. And, as I watched him, my heart stood still.

His suit, shoes and bowler hat vanished. In their place was a luxuriously long robe the colour of blood, with a black hood. As he turned to the side, I could see that his face had changed too. All parts of it had elongated and become hideously demonic. His complexion had turned so pale it looked silver. A thin, sharply angled blood-red beard now covered the lower part of his chin. He looked like a vulture with a man's body.

He began walking and I followed him, taking in as much as I could.

The walls and floors were stone, cold to the touch, and indeed an icy chill seemed to radiate from them. The corridor was ill lit, casting flickering shadows here and there. Dozens of corridors snaked off the main one I was on, and blackened and bolted doors lined the hall. My mind conjured images of prisoners behind each of them, awaiting their doom.

Next instant I heard a low moan followed by a scream emanating from deep inside the bowels of the place, which gave credence to my thoughts. I shivered and drew my cloak closer around me.

Endemen had picked up his pace, striding purposefully down the centre of the wide, darkened corridor, and I hurried after.

I heard it before I saw it. I knew that sound well. Slithering, followed by screeching.

A second later, the creature turned the corner and came into full, towering, terrifying view.

It was a jabbit, an enormous serpent with at least two hundred and fifty heads (no one faced with one had ever lived long enough to properly count them). One bite from a single venomous head was enough to drop a two-ton creta.

Endemen lazily held up his wand, and the jabbit stopped dead in its tracks. As he walked past, Endemen casually patted one of its venomous heads.

Endemen walked on, leaving the jabbit blocking the corridor in front of me. All Wugs had been taught to fear the jabbit above every other beast, and I was no exception. Before I could move, the trunk of the serpent passed right next to me. One of its poisonous heads actually brushed my cloak.

The thing froze. And so did I.

Each of its heads twitched back and forth.

They were *smelling* me!

I was afraid to move, terrified to even breathe.

I stared at the awful creature as it swayed back and forth next to me. I willed it to move on. For one agonizing moment, my gaze locked with one of the pairs of eyes. Invisible though I was, I was sure it could see me.

Go away. Please.

And then the most amazing thing happened.

The jabbit slithered away and disappeared down the corridor.

I let out my breath, shaking and nauseous with relief. I looked wildly around.

Endemen was gone.

16

PEOPLE OF THE GLASS

I hurried down the stone passageway until I reached a large chamber that had multiple corridors fanning off it. I had no idea which one, if any, Endemen had passed down.

Footsteps sounded in the distance and I quickly picked one option and shot down it.

There were a number of doors along this way, also all shut. As I hesitated, a door across the passage opened and a short, brutish man with a trim beard and only a single eye (the other socket being empty) walked out. Like Endemen he was dressed in a long black cloak with a red hood.

Without thinking, I shot my invisible self past him and into the room before the door closed.

I huddled back against the wall and tried to catch my breath.

That's when I heard the voice.

'Please,' it wailed. 'Please, don't.'

It was a woman's voice, ragged with pain. I gripped my wand and ran round the corner.

What I saw staggered me.

There was a line of looking glasses hanging on one wall. Inside each glass was a person. They were clothed in filthy rags. A mother and daughter were trapped in looking glasses hung side by side, crying desperately. Their hair was black and hung down around their shoulders.

On the other side of the room stood a man with a wand. He was leisurely pointing it at the people in the glass.

Unlike the bloke I'd seen leaving earlier, this man was tall and broad-shouldered, with a massive, veined neck. His face was flushed and his eyes were set too close together, giving him a permanently overfocused, menacing expression. His beard was large and bushy. He wore the same black-and-red cloak.

He lifted his wand and his mouth twisted into a malicious smile.

He fired another spell at one of the looking glasses, and the person trapped there doubled over and screamed.

As I looked on in horror, I saw what appeared to be sparkling dust falling from inside the glass and gathering in a bottle that had been placed on the floor directly below it. There were bottles lined up under each glass. All of them held some measure of the sparkling dust.

'Please, don't,' screamed a woman.

'Mercy,' pleaded a man behind the glass.

'Have p-pity,' moaned another man, who was on his knees, hunched over in agony.

I saw the bearded man's cruel smile deepen.

Lined up in deep niches on the walls behind him were glass bottles, all filled with the sparkling dust. And each bottle was stoutly corked.

The bearded man called out to one poor bloke trapped in the looking glass. 'Here now. You're going to love being an Ordinary, eh?'

An *Ordinary*? What did that mean?

When he raised his wand again, I matched this movement, readying an incantation of attack.

But then I hesitated. If I performed magic, I would reveal myself. And yet, I had to stop him.

I willed my wand to become what it had been when I had first acquired it.

The Elemental.

It grew into a spear taller than me that was the colour of gold.

I hurled it at the man as he prepared another spell to cast.

The Elemental struck him full in the chest, lifting him off his feet and sending him sailing against the far wall.

He hit the stone with a heavy thud. Two of the glass bottles were dislodged and fell on top of him, but the glass didn't break.

The Elemental automatically returned to my hand as the man slid to the floor, unconscious.

His wand had fallen from his hand and rolled across the floor.

I stooped and picked it up. It was made of blackened wood, as though it had once been afire.

I slipped it into my pocket and turned to the people in the looking glasses.

'Hello?' I said quietly. 'Can you tell me who you are?'

They were silent and I realized I was invisible.

I turned my ring the right way round and my invisibility vanished. I edged closer still.

As I did so, one man slammed himself against the glass, scratching and clawing at the surface in an attempt to escape.

I watched in horror as he slumped down and curled into a ball, his body shaking.

I backed away and looked down at the glass bottle under him. It was over half full with the dust.

I glanced at the looking glass that held the young girl.

She turned her face to me, and with a stab of horror I saw that her eyes were nearly blank. I looked at the woman in the glass beside her. Her mother. Her eyes were completely blank.

I looked down at the bottle underneath her looking glass. It was very nearly full.

I hesitated, torn. I had no idea how to free these people; but if I left them, they would end up as slaves in Greater True. For now I realized: slaves was what they were.

'Oi! Who the blazes are you?'

I looked around to see the man I'd slipped past earlier, standing there, staring dead at me with his one eye.

He raised his wand and fired a spell at me.

I deflected it with my Elemental, then hurled the Elemental right at him, willing the spear to do my bidding.

It hit him with such force that he simply vanished into nothing; the Elemental banked to the left and returned to me.

I looked at the burned hole in the floor where the man had been. I had just killed a Maladon.

I could hear voices. Instinctively, I raced over and picked up the bottle of dust underneath the mother's looking glass, stoppered it and shoved it into my pocket. I reversed my ring and turned invisible once more.

I ran to the door, eased it open and saw that the hall was clear.

I slipped out and ran down the passageway in the opposite direction from which I'd come.

I turned the corner and had to slam myself against the wall as a half dozen cloaked Maladons raced past me, wands raised and ready.

I waited for them to be well out of sight before I hurried off, stopping dead once I rounded the next corner.

The garm was only twenty feet from me. But I had never seen a garm like this before. Like the others of its breed, it had four huge legs, armoured skin, a mouth that breathed fire, and blood that ran perpetually down its massive chest.

Yet there was one significant difference.

This garm was tethered to a huge leash made of chain links. It was sniffing the cobbles and was being led down the corridor by an enormous man.

This was not good. Garms could pick up a scent from miles away. They must have figured out I was invisible. As I watched, paralysed with fear, it slowly lifted its head.

I pushed open the door closest to me, leaped inside and bolted it behind me.

Only just in time. The garm smashed into the door, growling and snarling.

I tapped my right leg with my wand and said, 'Pass-pusay.'

Absolutely nothing happened. I was still rooted to the

spot. There had to be something here that blocked that magical exit. So now what the Hel should I do?

I looked at the Elemental, still fully formed in my hand. Then I looked at the opposite wall.

I had never attempted what I was about to try. But I really didn't have any other option.

I gripped the Elemental tightly, willing it to do what I wanted it to. I thought back to what Alice had told me on that battlefield long ago.

When you have no other friends, it will be there for you.

The garm hit the door with another blow and this time it toppled inward. The beast and the man leading it burst into the room.

It was now or never.

I threw the Elemental directly at the far wall.

But this time I didn't let go!

I was lifted off my feet and the tip of the Elemental slammed into the wall, dissolved the stone and, together, we hurtled through the fresh opening.

We shot through another room, smashed through another wall, and passed into another chamber.

We hit and exploded through one more wall and I felt my heels hit the floor.

The room we had just landed in was truly enormous.

I could barely see the ceiling, which was made of glass. There were colourful banners covering the walls. They all held the symbol I had seen earlier. The five-pointed star with the terrifying pair of eyes.

And then my gaze alighted on what looked very much like a throne. It was huge and made of what appeared to be solid gold with a curved armrest. It had a high back emblazoned with the same awful star symbol.

There was a man sitting on it.

He was shrouded all in red, including the hood covering his head. His hands poked out from the sleeves and they were unnaturally elongated and curved.

And standing in front of him, in his own long robes, was Endemen.

My entrance had not been quiet. Both of them were staring in my direction. And though I was still invisible, they well knew, by the destruction that had unfolded, that someone was there.

Endemen had his wand out and pointed it towards me.

But the creature on the throne simply waved his hand, and I felt the very air around me begin to harden.

I couldn't move.

And something else happened.

In my head came a voice.

Go now. Go now or you are lost.

With what felt like a superhuman effort, I pointed the Elemental up and, like a fired morta, I soared up, up until I smashed right through the ceiling, sending huge chunks of glass plummeting.

Free.

Or so I thought.

17

HOME AGAIN

I lay prone in the air, clutching the Elemental, willing Destin to fly faster than it ever had before.

When I looked back, I saw no fewer than six Maladons soaring after me, led by the lethal Endemen.

I knew they couldn't see me. But somehow they could track me.

Spells blasted towards me. I rolled and dived and then shot upward, dodging them all.

Frantic thoughts ripped through my mind. My wand was my Elemental and vice versa. Well, why couldn't it be *both at the same time?*

I attached a magical tether to the Elemental. I hurled it directly at the Maladons. It blasted forward like a runaway train. They were heading right for it though they couldn't see it.

When it was ten feet from them, I muttered, '*Impacto.*'

A white light blasted from the Elemental and smashed into the Maladons, flinging them out of the sky.

Endemen and two of the Maladons had managed to

somehow avoid my spell. They followed in grim pursuit, as though they knew my every move. But how?

Then it struck me. *The wand!*

The blackened wand I had taken from the man in the room of glass. I groped in my pocket and pulled it out, snapping it in half and dropping the pieces to the ground. Then I swooped upward, praying that my hunch was right.

I looked back.

Sure enough, Endemen and his group were still heading downward.

They touched down, and I saw Endemen pick up the broken pieces of the wand and look around.

Then he looked up and screamed the bloodiest scream I'd ever heard. Even the shriek of the jabbits had never inspired such terror in me. I shuddered and urged Destin onward.

Reaching for my wand, I tapped my leg and said, *'Pass-pusay.'*

I had one destination in mind.

A moment later my feet hit something solid. I staggered a bit and then stood upright.

I was on the doorstep of Empyrean.

I turned my ring around and waved my wand; the door opened and I passed quickly through.

With another wave of my wand, the door shut and bolted.

The next instant someone lifted me into the air. Delph.

'Vega Jane!' he shouted in my ear, nearly deafening me. 'You're alive.'

121

'Blimey,' I said. 'I'm right next to you, Delph. I could hear fine until you screamed in my ear.'

But I smiled and hugged him back.

Around his feet danced Harry Two, barking his head off.

Over Delph's shoulder I could see what looked like most of the staff of Empyrean, with Pillsbury and Mrs Jolly at the head. There was an assortment of floor lamps, coatracks, the rake, the wheelbarrow and two marble statues, one a man in chain mail and the other a sinewy horse.

Pillsbury, his armour squeaking slightly, lurched forward.

''Tis good to see you, Mistress Vega,' he said. 'Master Delph told us that you were off to . . . We thought, well, we thought perhaps . . .'

'Me too, Pillsbury. But I'm back, safe and sound.' I looked around. 'Where's Petra?' I asked.

'In her room,' Delph said. He wouldn't meet my eye.

'I have lots to tell you,' I said.

'And I want to hear all of it,' Delph replied. 'But I think you should go and change first. And maybe wash.'

I realized what a state I must look. While Mrs Jolly prepared a meal, I went to my room, took off my dirty garments, cleaned up, put on fresh clothes and headed back downstairs.

Delph was already waiting for me in the kitchen. While we ate, I told him all that had happened to me.

He looked very thoughtful. 'This bloke on the big throne. The one Endemen was summoned by. Did you get a look at him?'

I shook my head. 'But he was very powerful, Delph. I felt the entire air around me hardening. Another moment and I don't think I could have escaped.'

Delph rubbed his jaw and thought about this. I could almost see the gears in his head whirring as I sipped my tea.

'Show me the bottle you took.'

I had brought the bottle of sparkling dust down with me and now I pulled it out for Delph to see.

He took the bottle from me and held it up to the light.

'Delph, the man was taking it from the prisoners. He said to one of the men . . . that he was going to become an *Ordinary*.'

'That must be what they call non-magical folks. Ordinary.' His expression was one of unbridled disgust. 'The Maladons are vile, Vega Jane. I'd take an army of jabbits over them.' He stood. 'Wait here. There's something I want to show you.'

A minute later he returned carrying a large book. He set it down in front of me.

'While you were gone, I found this in the library, behind a panel.'

'How'd you find the panel?'

'It was an accident. Hit it with my elbow.'

I looked down at the book. It had no title.

'Turn to page two twenty-four,' said Delph, a bit ominously.

I flipped to the page. It was a chapter heading, in ornate writing.

'*Incada Masacarro?*'

'It's a spell. A wicked one, and it looks mighty tricky to

manage. It tells how you can remove the magical powers of another. It's done through a series of torture incantations. It leaves the person with nothing inside.'

I turned the pages of the chapter – Delph was right. The pages were full of incantations and terrible drawings.

'This is horrible, Delph. So what happens to the person after this is done to them?'

'That's the other awful part. Since there's nothing there, they can be filled up with anything you want. Make 'em slaves for life. That part's at the end.'

I read this section and drew a quick breath. 'Delph, when I was in Greater True, I saw servants with blank eyes, like the people in the looking glasses back at the castle.'

He nodded, his gaze on the page I was reading.

'I think you saw the result of a full bottle taken, then, Vega Jane,' he said grimly. 'A sorcerer or sorceress turned into an Ordinary and then enslaved.'

I swallowed. Was that to be the fate of all those back at the castle?

All those you left behind, Vega?

I thought of the full bottles in the niches along that wall. Each bottle represented a person who used to be magical, but was now a slave.

I glanced at the spine of the book, where there was something printed in faded letters. My eyes widened in disbelief.

'Delph, look who wrote it!' I exclaimed. 'Colin *Sonnet*! Now, how much coin would you wager that he's related to Petra?'

He nodded slowly. 'I already saw that.'

I frowned. 'That means Colin Sonnet had to be a Maladon!'

'We don't know that. And remember, the book belonged to Jasper Jane. You saying he's a Maladon too?'

'Of course he wasn't a Maladon. He needed to know about the dark forces so he could better fight them.' I tapped the name on the spine of the book. 'Like this evil bloke.'

'Vega Jane,' he began in a weary tone. 'We don't know he was evil and we don't know that Pet is either.'

I hesitated, then told him what I had seen – Petra, casting dark spells in her bedroom.

To my surprise, he shrugged. 'So what? Like Jasper Jane, maybe Petra was studying those spells so she could better fight the Maladons, eh?'

'Why do you keep defending her?' I said suspiciously.

'Because she's proved time and again that she's on our side.'

I studied his features and thought, *Or maybe for another reason entirely.*

'You didn't see how . . . *happy* she was to be casting these dark spells, Delph,' I said. 'If she turns against us, we need to be ready.'

He rose. 'Fine. Let's go and talk to her then.'

I gaped. 'Delph, no, we shouldn't do that.'

'Vega Jane, I believe in Petra, but you obviously don't. So we need to put this to rest once and for all. Otherwise, you're going to be looking over your shoulder all the time, and what will that help?'

'If she is our enemy, she won't admit it.'

'Leave that part to me, Vega Jane. But we can't take Harry Two with us.'

'Why not?'

'You'll see.'

18

A BLOOD OATH

We knocked on Petra's door. At first there was no answer. We knocked again, harder; Delph actually pounded with his fist against the stout wood.

'Who is it?'

Petra's voice sounded tight and unnatural.

Delph said, 'Me and Vega Jane. She's back. We need to fill you in on what she found out. About the accursed *Maladons*! You might find it interesting, them being your kind and all.'

I glanced at him, confused. He was being antagonistic, when a moment ago he had fiercely defended Petra.

We heard hesitant footsteps coming towards the door.

It opened and there she was.

She was dressed in her nightshirt though it was well into the day and her hair was damp and tousled.

In her right hand was her wand.

I slipped my hand into my pocket and gripped mine. Just in case.

'So you're back,' she said, shooting me an odd look.

'You've been gone long enough.'

'I heard you haven't come out of your room,' I said. I hesitated. Delph was right; I might as well find out. 'I know you took those pages from Jasper's room. They were from the book on dark incantations.'

Petra instinctively shot a glance at the nightstand next to her bed. 'Have you been spying on me?' she said.

Delph pushed past her and into the room. I followed and closed the door behind us.

'What's going on?' Petra said. She crossed her arms across her chest and scowled at us.

Delph said, 'Vega Jane found out quite a bit 'bout them Maladon blokes.' He turned to me. 'You want to start filling her in?'

'OK,' I said hesitantly. I still had no idea what Delph was up to.

I had only just opened my mouth to begin when, with a sudden yell, Delph ripped a broadaxe off the wall and swung it towards me.

I was so stunned that I had no chance to protect myself.

'*Embattlemento*,' Petra cried out.

The force of her spell was so strong that Delph and his axe were tossed ten feet backwards and he crashed against the wall.

'What the Hel!' shouted Petra, her wand aimed at Delph's chest.

I stared at him, stunned. '*That* was your plan?' I shouted. 'Almost getting yourself killed?'

Delph dusted himself off, put the axe back on the wall and shook his head.

'See?' he said. 'On your side. Whatever that book says.'

Delph pulled the book from his pocket and passed it across. Petra saw the author's name and her face paled.

She looked up at both of us. 'I don't know who this is.'

'I'm sure you don't. But he's probably an ancestor.'

Petra bit her lip. 'You still don't trust me,' she said. 'After all this, you still don't trust me. What do I have to do? Tell me, what?'

'You can stop practising dark spells behind closed doors without telling either of us!' I said.

There was a long, uncomfortable silence. Petra shook her head. 'I thought we were friends,' she said quietly.

'Petra—' I began.

She held up a hand. 'Just don't. I don't want to hear it. Not now.'

'We *want* to trust you. But the Maladons are evil.'

'And because their blood runs in me I must be evil too, eh?' she snapped.

'I've seen what they can do,' I said. 'I've seen what they do to people. How they turn them to . . . well, nothing. Take their powers away and collect them in bottles. And then enslave what's left, little though it is.'

'They . . . th-they d-do that?' Petra said, her voice cracking.

I held up the bottle of dust. 'This is what they take from them. Their magic, their souls, everything that makes them who they really are.' I added bitterly, 'They leave nothing behind except a blank-eyed slave.'

Delph held up the book. 'The spell that does it is in here. Written by your ancestor.'

'But I'm not my ancestor, am I?' she yelled.

A silence fell. Then Delph said, 'There is something, something that each of you can do, to put this matter to rest once and for all.'

We looked at him.

'What?' I asked.

He held open another page in the book. We stared at the writing there.

'*The Oath of Oblivion?*' I read out.

Delph nodded. 'You each take a bit of your blood and give it to the other. Then you swear allegiance to each other, touch your wands together, say the spell at the same time and a bit of your blood is magically transferred to the other.'

'And if we don't keep our promise?' I asked.

'Then you go into oblivion,' said Delph. 'And from the pictures in the book, you *don't* want to go there.'

Petra and I stared at each other.

I said, 'I . . . I don't know.'

'Me neither,' said Petra.

'Well, then that's a bit of a problem,' said Delph, his features unusually dark. 'Because, Vega Jane, I'm getting tired of having to come back to this question of Petra being loyal or not.'

I flinched and glanced at Petra, who had the trace of a smile on her face. Irritation rose, but Delph wasn't finished.

'And you, Petra. I'm sick of you always complaining that everyone is against you. You're not the only one who's had it rough.'

The smile on Petra's face vanished. We both just stood

there glaring at Delph.

He barked, 'There's a whole world out there we have to confront, and it's got plenty enough evil in it, I reckon. Too much for us to have to worry about whether we trust each other. So it has to end. Now!'

He abruptly stopped and glared right back at us.

'Well?' he prompted.

'Shall we have a go at it, then?' I finally said to Petra in a small voice.

Petra seemed to roll this around in her head, too long to suit me, but she said at last, 'OK. I guess.'

Delph guided us through the spell.

We said the oath first, together, and then we ever so carefully touched wands.

As soon as the wood of our wands touched, they held fast to each other, like they had been sealed together. Petra gasped, and I heard myself do the same. The astonished look on her face, I'm sure, simply mirrored the one on mine.

'Now, the spell,' said Delph.

We read off the words, speaking in unison. As we spoke the last word, we both yelped in pain.

Gashes had opened on our foreheads. Blood poured down Petra's face, leaped from her skin to her wand, then on to my wand, and from there it catapulted directly to the wound on my face. The blood seemed to disappear inside me. I felt a sudden chill and then a comforting surge of warmth. I could sense the skin closing up and the wound healing. The exact same thing had just happened to Petra.

Our wands parted and we instinctively stepped back.

We were both breathing heavily, as though we had just fought some duel or run a long distance.

We simply stared at each other. I couldn't find words, and apparently neither could Petra.

Delph stepped between us and said, 'The oath is done. You two, I reckon, are in this together, for as long as it takes. So, no more fighting between you.'

I slowly lowered my wand and gazed at it. When I looked closely enough, I saw a new indentation there. It was crimson. Apparently not all of Petra's blood had entered my body. A bit was still on my wand.

Petra said, 'If you must know, I found the incantation book. I was curious. I knew the spells were dark, but I still wanted to attempt them. It just seemed like a good idea. To know how the other side fights.'

I said, 'My ancestor Jasper Jane thought the very same thing. So it probably *is* a good thing. I'm sorry if I thought otherwise.'

'There's something else,' said Petra. Her face was flushed and her voice was unsteady. 'There was something in those spells that . . .' She faltered for a moment. 'That seemed natural to me. They were compelling me to try to perform them.' She drew a deep, tortured breath and looked directly at me. 'So I'm glad we took the oath, Vega. I would never want to do anything to hurt you.'

'I know,' I said.

A moment later I could feel Delph's arm around my shoulder. His other one went around Petra, and he drew the three of us together into an embrace that lasted for a long moment.

When we parted, I was smiling, and so were Delph and Petra.

I looked at Delph and said, 'Thanks.'

'Yes, thanks, Delph,' echoed Petra, her look one of grudging admiration.

'Wait a mo'. Why didn't you want Harry Two to come along?' I asked him.

'Are you mad? When I attacked you, he would've torn me apart.'

I laughed. 'I think you're right about that.'

Delph said, 'Are we all good now?'

We both nodded.

'And now we need to figure out where we go from here,' he said.

I shivered at his words. I well knew where we would need to go.

Directly into the black hearts of the Maladons.

And we might never get back out.

19

BIMBLETON STATION

Later that morning, Mrs Jolly put together a wonderful meal and brought it into the library for all of us.

I had to get something off my chest.

'Delph, I don't know how to get back to the castle. I followed Endemen there, but I wasn't paying attention to directions, then I used the *Pass-pusay* spell to get out.'

'Why not use the *Pass-pusay* spell to go back then?' suggested Petra.

'I don't think I can. When I tried to leave by incanting, it didn't work. I had to use the Elemental to break out. Besides, even if I could, we might land in a mess of garms and jabbits and Maladons!'

'That's all right, Vega Jane,' Delph replied. 'I don't think we need to go to the castle; at least not yet.'

'What are you talking about?' I snapped. 'Not go to the castle?'

'I think *first* we need to go back to the beginning,' he said, his voice calm.

'To the beginning?' I retorted. 'What, the beginning of

the Quag?'

'Not that,' he said. 'I meant we should go back to True.'

Well, this brought me up short. 'What is there in True?' I asked.

'The people on the train. The ones who are taken. We need to find out where are they taken *from*. I was thinking that maybe by going to the source, we could help all of *them*.'

I let out a long sigh. Leave it to Delph to come up with a noble plan to help others.

We set off the next night. Pillsbury and Mrs Jolly saw us off.

We stepped outside the front door, which Pillsbury firmly closed behind us.

'Are you ready?' I asked Delph and Petra.

They both nodded, and Harry Two, who dangled in his harness, licked my hand.

I tethered all of us together with my *Lassado* incantation and then reversed my grandfather's ring, making us invisible.

'Are you going to use the *Pass-pusay* spell?' Delph asked.

I shook my head. 'Astrea never said it was meant for more than one person to use. I'm afraid something might go wrong.'

We kicked off and soared upward, Delph on my right and Petra on my left, like a pair of wings.

We all kept our gazes swivelling, looking for any sign of Endemen or his cohorts.

We flew over the trees, and I tacked back in the direction of where he had been travelling on the train.

I kept my gaze pointed down searching for it, but Petra

saw it first.

'There,' she said.

I looked where she was pointing and saw the train tracks.

I nodded and took a moment to get my bearings.

I peered around, looking for a landmark that might be helpful to orient me better, and I found it in a bluish hill to my left. We had passed that coming from True. That meant True was to the left and Greater True was located off in the distance to my right.

I turned to the left, changing our flight path to match the route of the tracks.

'Petra,' I said. 'Use your wand to do the magnification spell.'

She looked at me strangely but pulled out her wand, pointed it downward and spoke the pair of words.

Instantly the tracks were right in front of us and we followed them easily, all the way back to True.

Although we had travelled quite a way, it was still night-time when we arrived in True. With the aid of the spell, I could see a couple of people walking and one motor passing down an otherwise quiet street.

Then True was behind us as we continued to follow the train tracks.

We passed a number of towns and smaller villages, none near the size of True or Greater True. We kept going until Delph said, 'There!'

The train tracks ended, and there was a structure.

I descended slowly, scanning the area to see if anyone was around, but the place looked deserted.

We alighted at a spot about a hundred yards distant

from the structure. I could see that it was small and wooden with a metal roof and was open to the elements on all four sides.

'It's just a shelter really,' whispered Delph. 'For folks to gather under and wait for the train.'

Still invisible, we drew closer. There was a sign hanging from one of the support posts.

'*Bimbleton Station*,' I said. 'Apparently. Bit weird, isn't it? A station in the middle of nowhere.'

Petra nodded and said, 'I never saw that name on the schedule sign at True Station.'

Neither had I.

A moment later, a young boy dressed shabbily with dirt smudges on his face and no shoes on his feet came out of a nearby copse of trees. He was carrying a wooden basket.

As we watched from the shadows, he started picking berries off a bush and putting them in his basket. When the basket was fairly full, he walked around the shelter and stopped and gazed up at the sign.

He reached up on tiptoe and ran his finger along the letters spelling out the station name, then walked on.

'Let's go,' I said.

'Where?' asked Delph.

'Wherever he's going,' I replied.

We made up the ground quickly and soon gained sight of the boy. The walk through the woods took about twenty minutes, and I wondered at the boy's family allowing him to wander alone at night. Was this place safe?

Delph noticed it first.

'The light,' he whispered.

I looked up ahead, to where the boy was heading. Light was filling the sky there, only we didn't know what the source was.

I instinctively reached into my pocket and gripped my wand with my gloved hand. Out of the corner of my eye, I saw Petra do the same.

The boy disappeared around a bend in the path and we hurriedly followed.

When we cleared the curve, I stopped so fast that Delph bumped into me.

The lights we had glimpsed before were coming from wooden shacks, clustered around a small central patch of grass. Smoke was rising from stone chimneys. Maybe a hundred people or more were gathered around porches or walking along paths dimly lit by the shack lights.

They were of all different ages. Most were dressed poorly, like the boy, who had disappeared into one of the wooden houses with his basket of berries.

Delph whispered, 'What now?'

I whispered back, 'Let's watch and listen a bit.'

He nodded, and we drew closer to one group clustered on a crumbling porch.

'But when will it come again?' asked one young woman a little older than me. She wore corduroy trousers, a ripped and dirty coat and worn shoes. An old tuck was slung over her shoulder.

An old man in a slouch hat with a droopy moustache was seated on the top step busily whittling down a piece of wood with a small pocketknife.

'The *train*, you mean?' said the man. "Tis hard to say.' He scratched his forehead with a gnarled finger. 'I hear tell that other trains show up in other places. Not that I've been to those places, but I hear things from folks ambling down the road from time to time.'

'So there are other trains, then?' asked another man.

'Guess so,' said the first man. 'Lots of people, lots of trains.'

'Do they all go to the same place?' asked the man.

The man shook his head. 'Dunno. Now, *I can* tell you that it does show up at odd times. Nothing scheduled about it, you see. But you hear the whistle. And right after that, it appears.'

'And do they take everyone?' the dishevelled young woman asked.

The old man shook his head. 'No. Look at me. Been here a long time now. And I'm *still* here. And lots of you folks will still be here when the train leaves next; just the way it is.'

'How do they decide, then?' asked a young man who was standing next to the young woman. He held an old battered canvas bag in one hand.

The old man pointed his whittled stick at the fellow. 'No rhyme or reason that I can see. They just pick.'

'How many?' asked the man.

'Now, that varies too, don't it? Sometimes a lot. Sometimes not too many.'

'And it's a good place, that they go to?' asked the woman anxiously. 'Better than here?'

Another man said, 'No one's ever come back to complain, I can tell you that.'

'Course it's better,' bellowed the old man. He looked around. 'I mean what *wouldn't* be better than here? Work our fingers to the bone and for what? Imagine somewhere that looked after you. Roofs over your heads, food in your belly, medicine when you need it, education for the young ones. Who wouldn't want that?'

They all nodded. Apparently life for all of them was as hard as it had been for us in Wormwood. When I thought about what I'd seen in True and Greater True, it was like two different worlds. The 'have-alls' and the 'have-nothings'.

The old man said, 'I thought as much. So I mean to stay here until I gets on that damn train.'

'What does a train look like?' asked the young man.

'You'll know it when you see it,' said the old man. 'Long and metal and it runs on those little tracks you see at the station. Folks climb on, and off it goes. Fast it is. Gone in a blur.'

Many people looked around in wonderment, as though they couldn't believe what they were hearing. But then again, I had never known that a train existed until I got to True.

I noticed the young man and woman draw aside from the group. I nudged Delph.

'I'm going to become visible and follow those two. I want to talk to them. Find out where they came from.'

'This seems like a bad idea, Vega Jane,' Delph began to protest.

'Delph, I'm going to do this, OK?'

He frowned. And Petra glared at me. But I didn't care. I needed answers.

I slipped off the ring and passed it to Petra. She slid it on, making sure to keep the ring turned inward. Petra used her wand to maintain the magical link among the three of us. I headed off after the pair while the others, still invisible, followed.

It didn't take me long to catch up to them.

'Hello,' I said.

They both whirled around to stare at me.

'I'm sorry,' I said. 'I didn't mean to startle you. My name's Vega. I'm here for the train.'

The man said, 'I'm Russell, this is Daphne.'

'And where did you come in from?' I asked, trying to keep my voice casual.

Russell was about to answer when Daphne said, suspiciously, 'Why do you want to know?'

Russell said, 'Daph, she's just curious.'

Daphne folded her arms across her chest and said, 'OK, so am I. Where did *you* come in from?'

I folded my arms and glared back. 'Wormwood. And you?'

'I'm not telling,' she replied with a smirk.

'Daph,' said Russell.

'Shut it, Russ. For all we know she's going to bump us off the train. Less said, the better.'

'Fine,' I said. 'Good luck.' I turned and walked away.

'Oi, wait,' called out Russell.

But I heard Daphne exclaim, 'Oh, let her go. She's no bleedin' use to us. And I'm not going back to our village. I'm not, Russ.'

I walked back to the group gathered around the porch.

Delph, Petra and Harry Two were right behind me under the invisibility shield.

The people were still standing there, hands in pockets, talking among themselves. The old man who had been whittling had set down his work and was drinking from a pewter flask.

They all glanced at me before going back to their conversations.

I sat down next to the old gent. He lowered the flask from his lips, and I could smell sweet wine.

'Who be you?' he asked.

'I be Vega. And you?'

'Geoff. You just in?'

I nodded. 'And you?'

He capped the flask and chuckled. 'Oh, I've been here a while, missy. May be here a while still. One day I'll get on that train.'

He had on woollen gloves with the fingers cut off, revealing dirty fingers. He blew on his hands and stuck them in his pockets along with the flask.

'Geoff, how do you know the place the train goes to is a good one?'

He looked at me strangely. 'What?'

'Well, if no one ever comes back, how do you know?'

He laughed, took up his knife and began whittling again. 'You're a funny one.'

I could tell that he so very badly wanted to believe that a better life was just a train ride away that no logic I might employ would persuade him otherwise.

'How long have you been here?' I asked.

'Two years.'

'Why did you come here?'

He shrugged. 'Where I come from, there ain't much there. Been hard times for as long as I can remember.'

'Why is that?' I asked.

He shrugged again. 'Just has been. Since the old war. Not that I saw or fought in it. I'm old, but t'were long before my time. But it still lingers, you know. People never did get back on their feet. My little village, you can't rub two coins together. No work, people just getting by. No . . . hope. That's why I'm here, waiting for the train. Even if I don't ever get picked to go on it.'

'Why do you have to *wait* for it?' I asked curiously. 'Why don't you just follow the tracks to wherever it goes?'

Geoff snorted. 'I'm not stupid. I tried that.'

'What happened?'

'I was following the tracks, like you said, and . . .' He stopped, and his face took on a confused expression.

'And what?' I prompted.

'Well, I got lost. Couldn't find the tracks. Got turned around and ended up back here. Tried it another time and same thing happened.'

I looked around at some other people who were listening to this. They were nodding. One man said, 'Aye, me too.'

Of course. The Maladons had used a spell, maybe something like *Transdesa hypnotica*. We had encountered that in the Third Circle of the Quag. These people would never be able to find their way to True. The train was their only option.

'How did you know to come here?' I asked.

Geoff shrugged. 'Word gets around. Want a better life, get yourself to Bimbleton Station. Least, that's what I hears in my village.'

I looked around at the shacks. 'Who built these?'

'Dunno. They've always been here, least I think so. Nice place. Plenty of wood for the fires. Food in the woods. Fresh water from the river.'

'Why haven't you been picked to go on the train?'

He stopped whittling and considered this. 'Fact is, missy, I don't know why. It's not like they give you a reason.'

'They?' I pounced on this. 'Who is "they"?'

'Them blokes in fancy suits and hats. They must be rich. Odd chaps. But nice enough.'

Nice enough, I thought, *for barbaric murderers.*

He started whittling again.

'Yeah, right funny chaps. They decide who goes and who stays.'

'How does it work?'

He pointed around with the tip of his knife. 'Well, when we hears the whistle, we all rushes down to the station like. Now, them blokes in the funny hats, they get off the train and they looks round and they talks to folks. And they lines up those what's going on the train, they board and then off they goes.'

'And the others just wait here?'

'Some does. Others get fed up and just go back to wherever they came from. Not me, I ain't moving from here, 'less it's on the train.'

'But why—?'

'Well, aren't you the curious one?'

I glanced to my right and saw a strange man standing there. Behind him was Daphne.

I inwardly groaned.

'She was asking us questions too,' said Daphne huffily. 'And now she's pestering him the same.'

I said nothing.

My gaze remained on the stranger.

He had on a long coat, but I could see the lapel of the pinstriped suit beneath it. I wondered where his bowler hat was.

'You want to come with me, luv?' he said smoothly.

My gloved hand slid inside my pocket and curled around my wand.

'Not really, no.'

'Just over there,' he said firmly, pointing to his left. 'I can answer all your questions.'

My gaze drifted to the left, and I rose and said, 'All right.' I motioned for him to lead the way.

He did so, taking me round a corner. As soon as we were out of sight, he spun round, wand out.

But mine was already in my hand. I had been expecting this, and if my time in the Quag had taught me anything, it was to be prepared. I flew above him, lashed out and delivered a thundering kick to his head with my booted feet. He toppled over and hit the dirt, his wand flying away.

As he staggered to his feet, I said, '*Subservio.*'

A white light shot out from my wand and hit the bloke directly in the head. He slumped down.

I knelt next to him and spoke in low tones, erasing everything that he had heard in the last few minutes. I then dragged him deeper into the woods, placed him in a sitting position against a tree and put his wand back in his hand.

'Come on,' called Petra. 'Hurry.'

'Hang on,' I said. 'Might as well check his pockets.'

I began to dig through the man's coat pockets, searching for anything useful. I pulled out a picture and glanced at it.

My heart flew into my mouth.

The picture was of my parents.

20
ONWARD

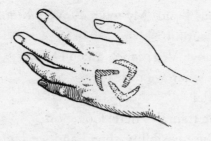

'Vega Jane?' whispered Delph.

I blinked. I hadn't realized I was holding my breath and it came out in a rush.

'Just give me a sliver,' I said desperately, my mind whirling.

I stared at the picture. It wasn't a drawing; the images seemed real, burned into the paper. I turned it over. There was something scrawled on the back, in bold writing.

Be on the lookout for these Campions.

I turned the paper back over and stared at the images of my mother and father. I thought back to that awful night at the Care in Wormwood, when my parents had been engulfed in flames and then had disappeared. I traced their features with my shaky finger.

Mum? Dad? Where are you? How can I find you?

'Vega Jane?' hissed Delph. 'Are you all right?'

I held out the picture. 'He had a picture of my parents.'

'Your parents?' said Delph in disbelief. 'But how can that be?'

'You look like your mum,' said Petra, studying the image. 'She was very beautiful.'

I looked at her in surprise.

'Thank you,' I said. 'My mum *was* very beautiful. I mean, she *is* very beautiful.'

'So what now, Vega Jane?' asked Delph.

And that's when we heard it.

The whistle!

I said, 'The train. It's here! Come on.'

I joined the invisibility shield and we ran as fast as we could back to the shacks. They were deserted. We kept on running until we reached Bimbleton Station.

This was probably a mistake, I thought. The Bowler Hats would be here and perhaps Endemen too. But we didn't have much choice.

The humble train station was transformed from earlier. A shiny black train had arrived. And where before there had been only one small boy, now the place was jammed with what I estimated to be hundreds of people jostling one another to get closer to the train.

Then one of the carriage doors opened and he appeared.

The four of us took a collective step backwards.

It was Endemen.

He smiled and doffed his hat, and the crowds around the train instantly quieted.

'Hello,' he said. 'I welcome all of you to Bimbleton Station. I do hope we can take as many of you with us as possible. But first, my associates will need to ask you all a few questions. Does that sound all right to you?'

He was being ever so polite, although I saw a wand up

his sleeve. The crowd waited meekly as his Bowler Hats began to move among them, taking certain people aside and conversing quietly. Endemen watched them, smiling faintly.

'Come on,' I whispered to the others.

We drew as close as we dared and found ourselves within a few feet of Russell and Daphne, the couple from earlier. They had been approached by a Bowler Hat with a shiny black moustache and flinty cheekbones.

'So you're the one what decides if we get on the train or not?' Daphne said.

The Bowler Hat said nothing at first, appraising her and then Russell.

'From where do you come?' he asked, his voice low and throaty.

'Clarendon on Hillshire,' replied Daphne. 'A long hike.'

'I can imagine,' the Bowler Hat said smoothly. 'And your surnames?'

'He's Everett and I'm Lloyd. We're going to get married. Our given names are Daphne and Russell for him.'

'Nice, very nice.'

The bloke pulled a book from his pocket, opened it and riffled through the pages.

'Lloyd, you say? Have you had others in your family take the train?'

'No. Least not that I'm aware of.'

The man swivelled his gaze to Russell. 'And you, Mr Everett?'

He nodded. 'My grandfather George – that was long ago of course, before I was born. We never heard from him again.'

'He went to a better life,' said the man. 'A *much* better life. Might I see the backs of your right hands, please?'

Daphne and Russell looked at each other. Russell was about to raise his when Daphne, with proper spirit, said, 'What does that have to do with anything?'

'It has to do with a great deal.'

Russell said, 'Daph, just do it.'

She sighed but raised her hand.

Russell's hand was blank. With a thrill of horror I saw a faint outline of a shape on the back of Daphne's. The mark of the three hooks!

'That mark on your hand?' the Bowler Hat said, looking expectantly at Daphne.

'What of it? It don't come off, case you're wondering. It's . . . it's like a birthmark, I guess. Had it always, I have. Ain't nothing wrong with it. Or me.'

She self-consciously covered it with her other hand.

'Well, I wouldn't exactly agree with *that*.'

The man did it so smoothly I almost missed it.

'*Subservio*,' he muttered. I saw the tip of his wand poking out of a hole in one of his pockets.

Daphne and Russell instantly went rigid and their eyelids fluttered.

'Now, Ms Daphne Lloyd, let's go to the train, shall we?' said the man. 'We have a very special carriage for you. Your friend will be riding on another one. My mate will be along presently to escort him. Come along, now.'

Daphne obediently followed him, while Russell simply stood there like a stone.

I glanced at Russell, waiting, and my plan came together

in an instant. I pointed my wand at him and said softly, 'You will go back to Clarendon on Hillshire and tell them that the train is a trap, an evil trap. It carries folks to their doom. Anyone with a mark on the back of their right hand is at particular risk. You must all go into hiding after spreading the word to never come to this place, do you understand me?'

Russell nodded dumbly.

I looked around. The Maladons were all occupied escorting people on to the train.

'Go now,' I said. 'As fast as you can.'

Russell turned and raced off. He was soon out of sight.

'Now what?' asked Petra.

'Now we get on the train and do what we can.'

Because I knew that Daphne Lloyd and others like her were headed to one place and one place only.

Maladon Castle.

21

CLARENDON ON HILLSHIRE

We snuck on at the last instant and shrank back against the wall of the vestibule connecting one car to its neighbour. I watched as Daphne Lloyd and the others were led to their seats and shackled. Under the *Subservio* spell they could offer no resistance.

This car had no windows, so no one outside could see what was happening. The passengers who were in other cars and not shackled were also under spells and could not fight back. The ones who had not been chosen had either walked back to the shacks or else started their journeys home.

I had to admit it was all very well planned. The Maladons had had centuries to perfect what they were doing: unobtrusively enslaving an entire people while at the same time destroying all those who could rise up against them.

I did wonder why some had been left behind.

I took out my wand and muttered the magnification spell. Instantly, I could see up and down the train carriages.

And now I knew how they chose whom they did.

The ones on the carriage without brands were all young, most under thirty. There was not one old person on the train.

Delph whispered, 'They just take the young and healthy. They mess with their minds and put them to work. Everyone else gets left behind.'

I nodded thoughtfully. I couldn't understand why they'd gone to all this trouble just to separate those with a mark from those without – the magic from the non-magic. When I thought about it, though, it was fiendishly clever. The Maladons didn't need to wage war or expend force. The magical simply came to them.

Then they could be quickly and quietly got out of the way. And their families would just believe they had gone on to a better life and would never think of attacking those who took them.

It really was quite brilliant. Not to mention, diabolically evil.

There were two guards in our car, one at either end. As we pulled out of the station, the one nearest us moved down the car and towards his companion. They began to chat far enough away that I felt comfortable whispering my concerns to Delph and Petra.

Petra hissed, 'How can we be sure they'll take all these blokes to Maladon Castle?'

'Because they need to steal their magic. That's where it happens,' I said.

'That's terrible,' she said in a hushed voice. She glanced at the shackled passengers. 'We can't let that happen to them.'

I felt the same, but if we tried to free them now, we could all be killed and no one would be saved. I didn't know how many Bowler Hats were on this train but we had seen at least thirteen.

I said, 'We can't fight them all, Petra. We'll lose. We need to keep quiet and see what happens.'

Delph said, 'Vega's right, Petra. We just have to see what happens.'

Petra scowled.

I looked at her, forcing her to meet my eyes. 'Do you want to win a single battle, Petra?' I asked. 'Or do you want to win the war? Because I don't reckon we can do both.'

She looked back at me. At first there was anger on her face. And then, surprisingly, understanding. 'I can see that, Vega,' she said. 'You're right.'

I never knew which Petra I was going to get. Crazy Petra or Rational Petra.

I said, 'The first stop will be True, and those without magic will be let off to have their minds erased. After that will come Greater True, or perhaps the train will take us directly to Maladon Castle.'

Delph asked, 'When you were at the castle, did you see a train or tracks running up to it?'

I shook my head. 'No. But I wasn't looking for them – I was keeping my eyes on Endemen.'

'Funny you should mention him,' muttered Delph. 'Look who's coming.'

I stiffened and we flattened ourselves against the wall as the very man entered the carriage from the other end.

Endemen was dressed in his usual attire, a pinstriped

suit with a waistcoat, a bowler hat and shiny shoes. A stark contrast to his true being. I wondered if all Maladons had a hideous self under their outer layer.

Endemen greeted each of the passengers in the carriage. Still under the spell, they mumbled their replies.

He looked them over and then knelt down next to Daphne, who was seated at the rear of the carriage only a few paces from where we were standing.

He pulled out his wand and gave it a little flick. Daphne blinked and focused on him.

Endemen said, 'Your village is Clarendon on Hillshire, correct?'

Daphne nodded. 'Yes.'

Endemen gripped her hand and held it up. 'Are there others who live there with this mark?'

Daphne looked at her hand as though seeing it for the first time.

'Yes. A few. I don't know how many.'

'Any in your family?'

'No. I'm the only one. What does it mean, this mark?'

Endemen smiled in a way that seized me with terror. Like a jabbit about to eat its dinner.

'Well, at the very least it means the end of you.' He let her hand drop and said, 'Now you will tell me exactly how to get to the village of Clarendon on Hillshire.'

She spoke the directions as Endemen used his wand to write her words visible in the air. Then he flicked his wand again and the images went directly into his head.

Without another word, he turned and walked over to one of the Bowler Hats.

The man said, 'Do you want to leave immediately for this village, Mr Endemen?'

'There's no particular rush. When we've finished what we need to do here.'

'Hel,' said Delph. 'The Maladons are going to that village and they're going to kill everyone there!'

'We have to stop them,' I said. 'Now.'

Petra said, 'You already sent that bloke Russell to warn them. What happened to winning the battle but losing the war?'

'I have no idea if the folks in the village will listen to him, or if they do, how fast they'll flee. Besides, I have my reasons.'

And my expression was so ferocious, I suppose, that Petra turned away.

'We don't know how to get there,' said Petra.

'Yes, we do,' said Delph.

We both looked at him and in unison said, 'We do?'

He nodded. 'She told that bloke Endemen. Didn't you hear?' He tapped his head. 'All up here.'

Petra looked at me.

I smiled. 'Delph has always been good with directions.'

'OK, so how do we get off the train?' asked Petra.

I had no choice but to try the spell with all of us together. It would either work, or we'd be lost in oblivion. I didn't really have time to think about it.

I tapped my wand against my leg, thought of the train station at Bimbleton, and said, 'Pass-pusay.'

In an instant we were back at the train station.

From there we rose into the air and headed west,

following Delph's instructions.

It took us a while, because there were four of us.

At last, I looked down and saw it. A tiny hamlet set on the side of a grassy hill.

'Is that it?' I called to Delph, who nodded.

We alighted silently a bit to the east of the hamlet and looked around.

'Do you see anything?' I asked, my wand at the ready.

Petra had her wand pointed ahead of her but shook her head. 'Nothing.'

'I don't see no bodies lying around, or houses blown up,' added Delph.

Petra hissed, 'Look.'

It was Russell, sprinting through the streets, pounding on doors. When they opened, I heard him telling the people there what I had told him to say. The fear in their eyes told me that his warnings had been believed. People were already emerging from their houses, holding bags.

'I wonder where they'll go that will be safe?' asked Petra.

'It's too late. They're here,' exclaimed Delph.

Endemen and five Bowler Hats had appeared on the edge of the small village square.

The villagers looked back in terror.

Endemen smiled and raised his wand. In unison, so did the other Maladons.

The villagers were so stunned they were rooted to the spot.

'*Embattlemento*,' I said, my wand pointed between the Maladons and the villagers.

Their spells hit my shield and the explosion was so fierce

that all the villagers were nearly knocked off their feet.

'Run!' I shouted.

Russell echoed this command. 'Run. Run!'

The villagers turned and raced off, fleeing towards the woods beyond, dragging their children and hastily gathered belongings behind them.

Endemen was not focused on them. He was looking around for the source of the spell that had blocked his.

I lifted off the ground, pulling the others with me as Endemen and his men spread out and charged ahead.

They passed directly underneath us.

We followed the path of the villagers down below as they raced towards the dense forest that we had passed on our way here.

I looked back in time to see Endemen and his men take to the air and give chase.

I glanced at Petra and we both raised our wands.

'Impacto,' we cried out at the exact same time.

Our combined spells hit the blokes with a thunderous blow; they were all blasted out of the air and landed unconscious in a massive heap.

We landed next to the fallen Maladons.

'Help me search them,' I said to Delph and Petra.

Delph said warily, 'But what if they wake up?'

I raised my wand and made whirling motions with it around the fallen Maladons. 'Ensnario.'

Thick golden cords spilt from my wand tip, and soon all of them were bound tightly. Then I used my wand to drive the ends of the cords deeply into the ground.

We all worked fast, searching the pockets of the

Maladons. I searched Endemen. In his hat I found a bit of looking glass attached to the very top of the interior. This must have been what he was looking at back in Greater True when he said he'd been *summoned*. It somehow allowed communication from a great distance. I pondered whether to take it, but then thought better of it. They would know it was gone and might use it to track us somehow.

As I stared into the glass it became smoky and an image started to appear. The foulest face I had ever seen. I dropped the hat.

It wasn't a person. It wasn't even a corpse. It was worse than dead, if that was possible.

Then I became worried. If Endemen didn't answer what might have been a command from this bloke, legions of Maladons might start popping up all over Clarendon on Hillshire.

'I'll be right back,' I told the others.

I soared into the air and towards the woods, where I found the villagers shaking and whimpering. I landed in their midst.

'You!' exclaimed Russell.

One man raised a knife and started towards me. 'You're one of them lot.'

'Kill her!' screamed several others together.

Russell got between us. 'No. She was the one who warned me. You saw what happened back there. She protected us.'

The man with the knife lowered it. 'Sorry, missy.'

'You need to keep going,' I said. 'Those blokes back there are the Maladons. They use Bimbleton Station and others like it to entrap and then enslave all who board the trains. They take mostly young people.' I looked around. 'Who here has a mark on the back of their hands? Of the three hooks?' When none stepped forward, I urged, 'Please. It's important.'

Two men and a young woman stepped forward. 'We three do,' said the woman. 'But we don't know what it means.'

'It means you are magical, like I am. And it also means you could be tracked by it. Hold out your hands.'

They did, and sure enough, there was the faint mark.

I raised my wand, pointed it in turn at their hands and said, *'Embattlemento.'*

A glow covered the mark and then sank into their skins.

It might hide them for a while, I thought. But as they grew older, their marks would become stronger and more visible.

I looked at all of them. 'You must warn everyone you come across of the Maladons' plan. They want to rule all of you. And they will kill anyone who tries to stop them.'

Russell looked at me. 'They . . . they took Daphne. She had that mark on her.'

I nodded. 'I know. She's on the train right now. And I promise I will try to save her, Russell. I give you my word.'

He nodded, tears in his eyes.

The man who had held the knife said, 'You're going to try to stop them?'

'Yes, I am.'

'If it's just the one of you, what chance have you got?'

'I'm not alone,' I said. 'But one day I might come and find you and ask for your help in defeating them.'

Russell glanced at his mates and then back at me. 'And we'll be willing and ready when you do.'

I thanked him with a smile. 'Now go. Quickly!'

They all turned and raced away.

I returned to the others. 'Did you find anything?' I asked.

'Nothing of interest,' Delph said.

'Right. Well we need to get going,' I said. 'We need to try and help the ones on the train.'

'So we kill 'em, right?' said Petra. She held her wand at the ready, her expression steely.

I shot Delph a glance, then back at Petra.

'Like they wouldn't kill us given the chance,' she snapped.

Petra was right. We might never get another chance like this again. I took a deep breath and pointed my wand at Endemen's chest. It would be over in a sliver, and would mean one of our strongest enemies had been vanquished.

But, as I stood there I realized I could not kill someone in cold blood. If he were trying to kill me, yes. But not this way. I lowered my wand.

I glanced up. Delph looked relieved; Petra, simply disappointed.

'So what, then?' she demanded. 'Just leave them here so they can wake up and keep killing?'

'I have another idea.'

I snatched up all their wands and blasted a deep hole in the ground, dropped the wands in it and then used another incantation to cover the hole back up such that the ground looked completely undisturbed.

'All right?' I said.

Petra nodded grudgingly.

I tethered us together, tapped my leg with my wand, said, 'Pass-pusay,' and we were instantly transported back to the train, roaring on its way to True.

We had done a right good job back there, I thought.

I didn't yet understand how far out of my league I truly was.

But I would, soon enough.

And then I would very much regret not taking Petra's advice and killing Endemen while I had the chance.

22
THE BATTLE BEGINS

The train pulled into True as it had before, in the middle of the darkness with a belch of smoke and a rasp of brakes. We were all alert as the train came to a full stop.

We heard the sound of doors opening but not in the car we were on. This did not much surprise me. I didn't expect any of the 'branded' ones to get off here.

Petra and Delph looked at me questioningly.

I was torn. I knew that the people taken off here would have their minds altered by the Mesmerizer. But I also knew that whatever happened to the people getting off in True, it would pale in comparison to what would happen to the poor devils who would continue on to the castle.

There were no windows on this train car, so I couldn't tell if it was still night or if the sun had come up. I wondered whether Endemen and the others had woken up yet and managed to retrieve their wands.

You should have listened to Petra, you fool.

I shook my head, trying to clear it. Obviously I could do nothing about Endemen now. Instead, I turned my attention to the other passengers in the car.

There were five of them, including Daphne. They all sat rigid in their seats, staring at nothing, oblivious to the awful fate that awaited them.

I looked behind us. 'Come on. I want to go into the next car and see what's happening.'

We rose quietly, and I led the way towards the car attached to this one.

We passed by the guard at that end. He made no sign of having seen or heard us. I looked over my shoulder to make sure the other guard wasn't looking and then I quietly opened the door into the next car. We passed through and Petra closed it behind us.

The car was quiet, as I knew it would be. The people there were not restrained, but they were all under the *Subservio* spell and could do nothing to escape. As we watched hopelessly, the doors to the car opened and a Maladon entered. He waved his wand and all the passengers rose as one and started to file out.

When the train car was empty, the doors closed and we started moving again. We would be heading on to Greater True now, I thought. Just then, the train came to a jolting halt.

'What the Hel?' exclaimed Petra.

We next heard a gnashing of metal on metal, and then came another jolt.

Delph realized what was happening first.

'They're disconnecting the train cars,' he said.

'Oh my holy Steeples,' I cried. 'Quick!'

I rushed back towards the windowless train car and

opened the door in time to see it start to rise into the air. I grabbed Harry Two and leaped, gripping a handrail on the exterior of the train car. The others leaped after me and clung to the car.

The car soared into the air and then shot forward with such velocity that had we not been holding on tight and tethered together, we would have assuredly plummeted.

It was freezing up here, moving at such speed, and my teeth chattered.

After what seemed like forever, we began to slow and then descend. It was still dark, but I perceived the lights down below.

I said over my shoulder, 'I . . . I think it's Maladon Castle.'

As we flew lower and lower, my fears rose higher and higher.

We were directly over the castle now, and as we hovered in mid-air, a huge dome that I had not noticed on my previous visit started to open. The train car began to lower inside.

The train car landed with a hard jolt on the floor of the castle and I immediately looked around. The space we were in was large and open and lighted by torches lining the stone walls.

A large door set against one of the walls opened.

And there he was.

Endemen.

He was leading a tethered garm. As he drew more fully into the torchlight, I saw with some satisfaction that his suit was dirty, his sleeve torn and his hair dishevelled. He had a large lump over one eye, no doubt due to my *Impacto* spell.

He looked murderous.

In his other hand he held his wand.

Why hadn't I destroyed them when I had the chance? I shot Petra a glance. She was glaring at me in a way that said, *I told you so*.

Endemen was followed into the room by the Bowler Hats, who looked as rumpled and angry as he did.

I let go of the train and beckoned the others to follow me. We paused at the door and looked back.

The train car door opened, and in went Endemen and the garm. No doubt they were going to use the garm to sniff us out before blasting us to smithereens.

We stepped through the door Endemen had come through and then peeked back around the corner, watching.

Minutes passed. Nothing happened. There were no spell blasts.

Next thing the branded folks were being led off the train car.

'Quick,' I said. 'I know where they're going. And we can't let the garm close enough to smell us.'

We retreated down the passageway. Finally, we reached a part of the castle that I recognized, and, gaining my bearings, I led the others towards the room where the branded ones would be taken to rob them of their magic.

The door to this room was open, no doubt because they knew the fresh batch of victims were on their way. We slipped inside and then over to a far corner.

I showed the others the looking glasses on the wall.

They were now all empty, and my heart ached at what this represented. All those people were now slaves in Greater True.

'Their magic is stored in these,' I explained, pointing out the bottles with the fine dust in them.

Delph and Petra looked closely, pale with the horror of it.

'Vega Jane, look, the bottles are *labelled*,' said Delph.

I looked more closely and saw what I had not seen before. Each bottle was engraved with the name of the person, I assumed, from whom the dust had been taken. An idea occurred to me.

I pointed my wand at the bottles and said, '*Minamite.*'

All the glass bottles instantly shrank so they could fit in the palm of my hand. I scooped them up and thrust them into my cloak pocket.

'But, Vega Jane,' said Delph. 'They'll certainly notice they're gone.'

Petra had opened a trunk that sat against one wall.

'Look here.'

It was full of empty bottles.

I looked wildly around. We needed something to fill them with.

Then I saw it. The large hole in the wall from my previous battle was still there.

'Delph, grab that bucket over there and hold it under that hole.'

He did so.

I pointed my wand at the hole and said, '*Springato erupticus.*'

The spell was usually used for tapping water, but it

would unleash whatever was inside something. A moment later, fine grains of sand started pouring out of the wall and into the bucket.

When it was full up, I used my wand to quickly fill all the bottles with the sand and then corked them.

'The names,' said Delph. 'Don't forget the names.'

Petra and I used our wands and began magically engraving names on the bottles. We had only done the front row when Delph said warningly, 'They're coming.'

The door opened all the way, and in marched the branded ones along with their captors, including Endemen. Thankfully, he had left the garm behind.

Still, we shrank back into the furthest corner and watched, our breaths held tightly as we tried to stay perfectly still.

Daphne and the others dutifully lined up against one of the walls and stared at nothing as Endemen paced back and forth in front of them.

I clutched my wand, and I observed that Petra was doing the same.

Delph had balled his hands into fists.

Endemen finally turned to face the group.

He lifted his wand and pointed it at Daphne. A light shot out and plunged directly into Daphne's chest.

She stiffened even more, and her rigid gaze focused on Endemen.

'Did you meet a stranger at Bimbleton Station?' he asked.

Daphne nodded. 'It was a young woman.'

'Her name?'

'Vega.'

Endemen shot one of the Bowler Hats a glance and then returned his gaze to Daphne.

'What else can you tell me about her?'

'She was asking questions. Who we were and where we were from. Very nosy, she was.'

I frowned as I watched Endemen ponder this.

'Did she say where she was from?'

'A place called Wormwood.'

Endemen froze for an instant. 'Well, well,' he said, smiling.

I felt my panic rising. I never should have told Daphne where I was really from. I should have lied. I inwardly groaned at my stupidity.

'What else?' queried Endemen.

'That's all.'

'You lie!'

He snapped his wand at her and she fell to the floor, screaming in agony.

Petra raised her wand but I grabbed her hand.

'Tell me the truth,' Endemen said.

'I am, I swear,' Daphne sobbed. 'I was afraid she was trying to get on the train ahead of us, so I left her.'

'But you told her how to get to Clarendon on Hillshire.'

'No, I didn't. I swear it.'

'You lie.' He looked at the others. 'You all lie.'

Then suddenly, he shouted, '*Rigamorte*,' while giving a backward slash of his wand. A black light shot out of it and slammed into all of them.

They toppled to the floor as though roped together. We all stood there, stunned. I looked down at Daphne.

Her eyes were open and fixed.

Endemen had just killed her.

He had just *murdered* her.

I looked at the others. He had just murdered them all.

Without a backward glance, Endemen and his cronies vanished through the doorway.

I stood there, my chest heaving, my eyes filling with tears as I stared over at dead Daphne, and then at the others. They were all young, barely older than me. And their lives were already over, because of a mark on their hands, and a madman who liked nothing better than to kill.

I fingered the Adder Stone in my pocket. I knew it could not regrow limbs. I believed it could not bring back the dead. But it had brought Harry Two back from *near* death twice. So there was the possibility . . .

I took it out, waved it over Daphne's body and thought the best thoughts I could.

She remained as still and lifeless as ever.

I tried again and again. I finally felt something tug on my sleeve. It was Delph. He shook his head sadly. I slowly put the Stone away.

I had lied to Russell. I had done nothing to save Daphne. I had done nothing to save any of them.

The guilt and shame would never leave me. But there was no time.

I took several long breaths, steeled myself and marched out the door with the others behind me.

I told myself that if I ever had another chance to kill Endemen, I would not hesitate.

23

THE THING IN THE TOWER

We skittered down a hall and turned a corner. And there good fortune finally found us.

Before us was a Maladon in a cloak. Behind him, attired in elegant clothes but with blank eyes, was a tall man.

There was no one else around, and I whispered to Petra what I needed her to do. She nodded and we raised our wands together.

'*Impacto*,' I said. My spell struck the Maladon full in the chest and he slumped to the stone floor.

'*Subservio*,' said Petra, and her spell hit the tall, eyeless man, who instantly became rigid.

I performed the magnification spell and saw that a room across the corridor was empty.

Delph dragged the stunned Maladon into the empty room. I used my wand to bind the Maladon tightly.

Then we turned our attention to the eyeless man.

His clothes were shiny and neatly pressed and looked to be of the best quality. I wondered, and not for the first time, why the Maladons would dress slaves in such finery.

I released the invisibility shield by turning my ring around.

'Can you see us?' I asked.

The man nodded.

So despite the blank eyes he still retained his sight.

I said, 'What is your name?'

'I have no name. I am a Victus.'

I thought back to the labels on the bottles. I hadn't seen a *Victus*, but then I hadn't had time to look at them all.

I looked back at Victus. 'How came you to be here?'

'I do not know. I just am here.'

I sighed. This bloke wasn't being much help.

Delph whispered, 'Vega Jane, they've probably removed his memories. Ask him about now. What he's learned about being here.'

I nodded. 'OK, Victus, what can you tell us about Mr Endemen?'

'He is one of my masters. A great sorcerer.'

'And does *he* have a master here?' I asked sharply. 'The man in the cloak who sits on the throne in the big room?'

'That is our king. Necro. The ruler of everything there is.'

I looked at Delph. ' Necro.'

My greatest fear had just been realized. The evil bloke who'd defeated my ancestors was still *alive*.

'Victus,' I said, 'have you heard of anyone named Virgil here? Or Hector, or Helen?'

He shook his head. 'No. No one with those names.'

'How many Maladons are in the castle?'

'Hundreds. This is where most of my masters live.'

172

'Have you been to True or Greater True?'

'I served my masters in Greater True before coming here.'

'They keep garms and jabbits here. Any other creatures?'

'No.' He paused. 'But I have not been to all parts of the castle. There is the Tower Room.'

'Do you know what's in the Tower Room?' Petra asked.

He shook his head. 'I do know it's heavily guarded.'

'By what?' I asked.

'Two jabbits, for one thing. Magic, for another.'

'Would you like to ever leave this place, Victus?' I asked.

He shook his head. 'Never. This is my home. 'Tis an honour to serve my masters.'

'Even though they don't treat you well? They hit you and curse at you, don't they?'

"Tis my fault when they do. For I have displeased them somehow. They are fair and just.'

I sighed. The bloke's mind was simply too damaged for him to see the truth any longer. Now my thoughts turned to what could possibly be in the Tower Room.

I looked at Victus. 'Do you know how to get to the Tower?'

He hesitated. 'Why do you want to go there?'

'Please, Victus, just tell me. I'd really appreciate it.'

To my surprise, his lips quivered.

'Yes, miss, of course, miss.'

And he told us.

I looked down at the bound Maladon before glancing up at Petra. I know what she wanted to do: kill him. And a large part of me wanted to strike as well. But my practical side took over.

173

'If they find him dead, it will alert the whole castle,' I told her.

She slowly nodded but didn't look pleased.

I removed the bindings from the Maladon and cast a *Confusio* spell over him to muddle his mind enough to where he would not know what had happened. And, most important, would not blame Victus for anything.

I turned once more to Victus and explained what I had done and why.

'I don't want you getting into any trouble for helping us,' I said.

His lips quivered once more.

I put out my hand. 'I want to thank you so much for helping us, Victus.'

He slowly reached out and shook my hand. For a brief moment I thought I saw something else in his blank eyes, something that perhaps had always been there until it was buried so deep Victus had been unable to find it.

I performed the incantation to release him from the *Subservio* spell. His expression didn't really change. But I thought there was an emotion I recognized somewhere deep in his features: gratitude.

We left them behind and, safely under the invisibility shield, made our way cautiously towards the Tower.

We rose higher and higher, following Victus's directions, climbing stone stairs and wooden ladders and winding steel steps.

Then we reached a corridor and I knew we had arrived.

I knew that by the sounds.

A pair of jabbits was screeching.

We rounded the last corner and there they were.

Each was poised on either side of a large metal door. Inside that door was the Tower Room, along with whatever was so important that it required twin jabbits to guard it.

The serpents were swaying back and forth, their hundreds of eyes surveying the hall in front of them. Luckily they couldn't see us, but it wouldn't be long before they smelt us.

'How are we going to do this?' whispered Delph.

We had dealt with jabbits before. But this was tricky. We couldn't have a pitched battle in here. The noise would summon every Maladon in the castle.

I looked at Petra and told her the spell to cast.

She nodded and took aim at the serpent on the right while I focused my attention on the one on the left.

Delph and Harry Two stepped back and waited.

'*Paralycto*,' Petra and I said simultaneously.

The spells shot out and hit the jabbits right in the chest.

They froze mid-screech.

We lowered our wands and glanced appreciatively at each other.

'Right good one,' said Delph.

Harry Two licked my wand hand.

We cautiously moved forward. Victus had said that magic also guarded the Tower Room, but I had no idea what shape this defence would take.

We reached the door safely, though my heart was beating uncommonly fast. It was unnerving to be so close to the vile jabbits, paralysed or not.

I looked at the door, studying the lock. Astrea Prine

had shown me several spells that would open locked doors. *Ingressio* would be too simple. I tried another.

I raised my wand and said, '*Securius terminus.*'

The door swung open.

Suspicion and fear swept over me; this was all far too easy.

I eased the door open and we stepped through.

Delph said, 'We need to hurry, Vega Jane. Someone might come along and see the jabbits all frozen-like.'

The room was not large. The walls were stone. There were openings in the Tower Room about six inches wide, too narrow for anyone to pass through, but they did provide some light and air. It was chilly in here, and I wrapped my coat more closely around me as we crept forward.

I glanced at Delph, who took a long knife from his belt.

Harry Two's hackles rose, and a low growl emitted from his throat.

I used my wand tip to illuminate the centre of the room.

I gasped.

Sitting in a wooden armchair was a crumpled creature dressed in rags. It was tall and painfully thin, its atrophied muscles taut against the bone. The head was overflowing with long white hair and was bowed until it was almost touching a bony knee.

The thing, no doubt seeing my light, turned its head in our direction.

It was all I could do not to scream.

It had no face. No eyes, no nose, no mouth. It was just flat skin so pale that I couldn't believe that it was alive. I was frozen with fear and pity.

Even though it had no eyes, I felt that the thing could see us.

Petra gasped, 'What is that?'

It turned back around and its head once more bent down. I put out my wand light.

'Why would they keep this thing up here under such heavy guard?' asked Delph. 'Why is it so important?'

I edged to one of the slits in the wall and looked out at the countryside. Then I turned to the others. 'We need to get out of here,' I said. 'Now.'

I couldn't explain why, but I knew that something was very, very wrong.

I hurried over to the door and tugged on it.

It wouldn't budge.

I cast my spell to unlock it. It didn't work. I tried every spell I could think of to open that door and not a single one worked.

I put my ear to the metal. I was listening for any sound from the jabbits, but I heard nothing.

'The magic,' said Delph. 'Victus said there was magic guarding this room. I reckon if you get past the jabbits and get in here, they got spells that make sure you don't get *out*.'

I pointed my wand at the slit in the wall. If I could enlarge it, maybe . . . I cast my spell. It immediately rebounded on me and knocked me head over heels across the room.

I slowly rose, rubbing at a painful newly risen knot on my head.

'Hel,' I said.

As I took a step back across the room, the creature shot out a hand and grabbed my wrist. Though terribly emaciated, it was ridiculously strong. I dug my fingers into its flesh to make it let go, but its grip was like iron shackles.

Delph came to my aid, but even with his immense strength, he could not break the creature's grip.

Petra pointed her wand at it and said, '*Impacto.*'

Her spell ricocheted off the thing and she had to duck to avoid being hit.

'Uh, Vega Jane,' said Delph.

'What?' I barked, still struggling to free myself.

'Is it my imagination, or is this room getting smaller?'

I looked wildly around.

He was absolutely right.

The walls were moving towards us. Already the room was half as large as it had been.

I tugged with all the strength that Destin provided me and still I could not break the creature's grip. And the walls were barely two feet from us and were closing in with alarming speed now.

'Let go!' I screamed.

The walls were barely six inches from us, and in a few more seconds we would be smashed flat. I felt one wall hit me in the back.

Delph was pushing back against another wall with all his strength, but it was useless. It pushed him right into me. Petra was next to me and Harry Two on the other side. The walls would be touching within a few seconds. As we watched, the wooden arm of the chair splintered.

It was over. We were done for.

And then Harry Two jumped up and licked the creature's arm.

It immediately let me go.

Frantically, I pointed my wand at the oncoming walls.

'Embattlemento.'

My shield spell sprang out all around us. When the walls hit it, they ground to a halt.

But only for a moment. Then they started moving forward again, but at a much slower pace.

The walls pushed us closer. My lungs were constricted as Delph, Petra and Harry Two were shoved more tightly into me. I could feel the creature's rank breath on my cheek, so close was I to it. Our faces were now an inch apart. There was no room left to even breathe.

As panic set in, I felt my wand hand jerk.

Of course!

I willed my wand to return to its form as the Elemental.

'Everyone hold on!' I shouted.

As I spoke, the door to the Tower Room was vaporized, and Endemen stood in the doorway.

I knew he couldn't see us, but he knew we were there.

He pointed his wand at the narrow space that was all that was left of the Tower Room.

As I had before, I tossed the Elemental upward, but held on.

We were all immediately ripped off our feet, bound together as we were by the magical tether.

The Elemental hit the stone ceiling and blasted right through it.

We were out in the open.

I gulped in several large breaths as we flew, and knew the others were doing the same. I turned back. Endemen was behind us, astride one of the jabbits, which, as it turned out, was of the *flying* jabbit variety, as I had seen from my brief journey back in time when I lived in Wormwood.

Behind him were a dozen Bowler Hats.

Well, I had managed to lose them before. Perhaps I could again.

I zigzagged across the sky, but they matched me move for move, as though they could actually see me.

The jabbit put on a burst of speed and came so close to me that one of the heads tried to bite my boot. I kicked it away in the nick of time.

Then Delph cried out, 'It's the jabbit. It can *smell* us.'

I knew if we attempted to fire spells at Endemen and his cohorts, it would truly give away our positions. I put on a burst of speed and pulled away, but I sensed that Destin could not keep up this pace.

Next instant I saw that Endemen and the jabbit had closed the gap by half and were moving up fast.

'We can't outfly them, Vega,' cried out Petra.

'Then we'll just do this!'

I turned so sharply that the others were swung out wide on the tether.

Now I was heading right for Endemen and the jabbit, though they couldn't see us.

But the jabbit could smell us, and I could tell from its hundreds of confused expressions that it didn't know quite what to make of its prey coming so willingly to the slaughter.

I readied my wand, but Delph shook his head. 'Spell cast will give us clear away,' he said. He pulled out his long knife. 'I'll kill it with this, Vega Jane.'

Petra exclaimed, 'A knife? Against that! Are you barmy or what?'

Delph said, 'My dad told me once that the underbelly of a jabbit is the softest spot on it. And my dad never told an untruth in his life.'

He gripped his blade and readied himself as we roared towards the hideous flying serpent.

Endemen was barely ten feet from us. At our combined speeds, we would crash into each other in another few seconds.

I counted one, then two.

The screech of the jabbit was ear-shattering. I could see every mouth open, all the venomous teeth about to tear into us.

'Vega!' screamed Petra.

I felt Harry Two go rigid in his harness.

They were right on us. I could see the darkened pupils of Endemen's eyes.

'Now,' I shouted.

I dived.

We soared directly under the jabbit.

'Now, Delph, now!'

He pointed the blade straight up.

It ripped into the serpent's underbelly.

Jabbit blood spattered us and the great beast tumbled from the sky, bringing Endemen and his crew down with it.

I turned back around and accelerated to Destin's top speed. I felt the links of the chain against my skin. They were like ice. It was as though my chain instinctively knew that our very survival was at stake. It was giving our escape every bit of power it could provide.

We were far enough away now.

I raised my wand, tapped my leg and cried out, 'Pass-pusay.'

The image of wonderful, safe Empyrean was firmly in my mind.

The next moment we landed at the front door of the place.

I lunged for the huge doorknob, opened the portal, and we all fell inside.

Delph leaped up and slammed the door shut before he slumped to the floor alongside us.

We all just lay there panting and shaking.

As my head cleared, I looked up from the floor to see Pillsbury there.

'Mistress Vega, are you all right?'

I slowly stood with the others. We were all covered in jabbit yuck.

'No, Pillsbury. In fact, I doubt I'll ever be right again.'

24
BOTTLES OF RUIN

The sun was starting to come up as we headed for our respective rooms. I took off my soiled clothes and poured pitcher after pitcher of clean water over me. It magically replenished each time. I scrubbed every inch of me hard with a bar of soap. Then I did the same with Harry Two. I dried us both and I put on clean clothes that Pillsbury had placed in my cabinet.

When I got back downstairs, Petra and Delph were already there, looking somewhat revived in their clean clothes and skins. I could see the memory of what we'd gone through in their eyes; I'm sure it showed in mine.

'What *was* that thing in the Tower Room?' asked Petra. 'It . . . it had no face.'

'And what was so special about it that it needed such heavy guard?' asked Delph.

'I don't know,' I said. 'I know I couldn't make it let go of me.'

I looked at where it had clutched me.

Then I glanced at Harry Two. 'If not for Harry Two,

183

we'd be dead. He was the only thing to make that creature let go.'

I patted Harry Two's head, and he gave me an appreciative lick.

'Endemen killed Daphne and the others,' said Petra in a hollow tone. 'Like it was nothing.'

'We've seen him kill before,' I said. 'Those poor blokes on the train. He doesn't care who he kills, Petra.'

She turned on me, her eyes glittering. 'And yet you let him live back in Bimbleton! If you'd taken my advice, Daphne and the others would still be alive.'

'That's not fair,' Delph said defensively. 'Vega Jane had no way of knowing.'

'He's murderous, Delph,' snapped Petra. 'The point is how could she *not* know. Or how couldn't *you*, for that matter!'

I finally found my voice.

'To kill in cold blood takes a different sort of Wug,' I said quietly. 'And as much as it would truly be convenient to be so evil, I'm not that sort of a Wug. Neither is Delph.' I paused. 'Are you?'

'Maybe I am,' she retorted. 'Since I'm not a *Wug*!'

'So why didn't you just kill them yourself? You could have done.'

She started to answer but stopped.

'Why, Petra?'

'If I *had* killed them, that would have just been proof to you that I'm really and truly a Maladon.'

'Is that the only reason?' I asked. 'I don't think it is.'

'I don't care what you think,' Petra snapped. 'They

have an army! Magic far beyond our powers. If we leave Empyrean again, chances are we won't come back alive. But if we *don't* leave Empyrean, then we can't defeat the Maladons and turn things right again. So what was the point of us fighting our way through the damn Quag!' she positively shrieked.

I glared at her. But there was no getting away from it: she was right.

'I have no intention of spending the rest of my life safely within the lap of luxury here at Empyrean,' I said. 'I fought my way across the Quag to find my family. And to find the truth. Since I haven't discovered either yet, I intend to keep looking. You can do whatever the Hel you want, Petra Sonnet. I've no time or patience for cowards.'

She looked like I had punched her.

'And I reckon that's enough talk for one night,' said Delph, glancing nervously between us.

I ignored him and rolled my wand between my fingers. Petra did the same.

Delph must have noticed the tension. 'Well, I'm knackered,' he said, standing up. 'So I'm going to get some sleep.'

We watched him head up the stairs, and then Petra and I locked gazes once more. She eyed my wand and I hers.

'Do you really want to have a go at me, Petra?' I said coolly.

For just an instant I saw something familiar flicker in her eyes. I strained to think where I had seen it before.

I steeled myself for her attack.

But then she turned and stalked off up the stairs.

185

I let out a long breath.

I waited until she was out of sight, I wasn't sure why, and then I marched up the stairs too.

Poor Delph. If he thought Petra and me taking a blood oath and swearing allegiance to each other would completely solve our differences, well he just didn't understand females.

Though the sun was coming up I fell asleep almost immediately, with Harry Two right next to me. I awoke much later somehow feeling just as tired as I had when I'd gone to bed.

As I washed, I gazed at myself in the looking glass. It seemed that I looked older, more haggard and lost. My limbs were stiff and I had very little energy. I rubbed at a pain in my neck as I walked down the stairs.

Pillsbury was in the kitchen, where Mrs Jolly had laid out a truly sumptuous meal. A few moments later, Petra and Delph staggered in looking as lethargic as I felt. I wondered whether the jabbit venom had affected us somehow.

After Pillsbury and Mrs Jolly left us, we sat down and started to eat. None of us spoke a word or snatched a glance at one another. It was like we were each eating alone.

When I had finished eating, I started to feel a bit better. I set down my glass and looked over at Delph.

He finally gazed back at me, while Petra looked back and forth at us.

'We were almost goners last night about a dozen times,' he said.

I nodded weakly.

'I feel awful,' I said. 'You don't suppose we got some

jabbit venom in us somehow?'

Delph said, 'Vega Jane, if we'd done that, we'd be dead.'

'That's true,' I said thoughtfully. 'What was that thing in the Tower?'

'It seems to me it was a prisoner there,' said Delph. 'And if it was, maybe it's an enemy of the Maladons.'

I shot him a glance. 'Then that might make that thing an ally of ours.'

He nodded. 'That's what I was thinking. We could try and rescue it . . .'

I shook my head. 'Too risky. Don't forget that the damn thing nearly got us killed. The Maladons are tricky. It might have been a trap.'

Delph nodded. ''Tis true enough.'

I slapped my forehead and leaped up.

I ran upstairs, grabbed the coat I had worn the night before and ran back into the kitchen. I put my hand in the pocket and drew out the miniaturized bottles.

'Hel,' said Delph. 'I'd forgotten all about them.'

I set the bottles on the floor, drew out my wand and made the reverse incantation.

The bottles immediately returned to their full size.

'They're all slaves now,' I said in a hollow tone.

Petra glanced over at me. 'But why did the Maladons not just kill them, like they done to Daphne? Why keep them alive at all?'

'Because to them killing is nothing special,' I said. 'But to rob their enemies of their magic? To enslave them? Treat them like cow dung? Now, that would be something truly *special* for those monsters.'

My unspoken thought was, *Monsters — maybe like* you!

We all stared down at the bottles. Each represented a shattered life.

'We learned a lot last night,' I said. 'About how the Maladons operate, how they get their victims right where they want them. The layout of the castle.'

Delph said, 'We didn't see that bloke you talked about. The one on the throne.'

'And I'm glad we didn't. He makes Endemen look positively cute.'

I picked up one of the bottles and looked at the name engraved on it. 'I wonder where Clive Pippen is.'

'Why?' asked Petra.

'Because I'd like to return this to him.'

'You can do that?' she asked, her voice full of wonder with a smidge of disbelief.

'I don't know. Maybe.'

'Well, that's a big maybe, that is,' she retorted.

I agreed, but instead said, 'I think the first thing we need to do is write down all the names of the people on the bottles. We need parchment and ink . . .'

On cue, Pillsbury came in, carrying an ink stick, a bottle of ink and a small journal.

'I happened to hear what you required, Mistress Vega. Here it is.'

'Thank you, Pillsbury.'

The next moment he was gone.

'Helpful bloke, that one,' noted Petra.

Delph said, 'Vega Jane, you got nice handwriting from all your work at Stacks. So Petra and I will read off the names and you write 'em down like.'

I settled at the table, filled my ink stick from the bottle and let it hover over the first blank parchment page of the journal.

'I'm ready.'

They started reading off the names and I dutifully wrote them down.

Amicus Arnold, Pauline Paternas, Tobias Holmes, Reginald Magnus, Charlotte Tokken, Alabetus Trumbull, Clive Pippen, Dedo Datt, Aloysius Danbury, Cecilia Harkes, Sybill Hornbill, Miranda Weeks, Dennis O'Shaughnessy, James Throckmorton, Artemis Dale.

Then they both stopped.

I looked up, my ink stick poised over the parchment, and saw Delph holding an especially large glass bottle. He was staring at it, open-mouthed.

Petra was doing the very same thing.

'What is it?' I asked.

They both slowly turned to look at me.

'What is it?' I asked again.

Instead of answering, Delph simply handed over the bottle.

I took it, with a feeling of dread. Then I saw the name engraved on the glass and all other thoughts were struck clean from me.

VIRGIL ALFADIR JANE.

25

DELPH'S IDEA

I was so shocked that I nearly dropped the bottle. Then I gripped the glass so tightly that I was afraid I was going to crush it in my hand.

Finally, I set it down on the table and closed my eyes.

When I opened them the bottle was still there. Part of me was hoping we had all just imagined its existence.

'They've . . . they've got your grandfather,' said Delph. 'They've got Virgil.'

I looked down at my hands in my lap, lost for words. The mark of the hooks on the back of my hand was burning brightly.

'What is it, Vega Jane?' asked Delph, who was watching me closely.

'I don't know. My mark feels really odd. And it looks stronger than before, don't you think?'

He looked at it carefully. 'Maybe it does.'

Petra interjected, 'So what do we do? If they can beat your grandfather, a bleedin' Excalibur, what chance do we have?'

'It's not clear that they *have* beaten him,' I said defensively.

Petra gave me a look. 'Really? So what, he just gave up his magic all on his own?'

'All I'm saying is that we don't know for certain.'

'Well, it seems *certain* to me that he don't have no more magic,' she retorted. 'It's all in that bottle.'

As much as I didn't want to agree with her, I had to.

Delph said quietly, 'Do you think your grandfather is one of them slaves, maybe in Greater True?'

I picked up the bottle holding my grandfather's magic.

'I don't think so,' I said slowly. 'This bottle is larger than the others. That's a lot of magic. An Excalibur level of magic, I reckon.'

'So?' said Petra.

'So, I don't think they would treat him like all the others because he's *not* like all the others. They would give him extra-special treatment, and not in a good way. I mean punishment. Terrible punishment.'

Delph said, 'I'm not sure I know what you mean, Vega Jane.'

I took a deep breath. Even I was not totally sure what I meant, or I didn't want to be. 'I think my grandfather was the faceless creature in the Tower Room.'

I held up my arm.

'It touched me here and it burned like mad. But my mark also became more pronounced. And why else would it have let me go when Harry Two licked his arm?'

Petra did not look convinced. 'Why would they keep him alive? Why not kill him like they did Daphne?'

'I don't know. Maybe they want to keep him alive for

some other reason.'

'Like what?'

I slowly lowered my arm. 'I don't know!' I felt my face flush. 'You always have lots of questions, but never any answers!'

She gazed steadily at me. 'I came to this whole thing a lot later than you. I don't know anything about your grandfather, or Wormwood, or the Maladons or even magic really. I . . . don't like not knowing things. Maybe that's why I ask so many questions. But I guess it's not fair to always expect you to have all the answers.'

I thought that was as close as I'd ever likely get to an apology from Petra Sonnet.

Back in Wormwood I'd asked lots of questions too, because I also liked to know things. So maybe Petra and I were a lot more alike than I cared to admit.

Delph broke the silence. 'They could be trying to get information from him.'

'What sort of information?' I asked.

'Well, he's from Wormwood. Don't you think these Maladon blokes would just love to get to Wormwood and kill everybody there? I mean, we've all been in hiding there, though most of us didn't know it. They may believe that Virgil can tell them how to get there.'

'Through the Quag?' I said. 'Good luck with that.'

'But Virgil didn't go through the Quag, did he? He was able to bypass it somehow.'

I said, 'We don't know for sure what he did. We just know that he disappeared from Morrigone's home in a whirl of flames. And I believed that was the case when my parents disappeared from the Care too. I just later assumed that he had summoned them somehow. Maybe they were all captured.'

Delph shook his head. 'Remember, the Maladons are on the lookout for your parents. So I don't think they've been caught.'

Petra said, 'Unless they were captured but your parents somehow escaped.'

Delph shook his head. 'I'm not sure how likely that is.'

I was sorely confused now. 'All we know is *if* that creature in the Tower is Virgil, then the Maladons have my grandfather, but not my parents, since they're still looking for them. Perhaps my grandfather held off the Maladons while my parents got away.'

'Now, that's possible,' conceded Delph.

Petra added, 'So I wonder where your parents are now? If they are magical, we could certainly use a couple more wands.'

I sat there staring at the tabletop. I didn't know where my parents were. I had no idea if they *were* magical, or if they even had wands.

I took out the picture of them I had found in that bloke's pocket and looked down at it. The Maladons must have at least seen my parents somehow, otherwise how could they have made a picture of them?

And my grandfather. Was that really him up in the Tower Room? That faceless, shrunken, pitiable creature?

Had I been so close to Virgil that he had actually touched me on the arm? The Wugmort I had been searching for all this time might have been right next to me. And I had left him behind.

I rubbed my eyes. Despite my recent sleep I felt so weary I was afraid I might topple over.

But there was one fact staring me in the face. And it did not bode well for our chances of beating these fiends.

As Petra had said, if they could reduce a mighty Excalibur to that, what hope was there for us to prevail?

I looked up to see Delph staring at me. The way he looked, it was almost as if he could read my thoughts.

'You escaped from them, more'n once, Vega Jane. And you took Endemen's wand from him after blasting him with a spell. So don't short-change yourself in any fight with them blokes. Like I did back at the Duelum, I'd bet on you to win against them.'

'Thanks, Delph,' I said quietly.

When I looked at him, I saw something unexpected in his eyes that made my heart beat faster. I found myself flushing.

'I'd bet on you too, Vega,' added Petra, breaking the moment.

Delph coughed and looked away.

'Thanks,' I said.

I glanced at Delph. 'I thought the hard part was getting through the Quag. Now that seems the easiest bit of it.'

Delph said, 'Way I see it, we need help if we're going to beat the Maladons. Lot more of them than there are of us.'

'Agreed,' I said. 'But how do we change that?'

Delph pointed at the bottles sitting on the table.

'I think the answer lies there. We get the magic back to those people.'

'We don't even know where they are.'

'I think a lot of them are in Greater True. From what you said, that seems to be where the hoity-toity live.'

'OK, let's say they're in Greater True. Let's say we find some of them. Say we manage to get them back here and restore their magic. What good does that do? The Maladons will realize the magic is gone and their slaves are missing. They'll be on their guard and we'll never be able to free anyone else. They might just kill the lot, like Endemen did with Daphne and the others.'

In answer Delph held up a finger. 'We can start with one, Vega Jane. Just one. And we'll figure out a way so they won't know what we're doing. But we have to make sure that we *can* restore the magic. That's the point of all this.'

I shook my head, still confused. 'What exactly is the *point*?' I asked.

Delph glanced over at the bottles once more and then back at me.

'Why, they're going to be your *army* o'course.'

26

THE PATH AHEAD

That night I couldn't sleep. The thoughts in my head were swirling so fast it was like there was a blizzard in my brain.

Groaning, I rose from my bed, put on my cloak, snagged my wand and, leaving a sleeping Harry Two behind, made my way to the library. I shut the door behind me, conjured a fire in the fireplace and sat down in the desk chair facing the flames.

I opened the journal that I had put in a drawer there earlier. We had finished writing down all the names from the bottles, which were lined up on a broad shelf across from me.

I gazed at the bottles. To me they weren't simply glass and dust; they represented flesh-and-blood people whose lives had been savagely ripped from them.

I opened the journal and read down the list of names.

The problem was matching the names and the dust in the bottles to the actual people. How did we find them?

In frustration I slammed the journal shut and slumped back in my chair.

I rose and held the bottle with my grandfather's name on it, peering closely at the letters forming his name.

How had they known he was *Virgil Alfadir Jane*? Had he been forced to tell them?

I looked beyond the name to the dust contained in the bottle. Not only was the bottle different by virtue of its size, but the dust inside was slightly different as well.

I looked more closely. It was a fine texture, when the dust in the other bottles was a bit more granular.

Suddenly I had an idea. I raced back to my room and opened the drawer of my bedside cabinet where I kept my enchanted piece of parchment and pulled it out.

'Silenus?' I had discovered this odd bloke who lived on paper in the Quag.

His face instantly appeared on the page. 'Yes?'

'Silenus, I have a problem.'

He looked expectantly at me.

'Tell me, Vega.'

I explained to him what had happened at Greater True and then my two excursions to Maladon Castle. The possibility that my grandfather might be a prisoner there.

Then I held up the bottle and told Silenus what it contained and how it had got there.

He looked as repulsed by my tale as I felt telling it.

'The thing is, Silenus, we would like to be able to get this dust and all the other bottles back to their rightful owners. Only we have no way to track them down. And if we do find them, we don't know how to return the magic to the people. I know of no spell to do that.'

Silenus nodded. 'I can see how that would be a dilemma

of significant proportions,' he said sombrely.

'Right,' I said, a bit irritably, for I already knew *that*. 'Do you have any ideas on how we could do it?'

Silenus was silent for some time. I waited with increasing anxiety, never taking my gaze off him. If he didn't have an idea, what was I to do?

Finally, he said, 'You will recall, Vega, that we once spoke of the true purpose of magic; the probability of improbability, let us call it.'

I nodded. 'You told me that spell casting came out of necessity.'

'Yes, I did. What is magic but the will of the owner of such power to accomplish something which is desired? You say you want to match the bottles to the people? And then return the magic to them?'

'Yes, of course.'

Silenus now stared over at the bottle of dust containing my grandfather's magical remains. 'If that does indeed contain the magic that once flowed through the spirit of your grandfather, then all that you need is within those grains.'

I said, 'I'm not sure I understand.'

'You believe the creature in the Tower Room is Virgil Alfadir Jane?'

I nodded and said eagerly, 'Yes, I think so.'

'You are wrong.'

'Excuse me?' I said, half in anger, half in disbelief. 'I'm wrong about what?'

Silenus said, 'The creature in the Tower Room is simply a husk, the remains of an animal carcass; only in this case the carcass still breathes.' He eyed the bottle once more. 'There, in that vessel, is your grandfather. He is with you now.'

I looked at the bottle, feeling the first flickering of hope.

'So how do I get him out of the bottle?' I said.

'That is largely up to you. And your wand. But the key element, Vega, is that you must believe. Even a smidgen of doubt and it will not work.'

'How do you know that?'

'Because I have seen what doubt can do, Vega. It can wreck the best-laid plans.'

'I don't understand. Is it that hard to really believe in something?'

Silenus smiled the weary smile of someone who had seen this very thing over and over.

He said, 'It is actually the hardest thing of all.'

And with that, he vanished from the parchment.

I sighed.

Well, that was clear as dung.

Why couldn't the bloke give me a piece of uncomplicated advice just ONCE!

I looked at my wand and then at the bottle.

I raised my wand, pointed it at the bottle and said, 'Virgil Alfadir Jane, please come to me.'

Exactly nothing happened.

I refocused. I willed myself to believe that my grandfather truly was in that blasted bottle.

I waved my wand again, touching the tip of it against the glass of the bottle.

'Come back to me,' I said.

My eyes widened slightly when I saw just a little pop of light at the end of my wand, but then it quickly died out.

I tried several more times, but nothing else happened.

I put the bottle in my pocket and slid the journal in the drawer of my cabinet.

I went back to the library, walked over to the fireplace, gripped the edge of the stone mantel and bowed my head.

How was I supposed to have no doubt – when doubt was all I'd had ever since leaving Wormwood?

As I stared into the flames, I felt the tears creep to my eyes. I had fought so hard. Come so far. And now it appeared that I could go not one inch further.

I slumped down to the floor and curled up into a little ball.

As the timekeeper on the mantel ticked away, I just lay there, not moving.

This is not helping, Vega.

This is stupid.

You're stronger than this.

I rose and turned away from the fire.

I had to do something – anything – to feel like less of a failure.

I picked up the bottle with my grandfather's dust in it. I put my face right next to the glass. I closed my eyes and envisioned my grandfather as I had last seen him.

I opened my eyes and gasped.

My grandfather was in the bottle.

He was hovering in miniature above the pile of fine dust. Suspended in air.

When I blinked, he was gone.

I had only imagined it.

There was nothing there. There never had been.

I set the bottle down and sat back down in the chair.

Empyrean was very quiet. I knew Delph and Petra were asleep. I didn't know if Pillsbury actually slept; I wasn't sure that a suit of armour ever got tired.

As though in answer to my thoughts, Pillsbury appeared next to me, so fast that I nearly tumbled off my chair.

'Do you require anything, Mistress Vega?' he asked.

'What?' I gasped. 'No, I'm . . . I'm fine.'

His visor quivered just a bit.

'May I be somewhat impertinent, Mistress Vega?'

'I suppose so,' I replied uncertainly.

'You have a great deal of burden on your youthful shoulders. If you don't mind me saying, it would overwhelm someone far older and more experienced.'

'I guess so,' I said. 'But I can't use that as an excuse to fail, Pillsbury. I really can't. It's not like I'm going to get another chance to make it right.'

'I recall that Mistress Alice had a similar predicament when she lived here.'

I glanced up.

'What sort of predicament?' I asked.

'She knew that war was coming with the Maladons. I remember seeing her sitting in the very chair you're in now, far into the night, thinking and worrying, thinking and worrying.'

'Did she tell you what she was thinking about?'

Pillsbury nodded. 'I appeared before her, something I did not do lightly. She was a very forceful person, was

201

Mistress Alice. One did not like to intrude.'

He hesitated and rubbed his metal mitts together.

'Go on, Pillsbury, please.'

'Well, I could sense that she might need to talk to someone, or at least voice her concerns out loud. So I provided a way for her to do that.'

'But surely she had her husband, Gunther, to do that with.'

To my surprise, Pillsbury slowly shook his head.

'Master Gunther kept very much to himself on such matters.' He paused once more and then plunged on in a rush. 'He did not want war. Would have avoided it at all costs. *All* costs.'

I slowly revolved this around in my head. 'You mean, even if it meant the Maladons would take over and rule them?'

Pillsbury nodded.

'I could never imagine doing that!' I said forcefully. 'I would much rather die.'

'As would Mistress Alice. As she did,' he added sadly.

'Was she worried that Gunther might do something foolish regarding the Maladons? Something that might hurt Alice and her allies in the war to come?'

'I think she was worried about a great many things,' Pillsbury said diplomatically. 'And I daresay that might have been one of them.'

'You said that Necro came here before the war . . . How soon before the war started?'

'As recently as the night Master Gunther died,' said Pillsbury.

I slowly stood. 'Pillsbury, I have seen Gunther's body in the coffin here. His neck was slit. Are you telling me that . . . ?'

Pillsbury nodded, and I saw a solitary tear emerge from under the visor and meander down the metal skin.

'That foul Necro came here late that night. Mistress Alice didn't know. Necro told my master they would try and avert war. They met in this very room. Just the two of them. And when I came in later to see if they needed anything, there lay my poor master in a pool of his own blood. And the fiend Necro was nowhere to be seen.'

'He *murdered* Gunther?'

'Yes,' said Pillsbury. 'As sure as I'd seen him do it.'

'And what did Alice do?'

'She would have killed him, I'm sure of it, or tried to. But the Maladons declared war the very next day.'

'You said that the war started because Uma Cadmus and Necro's son, Jason, had fallen in love. And then Jason died.'

'That's only partly true. Necro blamed Jason's death on our side. Said that we'd had him murdered. That Uma had done it after bewitching Jason at the behest of her father. That Master Gunther was a coward who had slit his own throat because he knew his side could never defeat the Maladons.'

'What a pack of lies!' I snapped. 'Total rubbish.'

'Of course it was. But nevertheless, the Maladons wanted a war and they got it.'

'And they won it,' I reminded him miserably.

'Yes,' he said, his gaze on the floor.

We both stood there in silence for a bit.

'Pillsbury, there's going to be another war,' I said.

He didn't look at me, but his visor went up and down.

'Yes, Mistress Vega. I daresay there will be.'

'I can't guarantee the outcome. I don't know that we won't be beaten a second time, and utterly destroyed. But I can tell you that I will fight to the death. I don't want peace with the Maladons. I've seen what they're like. I'd rather die than have anything to do with that lot.'

Now he looked at me. I mean he *really* looked at me.

'If you're not the spitting image of Mistress Alice, then I don't know what you are.'

He left me on that note.

I sat back down and stared at the fire for a while. I thought about all that he had told me. It wasn't that I needed more reasons to hate the Maladons, but if I had, Pillsbury had supplied me with plenty more.

They had an army of well-trained sorcerers who could fly and fight and kill.

I had Petra, Delph, Harry Two and a bunch of bottles with dust in them.

Some army.

What I needed, I decided then and there, was my grandfather. A mighty sorcerer, an Excalibur.

I knew exactly what I had to do.

I had to travel back to Maladon Castle and rescue him.

27

A LOSS OF ONE

Maladon castle was directly in front of me.

Harry Two hung in his harness. I had ventured here without Petra and Delph. I had brought Harry Two because he seemingly had a connection with the creature in the Tower Room. Inside my pocket was the bottle with my grandfather's magical dust.

The castle rose from the darkness like a hideous mass.

As I drew even nearer, my jaw dropped.

I had assumed the castle would be quiet at night.

Instead I saw a scene of activity. Figures in cloaks were hustling to and fro. The castle was ablaze with light. The front gates were open.

What the Hel was going on?

I supposed that the chaotic scene I was witnessing did provide certain advantages.

I unbuckled Harry Two and attached him to me with a magical tether from my wand.

OK, here we go.

We set off at a trot towards the castle.

We quickly reached the circle of light thrown off by the entrance. To the left and right of us were Maladons in long red cloaks. I couldn't see their faces because their black hoods were drawn up.

For some strange reason I felt no fear being in the midst of my enemy. I felt, instead, a certain inexplicable calm.

We were ten feet from the open gates when I saw him.

Endemen burst forth from the entrance to Maladon Castle like a raging storm.

His hood was down and I could see his true, evil features. He had transformed into what he really was: that creature I had seen before. It was far more terrifying than the conjured face he normally wore.

He shouted to his fellow Maladons in some language I could not understand. His voice sounded urgent, but also strangely jubilant.

My feet started moving and I was past Endemen and through the open gate.

Harry Two and I darted off to a side corridor as I frantically tried to remember the directions to the Tower.

Oh, to Hel with it.

I drew my wand and muttered, *'Pass-pusay.'*

The Tower Room corridor was firmly in my mind.

An instant later we were outside of it.

The first thing I noted: There were no jabbits stationed outside.

The second thing I noted: There was no door.

They knew someone had been in the Tower Room before. So they had walled it up.

Now the question became: Was the prisoner still in there?

I pondered this for a few moments even as the sounds of whatever was going on down below reached my ears.

I drew close to the wall and put my ear against it. I could hear nothing.

But that wasn't good enough.

I pointed my wand and whispered, '*Crystilado magnifica.*'

Now I had my answer. The room was completely empty. Even the slits in the walls were gone.

They had moved him elsewhere. I frowned, thinking. They had kept him in the highest point of the castle. So what if they had moved him to the lowest? I turned around, and Harry Two and I made our way back down.

The activity had diminished quite a bit, and we didn't have to dodge Maladons flying through the corridors.

I spied the stairs heading down into the bowels of the castle. They didn't look the least bit appealing. Then I spotted someone familiar walking past me and carrying something.

'Victus,' I hissed.

He turned and looked around with his all-white eyes.

'It's me, Vega. I asked you before about the Tower Room, remember?'

He slowly nodded.

'I . . . I can't see you,' he said.

'I know. I'm invisible. What's going on around here? Why all the activity?'

'I do not know. Master has simply told us to prepare some things. Provisions and the like, for a journey.'

'A journey where?' I said.

He shook his head. 'Master has not said.'

I eyed him closely. 'Victus, do you remember who you used to be?'

He flinched for an instant.

I added, 'Because you were not always Victus. You were someone else entirely. And you were magical. Just like your masters.'

He shook his head sharply, but I could see in his tightened features that there was . . . something.

'No. I am simply Victus.'

I said, 'Will you be going with your master on this journey?'

He shook his head. 'Only the masters will go. We will remain behind.'

I nodded, thinking this over. 'Victus, the prisoner who was in the Tower Room. Do you know where they took him?'

'I cannot say.'

'Can't, or won't?'

''Tis the same to me.'

'I think not,' I said sharply.

He flinched once more.

I gripped his hand with mine. He instantly became invisible along with me. His skin was icy, but it began to warm under my touch.

'I think you could tell me if you really wanted to. That person is my grandfather, Victus. He is a prisoner here. I want to help him. But to do that I need your help. You helped me once before. Will you do so again?'

'You were very kind to me before, miss. You *thanked* me. I have never before heard those words here.'

'That's because your masters are evil and they don't care

208

about you. But I do. I want to free you, Victus. And all others like you. I hope you can see that.'

A moment passed as innumerable emotions seemed to flit across his sightless features.

He said in a hoarse voice, 'The person you require is not down below.'

'Where, then?' I asked.

'He is in the Great Hall with our one true master.'

My spirits collapsed. Necro. 'What's he doing in there?'

'I do not know. But I saw him there.'

'Is he in chains?'

Victus shook his head.

'Thank you, Victus. You've been very helpful.'

He bowed his head. 'I wish you luck, miss.' He paused and then added, 'Was I really magical, once?'

'You all were. And if I have anything to say about it, you'll be magical again.'

I let go of him, turned and rushed towards the Great Hall with Harry Two right next to me.

We finally reached the grand doorway leading into the even grander room, even if it had, at its epicentre, such a foul thing.

The one true master?

Rot. I gingerly put a foot over the threshold, and my dog followed.

I looked up and saw that the glass ceiling I had smashed through previously had been repaired.

The room was vast and empty.

Well, nearly so.

Up at the front I saw something. Something quite odd.

209

There was the throne. Seated in it was the ancient Necro.

In his hand was a wand. It was the blackest thing I had ever seen. It reminded me of the darkness I associated with Orco, of the world of the dead.

The wand was pointed at the pitiful person from the Tower Room. Something was emanating from the wand and piercing the body of the other. A ray of darkness, black as the wand and mostly hidden in the shadows of the room.

I drew my wand but was unsure what to do. As I hesitated, Necro lifted his wand and the black beam vanished. The poor faceless creature toppled from its stool and fell to the floor. With a flick of his wand, Necro vanished. I rushed forward and reached the spot where the creature lay. When I touched the skin it was cold and clammy.

Could this be my grandfather? Harry Two brushed past me and sniffed at the creature. Then he pushed his nuzzle against the cold hand, and I saw one finger twitch.

Harry Two stepped back and looked up at me as if to say, *There you go, mate – it's him.*

'Thanks, Harry Two,' I murmured.

I had Destin around me, which meant my strength was greatly multiplied.

I lifted the figure gently, and he became invisible.

'Grandfather,' I whispered into his ear. 'Are you OK? What did he do to you?'

I got no answer to my questions.

Carrying my grandfather, I hurried from the room.

The corridor outside was empty.

In my mind I assembled the floor plan for the castle and my method of escape. We hurried along the long corridors until we reached the main gate.

Two Maladons were stationed there, obviously guarding the exit.

I slipped past them, ran further on and then lifted into the air.

When I looked back down, the castle was as dark and silent as death.

Where had they all gone?

I had a sudden terrible thought. What if they had discovered Empyrean? When I returned home, would I find it destroyed? Delph, Petra, Pillsbury and Mrs Jolly and all the others dead? Was *that* where the Maladons had gone?

I tapped my wand, incanted my spell, and the next moment I was standing in front of my ancestral home. To my relief, it looked as normal.

Carrying my grandfather, I went inside, with Harry Two right behind me. I laid my grandfather down and turned my ring back around so that we became visible once more.

Pillsbury appeared in front of me, looking quite normal and unsurprised that a wretched, faceless creature was lying on his polished floor.

'Mistress Vega, can I be of assistance?'

'You can fetch Delph and Petra for me.'

'Of course.'

He vanished.

A few moments later I heard two pairs of feet hurtling down the stairs and the next instant Delph and Petra, still in their night things, were standing in front of me.

'Where have you—' Delph stopped when he saw the creature on the floor.

Petra gasped. 'You . . . you went back and got him?'

I slowly nodded. I could hardly believe that had all happened.

'How did you manage it?' spluttered Delph.

I ignored them. This was no time for questions.

I pointed my wand and said, '*Rejoinda* bottle of Virgil Alfadir Jane.' I curled my hand towards me and the next instant the large bottle came hurtling into the room. I neatly caught it in my free hand.

I looked at Delph. 'I have no idea how to get his magic back to him, but we need to figure it out, and fast. Maybe that book with the dark spells will have something about reversing it?'

Delph nodded and turned to get the book when Harry Two did the most extraordinary thing. He leaped up and knocked the bottle out of my hand.

We all watched, too stunned to move, as the bottle fell right towards the crumpled figure on the floor. At the last second, the stopper came off the bottle and the dust cascaded out, covering the body underneath it.

The dust didn't simply land on the body and stay there. It was absorbed into the skin. It was as though the thirsty body was greedily sucking up every last drop of it.

We all waited for what seemed like forever, but could have been only mere moments. Then a blinding flash of golden light seared across the room.

I shut my eyes. When I opened them, there was no huddled mass on the floor.

Standing in front of me, nearly as tall as Delph, and robust in every way, was a man I had not seen since I was six years old.

212

My grandfather, Virgil Alfadir Jane, stood before us. He seemed not to have aged a jot since I had last seen him.

My spirits soared. I wanted to leap into his arms.

'Grandfather, it's me, Vega!'

He looked at me. In those eyes I saw many things: love and sadness chief among them. I couldn't understand why he would look sad. Not now. Not when we had been reunited at last. Not after all that had happened in between.

He was here at last. My grandfather and I had been reunited.

He reached out his hand and took my fingers in his. They were cold. Yet the look in his eyes was full of warmth.

He smiled at me.

'Oh, Vega, my very, very dear grandchild.'

His words were faint, like a wisp of smoke, when I remembered his voice as a deep, powerful baritone. But I didn't care. A single tear emerged from his right eye and slid down his cheek.

'How I have longed to see you, Vega, over these many sessions.'

His hand went to my chin and stroked it. I gripped his hand with both of mine, the tears spilling on to my face, and I made no effort to wipe them away. I knew that Petra and Delph were waiting at a respectful distance and could see me crying, but I didn't care.

This man had been gone from my life for so long. Yet looking up at him, feeling his hand upon my skin, it was as though we had just recently parted.

'I . . . I missed you so much,' I stammered. 'I've been

trying to find you for so long. And now . . . now you're here. We're together.'

I hugged him tightly, burying my face in his chest, breathing his scent in, squeezing him so hard that he couldn't possibly ever leave me again.

He embraced me back with those strong arms that I remembered enveloping me when I was a child. When I was scared, he would comfort me. When I was joyful, he would rejoice with me. Every such memory came flooding back to me.

Then his grip suddenly weakened, and I felt him tremble.

'Grandfather?' I said, alarmed.

Gently, he guided me away from him, so we could look at each other. 'I always knew you were special, from the very night you were born,' he said quietly. 'You above all others. I knew it and felt it and I have not been disappointed in those beliefs.' His face crinkled into a smile.

I smiled up at him. 'Together, Grandfather, together we can manage this. We can defeat them. I know that we can do this. You're an Excalibur. And I'm, well, I can fight too. I think that—'

He held up a hand to quiet me.

'But our time together will be very short, I'm afraid, my dear, dear Vega.'

I froze. 'What? No! I just found you. You can't leave me. You can't!'

He paused for what seemed like an eternity as I stared up at him.

'I must. For you see, Vega, I am, unfortunately, already dead.'

214

There are times in everyone's life when loss strikes.

When one's heart breaks.

There are times when you truly feel as though you have no heart left, so shattered is it.

This was such a time for me.

I stared at my grandfather.

'You're . . . you're . . .' I could not say it. I could not say that word.

'He killed me, Vega,' my grandfather said simply.

'Necro,' I said, my eyes brimming with fresh tears.

I glanced back at Delph and Petra. They appeared to be cast in stone.

'He is a very powerful sorcerer,' said my grandfather. 'Who knows things that we never will. But we cannot dwell on that. We have things to discuss. You must have questions. Even as a young, you had more questions than every other Wug. So please, ask away, Vega.'

This was like a bad dream. Haltingly, I said, 'What . . . happened . . . after you left Wormwood? Where did you go?'

'I left to lead an uprising against those who had destroyed our ancestors.'

Now I said what I had to say. 'You . . . you left me behind.'

He reached out a hand for me but I stepped away from it.

There was a sound behind me. I looked around and noticed that Pillsbury and Mrs Jolly had entered the hall and were staring at us.

Pillsbury took a step forward. 'May I get you some refreshment, sir?'

Virgil glanced at me, and his eyes carried a twinkle. He turned to Pillsbury. 'I have quite enough refreshment being with my granddaughter, thank you, upset though she may be with me right now.'

'Your granddaughter? Then you are a Jane, sir?'

'Virgil Jane. I wish we could have met under better circumstances, but there you are.' He glanced around the room once more and said, 'What is this place?'

'It's our ancestral home, Empyrean,' I said. 'But surely you know of it. You're an Excalibur. You know all.'

'I know a great many things. But I do not know all, Vega. I never knew about this place.'

He looked at my pocket, where the end of my wand was sticking out. He pointed to it. 'Is that how you came to know of it?'

'Yes, it sort of pointed the way for me.'

'And how came you by your wand?'

'Alice Jane Adronis, the last Jane to live here. It was the Elemental and then it became my wand. Astrea Prine

216

trained me up in the Quag. Do you know her?'

'Alas, I do not, having not gone through the Quag myself.' He eyed my finger. 'I see that my ring made its way to you.'

'It was at Quentin Herms's cottage. Thansius gave it to me before I fled Wormwood. Quentin also left me a map and a book.'

He nodded. 'I know. Before I left, I asked him to do so, when you were of a proper age.'

I gaped. 'You . . . you asked him?'

'Yes. Herms was my trusted friend. Quite magical as well. On my instructions, he ventured into the Quag as far as possible and mapped it and took notes of all he saw.'

'And my parents? I know you summoned them. I was there when it happened. I could have gone with them,' I added, with a trace of bitterness.

'But I did *not* summon them, Vega.'

I stared at him. 'What! But if you didn't, how did they leave Wormwood?'

'I do not know. I had no idea they had left Wormwood. I have not seen them here. I hope with all my heart that they are safe.'

I took out the picture. 'I think they're out fighting the Maladons too,' I said proudly. 'I found this in a Maladon's pocket.'

His face crinkled into a smile. 'I am so pleased.'

'How were you captured?' I said. I had so many questions, and less time than I had hoped.

'I have spent the sessions since I left Wormwood collecting information, making contacts where I can, and causing as much strife for the Maladons as possible. Because of my efforts I believe they have given the insurrection a name.' He pointed to the wording on the back of the picture.

'The Campions?' I said.

He nodded. 'Of which your parents are apparently now members. I only wish I had been able to join them.' He paused for a moment, as though gathering his thoughts. 'Well, my efforts came with more and more risk. Finally, I found myself surrounded by fifty Maladons. While I am, or rather *was*, extraordinarily powerful, the odds were against me. I managed to kill a dozen of them before I was beaten.'

'Was Endemen there?'

'Yes. Him and his hatted men. They are the most elite fighters of the Maladons. They and I have spent much time together since I was captured. They lavished considerable attention on me,' he added drily. 'I am sorry I will not be able to return the favour. They wanted information. Information that I would not give them.'

'What information?' I asked.

Delph spoke up. 'They wanted a way through the Quag. So they could finish the job.'

Virgil glanced at him. 'It's Daniel, isn't it? You're Duff Delphia's son?'

'Yes, sir.'

Virgil studied Delph for a bit before saying, 'You're quite perceptive, Daniel. I remember you being the same way as a young.'

Delph gulped and said, 'Thanks.'

Virgil next turned his attention to Petra.

'And I don't believe we have met.'

Under his gaze, Petra flushed.

'I'm . . . I'm P-Petra , M-Mr Jane. I l-lived in the—'

'In the Quag,' Virgil finished for her. 'Yes, I have heard of such cases. The process was messy at the end. People were trapped between worlds, as it were. I'm very happy that you've survived and have joined this lot.'

'Are my parents Excaliburs, like you?' I asked.

'No. But they are magical. I shared much knowledge with them.'

'Which is why Morrigone cursed them into the Care,' I said spitefully.

'I did not know that.' Virgil studied me closely. 'If I had the power to summon Wugs from afar, Vega, I never would have left you behind. Do not believe for one sliver that I would have.' He paused. 'You were only six sessions old when I left. You needed to discover things on your own. As I did. I knew you were special, Vega, but it was the only way to see if you had the heart as well.'

'But the Maladons beat our ancestors in the war,' I noted.

'Evil can triumph over good. But that often has more to do with the failings of the good than the successes of the bad. Now,' he said briskly, 'I must convey to you what I know and what I have discovered.'

I noticed that his voice was growing weaker. We all of us drew closer to him.

'You've been to True and Greater True, then?'

I nodded.

'True is the place where they alter the minds of all who are non-magic. Then they labour there with smiles on their faces until they die.'

'We've seen how they do that,' I said. 'But can you explain Greater True? The young soldiers they have? And the arrogant people with the slaves?'

I saw my grandfather's face turn to a furious scowl.

'That is the genius of it, Vega. The pure genius of the Maladons.'

'What is?' I said breathlessly.

'The Maladons were very quick to see that there were relatively few of them, while there were a great many non-magicals, or "Ordinaries", as they derisively refer to them. So they came up with a diabolical plan.'

'They put some blokes on the top and other blokes on the bottom,' said Delph.

We all turned to him.

'Yes, Daniel,' replied Virgil. 'That is precisely what they did.'

Delph added, 'If some blokes have it better than others, with slaves and coin and all, they're content-like. They feel like their lives are good, so why would they want to change them. Eh?'

'Exactly,' said Virgil, looking pleased.

I looked at Delph with even greater respect. 'That's brilliant, Delph.'

'Yeah, brilliant,' echoed Petra.

Virgil said, 'Mark this carefully. True and Greater True are the largest towns I have been able to locate, and I have searched high and wide. The rest of this world is made up of smaller establishments, scattered villages, small homesteads, where those who live there labour hard for little. Word of these train stations is slowly spread among them. Trains that will take them to a better life.'

I nodded. 'We've been to Bimbleton Station. It was awful.'

'There is also a befuddlement incantation around the areas monitored by the Maladons. True, Greater True and the other towns of some size. No one unauthorized can ever find their way to any of those places.'

'Which means folks have to take the train,' I said.

'The Maladons didn't stop there. No brainwashing plan is perfect. People marry and have youngs and they grow up with certain independent thoughts in their heads. They might have grown up to resent those with more than them, or even the Maladons, though their presence is not widely known. So the Maladons came up with another plan.'

'What was that?' I asked.

'You mentioned the young soldiers with their uniforms and marching?'

I nodded.

'Well, aside from the Maladon army, they have a regular army as well, composed of males; the Elite Guard they're called. Male youngs are compelled to be part of military training as well, from an early age, until they are ready to serve their time in the ranks. To prepare to fight their enemy.'

'But who do they think their enemy is?' Delph asked.

'When you don't want those you rule to revolt against you, you have to give them something else to fear, to hate. Everyone under the rule of the Maladons has been taught from a young age that there is a great enemy out there just waiting to invade them. They focus all of their hatred and attention on that imaginary foe, and thus they never realize that they have already been enslaved.'

'But surely folks notice the enemy *never* attacks,' interjected Petra.

That was a good point, I thought.

Virgil responded, 'Oh, but they *do* attack. It's not the "enemy" of course, because there is none. No, the Maladons accomplish that any number of ways. They take innocent folks and implicate them in attacks that they themselves have performed. Or they use their magic to perform attacks against the people. These attacks are then repelled by the military might, and everyone ends up feeling absolutely wonderful at such grand victories. The Maladon parade those who have been enslaved as war criminals. They are dealt with summarily.'

We all fell silent. This was a great deal to take in, and I noted with growing alarm that my grandfather was looking weaker by the moment.

I held up my gloved hand. 'Underneath here is the mark that is on your hand. It was the Maladons' doing. It was burned into my flesh the instant I neared the end of the Quag. I keep the glove on it, otherwise the Maladons can track me.'

He nodded, his features sombre. 'I found that to be the case too. I had no glove. But I managed a particularly complex spell that rendered any Maladon who saw my mark temporarily blind.'

That was rather smart, I thought.

He pointed at the ring on my finger. *His* ring.

'Has this served you well?' he asked.

I nodded. 'Without it we would all be dead. So yes, it has served us very well. How did you come by it?'

'I travelled back in time through the portal at Stacks. Eon gave me a choice: the past or future. I chose the past. The ring was given to me by an interesting fellow: Colin Sonnet.'

We all gasped. I shot Petra a glance, to find her staring wide-eyed at my grandfather.

'How did you come to meet him?' I asked.

'When you go back in the past, there is not always rhyme or reason where you land. He owned a small shop with many interesting articles. He had also penned several books on sorcery.'

I know of at least one, I thought.

'But why did he give up the ring to you?' I asked, still watching Petra.

'He insisted that I take it. He seemed to think that a great war with the Maladons was nearing and he did not wish the ring to fall into their hands.'

'What was he like?' This came from Petra. She added nervously, 'See, my surname is Sonnet. Colin was . . . was my ancestor, I guess.'

'He was a good fellow. Solidly against the Maladons, though they had not yet adopted that name. Back then they were merely referred to as the worshippers of Necro.'

'Solidly against the Maladons,' repeated Petra.

Virgil nodded. 'He told me that the ring's origin was not incantation by sorcery, but rather the confluence of mystical powers coming together at just the right moment.

Quite a phenomenon of serendipity, but magic is often that way.'

A silence followed. Petra was now looking down at her bare feet.

I finally said, 'Alice Adronis gave me the Elemental as she lay dying on the battlefield. It's now my wand because we were family. But I can make it the Elemental whenever I want.'

'Transform it for me,' he said quietly.

I reached into my pocket and drew out my wand, then willed the Elemental to its full, golden size.

My grandfather stared at it reverently.

'I never met Alice Adronis. But I have learned of her past from various sources, and it was a tortured one. Her father was hard and cruel; he wanted only sons and never loved the daughter he had instead. He cast her out on her own one night and told her never to return. Between you and me, it seems that her father, even though a Jane, had more than a bit of the Maladon blood in him.'

Petra glanced at me. I could read her thoughts: *So how does it feel to perhaps have a bit of Maladon blood in you too?*

I turned back to my grandfather. 'What did Alice do?' I said breathlessly.

'One night, a terrible storm raged. She climbed to the highest peak in the land. On that peak was the tallest tree. She climbed to the very top of it, held out her hand as far as she could to the storm raging above and swore that if she was granted the wand she felt she deserved that she would always use it in defence of good, and to battle evil.'

Petra gasped, 'What happened?'

'A lightning spear shot down from the heavens and struck her right at the point of her finger. From that finger grew the Elemental. I don't know if you ever noticed that Alice only possessed four fingers on her right hand.'

I shook my head. 'She gave me her glove, which she said I had to wear in order to touch it. But Astrea Prine told me I needn't do so, and she was right.'

'Then you are the true inheritor of the thing,' pronounced Virgil. Next he groaned and clutched his head.

I knelt beside him. 'Is there nothing that can be done? I have a stone that heals almost all injuries.'

He looked up at me and managed a tortured smile. 'Nothing. Dear Vega. How I have thought about you all these many sessions. And to now be reunited for such a short period of time. It is hardly fair.'

'It's *not* fair,' I said, blinking back fresh tears.

'Such is life, I'm afraid.' He drew a long breath. 'The Maladons are everywhere. Of course at the castle, but also in True, Greater True and other places. They will look just like anyone else if they so desire. When they are at the castle they can revert to their natural form.'

I shuddered, remembering.

He sighed. 'I pity them, I do indeed.'

I said incredulously, 'You pity the Maladons? After all the evil they've done? After their leader has *killed* you?'

'Yes, Vega, I do. I suppose that is what separates us from them. We can feel compassion for others, whoever and whatever they might be. Regardless of what they might have done.'

He had now grown so pale that it was difficult to see him.

''Tis very near the end,' he said in a weak voice.

'Grandfather,' I cried out. 'I don't want you to leave me. I need you.'

'All you need, Vega, my dear child, you already possess. Please know that above all else, you will carry my love for you wherever you go. For I have loved you with all my heart, dear, dear Vega, since the moment of your birth.'

And with that he was gone.

29

FAREWELL

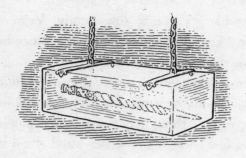

I did not come out of my room for the next two days.

When I finally did come downstairs with Harry Two by my side, Mrs Jolly had made a scrumptious breakfast, which Pillsbury served despite my protests that I could serve myself.

I was halfway through my meal when Delph and then Petra made their appearances. We sat and ate for a while in silence.

Finally, I said gloomily, 'Well, it's just us now.'

Delph laid aside his fork and looked at me. 'Virgil told us helpful things.'

'He prepared us, best he could,' said Petra. 'And it was good to know that my ancestor helped him.'

'Yes, it was,' I said.

If only I had managed to save my grandfather in the Tower. I had failed. And he had been finished off by the murderous Necro. How could I expect to lead others into a war when I couldn't even save one person?

Delph put a hand on my shoulder and said, 'I'm really

sorry, Vega Jane. Virgil was a great Wug.'

Petra put her hand on my other arm. I was surprised to see that there were tears in her eyes.

'I know what it's like to lose family, Vega,' she said slowly. 'And I know what it's like to . . . to not be able to save someone.'

I thought of her family being slaughtered by creatures of the Quag. Losing her uncle to a lycan attack and being unable to save him. I thought of her guilt in losing Lackland, of not being fast enough to use her wand when she could have done.

I had always thought that if I found my grandfather, he would lead and I could simply follow. That had always been in the back of my mind. Now, that was not possible. It all came down to me.

Petra said, 'You can't save everyone, can you? But the thing is, if you don't try, then you'll save no one. I've seen what you can do, Vega. I've seen how many times you've saved us. From jabbits and the Soul Takers and the like. I wouldn't be alive but for you, and neither would Delph. So if you're thinking you can't save blokes, well, you'd be wrong. Because you already have.'

She fell quiet and removed her hand.

We all sat there in silence for a time, not looking at one another.

Finally, I rose and said, 'If we're going to make a go of this, we need to make plans. We'll be surprised, no doubt, by what we'll be faced with, but we have to plan for that too. We must never again be so surprised that all we can do is flee.' I swallowed. 'We must never again leave someone behind.'

They both mutely nodded at this.

'Virgil told us a lot about this world. Some we knew and a great deal we didn't. The Maladons are well organized and powerful sorcerers. We can't underestimate any of them.'

'Vega Jane,' began Delph. 'Why do you think they picked now to . . . to kill Virgil?'

'I don't know, Delph. I suspect it had something to do with what was going on at the castle. There was a great deal of activity. We need to find out what it was about.'

'How do we do that?' asked Petra. 'Go back there?'

I shook my head. 'We've risked going back enough as it is. I think there might be a better way. We can find out more in Greater True.'

'Why?' asked Petra.

'Because that's where our army lies.'

'Do you want to leave now?' asked Petra.

'In a bit. I have a few things to do first.'

I marched up the stairs. There was nothing I needed to do, but I needed an excuse to gather myself. I couldn't fathom that my grandfather was gone.

I couldn't see how I would ever find my parents.

The thought of me leading an army to defeat the Maladons was ridiculous. I imagined telling Cletus Loon what I was expected to do and hearing him roar, 'Barking, you are. Why, you're only a *female*!'

I opened the door to my room and then looked behind me.

Harry Two had not followed me up. I wondered what that was about.

I closed my door and lay on my bed, looking at the ceiling.

It seemed like I had been running for my life ever since I stepped into the Quag, with no time to think things through.

Only, now I had to. I *had* to think.

I had set out from Wormwood – escaped, really – fought my way across the Quag, survived Endemen and his men, to find the truth. I had found it. And now I had to somehow fix it. But how?

My head was swimming. I closed my eyes and then reopened them.

And there she was.

Uma Cadmus was hovering right above me.

I sat up. 'My grandfather is dead,' I said. 'Virgil is dead.'

She nodded slowly.

'I'm expected to defeat the Maladons, but I don't know how to do so. My grandfather told me a lot, but he didn't tell me how to do that.'

Again, she nodded knowingly. 'He wouldn't have, would he?'

'Why not?'

'One can only defeat the Maladons by fighting them. It is through fighting them one comes up with ways and methods and strategies to do so. One cannot sit back and contemplate how to manage it. One must be engaged in the war.'

As she was speaking, she floated down from the ceiling to sit next to me.

I had to admit it was a bit disconcerting having, well, *regret* perched on my bed.

'Your father believed that Necro wanted peace,' I said a bit crossly. 'And instead he got a war.'

'My father was a good man who was fooled by a cleverer one,' she said with proper spirit. I could imagine myself defending my father in the same way.

'Well, your father and my ancestor Alice Adronis and Astrea Prine were all great magical beings. My grandfather was an Excalibur. And *they* couldn't beat the Maladons. I hardly see how I have any chance of victory.'

I watched as she stared off into the distance. There was so much hurt in her eyes that I seemed to feel it in my bones.

'You . . . you loved Jason very much, didn't you?'

She slowly turned to me. 'As much as one could love another,' she said simply.

'I haven't felt that way about anyone,' I said.

'Are you certain about that?'

I looked at her in confusion. 'What do you mean?'

'I have seen how you look at your friend Delph. And I see how he looks at you.'

I felt the blood rush to my face and I had to turn away.

'We're just friends.'

'Friendship often is and should be a precursor to love.'

I glanced back at her. 'You said you represent regret. Does that mean you regret loving Jason?'

'That is the only thing I do *not* regret.'

I took a deep breath. 'Uma, can you help me? I . . . know I must do this, but I'm not yet sixteen years old and . . . and I'm terrified that I'm going to fail and let everyone down.'

Uma reached out a hand and gripped mine.

This stunned me, for I had just assumed that she was not flesh and bone.

'Let me show you something,' she said.

She rose and drifted out of the room. I hurried after her.

I followed her ghostlike form down corridors and up staircases. We finally reached a passageway that I hadn't seen before.

At the end was a simple wooden door.

She passed right through it, whereas I was forced to use the doorknob.

When I entered, Uma was hovering next to the far wall.

The room was not large, but it was brightly lit by torches that came to life at my entry.

There wasn't a stick of furniture in the room. In fact, there was only one item in the entire space: a small glass box hanging from the wall.

In that box was a wand.

It was long and as golden in colour as the Elemental when fully formed.

Even though no one was holding it, it seemed to pulsate with power.

'Whose wand is that?' I asked.

'My father's.'

'That's Bastion Cadmus's wand?' I exclaimed.

'He was a tremendously powerful sorcerer. It was acknowledged by all that even Alice Adronis was second to him in ability.'

'But how did his wand come to be here?'

'Alice recovered it and brought it here after he was killed.'

'If he was so powerful, how exactly did he die? On the battlefield?'

'No. He was betrayed.'

'By whom?'

'Victoria, my mother and his wife.'

I gasped. 'How did that happen?'

'She didn't do it voluntarily. I was already dead, and the war had commenced. She was placed under the *Subservio* spell and she gave the Maladons information about my father – including when he would be home alone. She let them in and my father found himself surrounded by Maladons one night. There was no one to help him. He killed a dozen of them, but he had received a mortal wound. He died in the great hall of his beloved home.'

'I'm sorry, Uma,' I said.

'Necro did not want to face him on the battlefield. He knew my father would triumph. Yes, he never wanted war, and yes he may have gone too far in trying to appease the Maladons. But he was a tremendous warrior, which is why they decided to get to him by trickery, using my poor mother.'

'That's awful, Uma.'

'He was not simply my father, you know, but the father of *all* of our people. So when he died, much of the spirit went out of us,' said Uma wistfully. 'And the Maladons took full advantage of that. They fought even more fiercely. They could sense weakness. They smelt blood. They did terrible things.'

I looked at the box as she traced her fingers over the glass. Though it could have been my imagination, it seemed as though the wand sparked at her touch of the glass.

'I think that's why I remain here,' she said. 'To be somewhere that was happy, that was safe. That was free of the Maladons!' she concluded fiercely.

'What happened to Victoria — to your mother?'

'She came out of the spell, realized what she had done . . . and killed herself.'

I could think of nothing to say.

'Like mother, like daughter,' said Uma gloomily.

'You thought the love of your life was dead,' I said.

Delph's face shot through my mind.

What would I do if something happened to Delph? If he were killed?

She said, 'Do you know what the most powerful thing in the world is?'

I shook my head.

She took my hand and pressed it against my chest.

'That is the most powerful thing there is, Vega. All magic, all grand sorcery, pales next to it.'

'My heart?'

'And what it represents. It means desire, Vega. It means what you want more than anything else. But there are differences in feelings. In their potency.'

'How do you mean?' I asked.

'Some are fleeting, like fear and happiness. Others are more permanent. Like vanity or kindness. But in my brief life I found that there are only two that stand the test of time, that define who and what we are.' She paused. 'Love and hate.'

'Does that mean I will be soundly defeated as well?'

She again pressed my hand to my chest.

'The answer to that, Vega, lies right here.'

And in the next instant, she vanished.

I sat there for what seemed a very long time.

I nearly jumped when I felt something touch my hand.

I looked down, and there was Harry Two. He had finally decided to follow me. I was a bit cross, but when I looked down into his beautiful, mismatched eyes so full of love, my annoyance slipped away.

Love was indeed very powerful.

As I sat there thinking about that, and what Uma had said, a plan came together in my mind. A real plan, with precise steps and a goal at the end.

I stood and took out my wand.

I guess it all came down to whether I believed in myself or not.

I went back to my room, packed my tuck, threw it over my shoulder and headed down the stairs with Harry Two marching right next to me.

My dog looked as resolute as ever I'd seen him.

I met the others in the foyer of Empyrean.

They looked as ready as I did. Which was good, because we would need to be perfect to pull this off.

Mrs Jolly had prepared food for us. Delph put it in his tuck.

We stepped outside the front door tethered together.

We looked at one another.

'Well,' I said. 'This is it.'

'Do you really think we can do it?' asked Petra.

'Let's go and find out,' I said.

30

THE PLAN

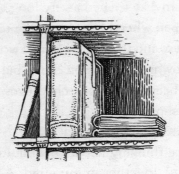

As soon as we were far enough away from Empyrean, I cast my *Pass-pusay* spell, and with the thought of the town in mind, we were instantly delivered to the centre of True.

It was midday, so folks were bustling around. Motors zipped past, people chatted away as they walked and shops were open, doing a thriving business. I watched women scrubbing the cobbles and men soaping up storefront windows.

They all looked pleasant and happy and oblivious to the fact that a terrible force had stolen their very lives from them.

Perhaps because of that, they would never know a bit of unhappiness or true sorrow or maybe even pain. Yet I thought that each of them, fully informed of the choice, would accept a real life of ups and downs over a manufactured one devoid of the whole spectrum of existence.

I desperately wanted to give them the chance.

Delph said, 'I thought we were going to Greater True?'

'We are. But we need something from here first.'

They followed me down the cobbles until we reached the place I had in mind. Our original hiding place on our first night in this new land. I could see the vast steeple and, inside, the huge bell.

'Why are we going there?' asked Delph as he followed my gaze.

The door opened and a group of people came out, all well dressed. One woman was carrying a baby draped all in white. The baby was screaming, while the mother was trying to calm it.

A christening ceremony. We did that with our newborns in Wormwood, christening them at Steeples.

We slipped through the door before it closed, and moved swiftly up the aisle.

The place was empty. The group that had left must have been the only one in the church.

The first night there we had headed upstairs. Instead, I led us down a corridor off to the right.

There was a wooden door partially open at the end of the corridor.

I peered through and saw a man sitting at a large desk, writing on a pad of paper.

It was the same man who had chased us when we'd been here before. He wore the same stiff white collar, but all the rest of his clothes were starkly black.

He paused in his writing, took off his spectacles and rubbed at his face, then turned and opened a book.

There was a wand sticking out of the open drawer of his desk. He had seen us that night. And reported us. That's why the other bloke had followed us. This man was a Maladon sent here to live among the 'Ordinaries'. Just as my grandfather had warned me about.

Well, now it was my turn to target *him*.

I raised my wand and said, *'Subservio.'*

The jet of light hit him directly in the back, and he instantly stiffened.

I kicked the door open and moved into the room with the others close behind.

I reached across his still form and snatched the wand out of the desk drawer.

Through the spell books we had discovered at Empyrean, I had added a number of incantations to my quiver. I was prepared to use one of them now.

I might as well make certain.

I pointed my wand at the man, gave it a long sweep and said, *'Origante.'*

The moment after my spell hit him, we all took a step back as the 'person' transformed into the Maladon that he was.

The face elongated. The hands became claws. The nose looked as sharp as a knife blade, the mouth cruel. When he turned to us, his eyes were large red drops of blood.

Petra screamed, but I gripped her by the shoulder.

'Keep quiet. He's under my spell.'

'What is that . . . that thing?' exclaimed Delph.

'A Maladon in its original form,' I replied. I glanced at Petra. She had a funny look on her face that took me a moment to interpret.

She's worried that if I use the spell on her, she will turn into something like that.

238

I looked back at our captive.

'What is your name?' I asked. 'Your real Maladon name,' I added.

When it opened its mouth to answer, I saw that, like the vile Orco's, its tongue was long and forked at the end.

The creature said, 'My name is Krill.'

Its voice was like a serpent's hiss and a banshee's shriek wedded at the vocal cords.

'And you work here to spy on the people living in True?'

'Yes.'

'How do you report to those at Maladon Castle?'

'Wand wire.'

'Wand wire?' This was a new term for me.

'We send messages using our wands. Like writing in the air. It leaves one wand and comes out through the wand of the intended recipient in the form of a thought in one's mind.'

Clever, I thought.

'Tell me the spell to accomplish that.'

He did so, and I tucked that away in my memory. I glanced inquiringly at Petra. She nodded, letting me know that she had done the same.

I turned back to Krill. 'There are people here who have had their magic taken from them. Do you have information on these people? Where they are living and what they are called?'

That was why I was here. I thought if there was one place where such records would be kept, it would be here. The place was called Saint Necro's, after all. His original followers had been called 'worshippers'.

Krill pointed to a large tome on a shelf above his desk. 'It is all in there.'

'Is that for only those in Greater True?'

'Greater True and Maladon Castle are the only places they are located. There are none in True.'

'You're positive?'

He nodded. 'Quite positive. These "things" are rewards for the most elite among the Ordinaries. They live in Greater True. And of course, a very few at Maladon Castle.'

'Why only a very few at Maladon Castle? I'd have thought the Maladons would love to be waited on hand and foot by the enslaved.'

'Because our masters do not like to be associated with filthy weaklings, regardless of how they are clothed.' He spat on the floor.

I bristled at his foul words, but I believed him. The Maladons *would* see us that way.

'Why do you keep these records at all?' Petra asked.

'We always keep records of *property*, however unsavoury.'

This statement made me want to curse him to dust.

Instead, I pointed my wand at the book, said the familiar spell and watched as it zoomed into my hand. I set it down, pointed my wand at it, said, *'Duplicado'* and an exact replica appeared in my free hand. I pocketed it and sent the original book zipping back on to the shelf.

I looked at Krill. 'Do the Maladons know that there are intruders among them? Has Mr Endemen spoken to you about it?'

Krill said, 'Mr Endemen does not speak to the likes of me. He uses intermediaries. But, yes, I have heard that there are those about who should not be here.'

I pointed my wand at Krill and reversed my *Origante* spell. Then I said to him, 'You will remember nothing of this, understood?'

He nodded. 'Nothing.'

'Turn around and go back to work.'

He did so while I freed him from the *Subservio* spell and then used the *Pass-pusay* spell to take us from this unholy place.

Invisible and back out on the street, Delph and Petra beamed at me.

'That was brilliant, Vega Jane,' exclaimed Delph, so loudly that I had to shush him.

I led them into an alley, took out the book and opened it to the first page.

I read down the page and said, 'These are all the people we must return magic to. We have their names and where they live now.'

'How many names on the list?' asked Petra.

I swiftly counted.

'Fifty-five. Fifty of them live in Greater True. The others are at Maladon Castle. One of them is Victus.'

'Blimey!' Delph said. 'Fifty names. Where do we start?' he added in a hopeless tone.

I placed my thumb over the first name on the ledger.

'Amicus Arnold. He lives on Goldofin Street in Greater True.'

'But what do we do when we get there?' asked Petra. 'We can't just free him without anyone knowing. Word will get out and everyone will be on guard.'

'I've thought of a way around that,' I said.

Next, I used the *Pass-pusay* spell to get us to Greater True. That was when we realized: we had no idea how to find our way around.

Then Delph exclaimed, 'Look there.'

We looked where he was pointing. It was a shop that sold maps!

We went to the shop door and I looked in through an open window. I could see a bloke at the counter helping a customer.

A moment later I spotted the map I wanted. I waited until the bloke had turned his back and did my incantation. The map flew through the window and into my hand.

We hurried around to an alley and I opened the map. It took a few moments, but I located Goldofin Street. It was only three streets over from where we were presently.

Number Forty-Seven was the one we wanted.

We quickly walked there and looked at the solidly built brick house attached to its neighbours on either side. There was a bright red door that reminded me of blood. The place was impeccable, the windows sparkling clean with not even a smidgen of dirt on the stone pavement in front.

As we watched from across the street, the red door opened and we saw a blank-eyed man appear there with a rag and bottle of liquid in hand.

This was undoubtedly the unfortunate if elegantly attired Amicus Arnold.

Elegantly attired!

I had wondered why these slaves were so beautifully dressed, and now I understood. It was a badge of humiliation.

A cruel joke, for all the 'elites' here knew that these people were slaves by their blank eyes. You could dress them up, but that didn't change the fact that they were owned by others. It was a heartless act.

That's exactly what the Maladons were: cruel and heartless.

Arnold began to dutifully polish the brass knocker. When it was gleaming, he went back inside.

My blood began to boil. This man had had his magic, his life and his honour taken from him.

Well, I meant to give them all back.

We waited, invisible, until it turned dark, and the streets emptied of both motors and people. Then we waited some more.

We quietly ate some of the provisions that Mrs Jolly had given us.

We spoke only in low tones because I had no reason to believe there weren't spies throughout this horrible place.

Finally, when we heard a tower clock chime the lateness of the hour, I pulled a tiny bottle of dust from my pocket. On the label was the name *Amicus Arnold*. I used my wand to return the bottle to its full size. Then I looked at the others.

'Ready?' I said.

They nodded.

Petra had her wand out.

Delph's hand hovered over the short-handled axe on his belt.

Harry Two's fangs were bared.

The red door opened with a spell cast, and we were inside.

I assumed that the owners would sleep in the upstairs rooms. That left the downstairs to their slave.

We passed through rooms that were lavishly furnished and past walls adorned with beautiful paintings. Our feet sank into thick rugs. Our eyes roamed over intricate wallpaper. As a former Finisher at Stacks, I had to marvel at the beauty I was seeing. But the foulness just underneath the surface made all I was viewing remarkably ugly.

We found the sleeping chamber of Amicus Arnold. It was just off the kitchen in what appeared to be a broom cupboard. He was curled up on the floor snoring softly, his beautiful, spotless livery hanging on hooks on the back of the door.

I realized with a start that I had seen this bloke before. He was the one who had been trailing behind the couple and caught the item the woman had dropped. He had been slapped for his troubles before I had blasted his 'masters' with an *Engulfiado* spell.

Harry Two had shown me the best way to accomplish our task tonight.

I spun my ring around so that we became visible.

Then I uncorked the bottle, turned it upside down and let the dust sprinkle over the sleeping man.

It didn't take long for each particle to be soaked right into him.

A few seconds went by as Arnold glowed brightly.

Then he sat bolt upright, blinked and his gaze fell upon us.

His eyes had come back. They were bright green and alert.

'What the—'

I held up my wand and said, 'You're Amicus Arnold.'

'I know I am.' He looked around. 'At least . . . at least *now* I do. It's all so muddy. How did I get here? Who are you lot?'

'My name is Vega Jane. This is Petra, Delph and my dog, Harry Two.'

'What the blazes are you doing here?'

I tried to convey an enormous amount of information as efficiently as I possibly could, talking rapidly. When I mentioned what I had done to his masters in the street, he smiled. 'I wondered about that. But I guess I was under their . . . their spell thing. The thing is, I don't remember being . . . magical.'

'Do you remember doing things that were inexplicable?'

He rubbed his jaw. 'Well, come to think, yeah. I could talk to my cat. My mum thought I had a fever or something. And I could make a coin spin as long as I wanted it to.'

'There you have it.'

'So you're saying I was lured on to the train and my magic stolen and I was made a servant to the people who live here?'

'Yes. Look. Your magic was kept in here.' I held up the bottle with his name on it.

He slowly traced the letters of his name with his finger.

'Blimey,' he said, tears creeping to the corners of his eyes. 'And you came here to save me?'

'You and a great many others,' said Delph.

I said, 'But you must go on being enslaved. For now anyway. Until we send the signal that it's time to go.'

He frowned. 'You really want to fight these . . . Maladons?'

I nodded grimly. 'To the death, I expect.'

Amicus shook his head sadly.

'I would join you, gladly. But I don't know how to fight. Not with magic.'

I glanced at Petra and Delph before replying. 'That's where we come in. We're going to train you. We're going to train all of you.'

He glanced at my wand. 'I don't have one of those.'

'You'll have a wand,' I said.

Petra and Delph looked at me in surprise. I had not told them about *that* part.

Amicus Arnold shook his head. 'Vega, I don't know if I can pretend to be enslaved now. When I see their faces I – I won't be able to help it, I'll turn on them. Punch them, or something. Then your plan will be ruined.'

'You won't have to pretend.'

I raised my wand.

'Do you trust me, Amicus?'

He slowly nodded. 'Yes, I do, Vega. After what you've done for me, I surely do.'

I performed the spell. He dropped to the floor and fell asleep.

I touched my wand to his eyes and said, *'Eraisio.'* Held firmly in my mind was what I wanted to happen. A spell of necessity, as Silenus would say.

His eyes turned blank once more.

Having to return Amicus Arnold to slavery was not easy, not after just freeing him. But I had a plan and I had to stick to it. Or else we would all end up as slaves to the Maladons.

Or dead more likely.

We left Amicus Arnold and moved on to the next one.

That night we freed eight people in total, an equal number of men and women. Each was much like Amicus Arnold: grateful, bewildered, uncertain and angry. They all swore to do what would be asked of them.

After that we retreated to the train station at Greater True. It was morning now but it was not busy. This town was for the elites, and there were not so many of them. As Petra and Delph fell asleep safely hidden behind our invisibility shield, I opened the book that I had duplicated back at the church in True. Using an ink stick, I ticked off the names of the people we had visited and freed.

Quite a few still to go.

I hoped we would survive to get to the last name.

And then, the *real* danger would begin.

31

ONE DEATH

The next night did not go nearly as smoothly.

We managed to successfully free a goodly number of people, including a bloke named Dennis O'Shaughnessy who wouldn't stop kissing me. He just about cried when I had to put him back under a spell until the time was right.

The next house after O'Shaughnessy's held an unexpected surprise.

The little girl I'd seen in the looking glass at Maladon Castle lay on her ragged bed in the bowels of a large house on Needles Court.

I gasped when I saw her. I had not known her name before. Now I did.

Miranda Weeks.

I returned her magical dust to her and she awoke. She stretched out her long thin limbs and then sat bolt upright. I explained what had happened to her. She took this all in, in a way that made her seem mature beyond her years. Then I told her what I had seen at the castle. Her mother and her in the looking glasses.

I said, 'We don't have another person with the surname Weeks on the list. Do you know what happened to your mother? I have her magical dust.' I drew the bottle from my pocket. 'I took it when I was at Maladon Castle.'

She leaned back against the wall. 'Now that you cleared my mind, I remember.' She paused, her face screwed up in pain. 'I heard them talking, these . . . these Maladons.' She paused again, and I could see her chin tremble. 'They said me mum died. They said that happens.' She fought back a sob. 'They said it didn't happen often enough. And then they laughed.'

I could only stare at her, horrified. Petra sat next to her and held her. Miranda wept into Petra's shoulder as Petra whispered soothing words into her ear.

Miranda finally stopped weeping, and Petra let her go and stood next to me. She really was the most perplexing person I had ever met.

I said, 'Miranda, I promise you that if you trust me, we will avenge your mum, OK?'

She nodded. I cast my spell, crafted blank eyes on her and turned to leave.

'Petra, what did you say to her?' I said.

She looked embarrassed. 'I . . . I just told her that I was her friend. That I would be there for her.'

'OK,' I said quietly. 'That was very nice.'

We headed off, my mind still awhirl at the conundrum of Petra Sonnet.

In the fourth house we visited was a gent named Dedo Datt. I had seen a number of people back in True who looked like him. He was of medium height and skinny, with black hair swept back off his brow. He was, unlike the others, not asleep. He was sitting up in the corner of his little room next to the basement stairs.

He made no movement when I twisted round my ring and became visible. He said nothing when we sprinkled the dust over him. But when the magic was readily absorbed into him and his eyes were no longer blank, they filled with tears.

'I have waited so long,' he said, rising and holding out his hand.

I was stunned. 'You were waiting?'

He nodded.

'So you remember what happened to you?'

'I remembered enough to know that I was not who I had become. But I was powerless to do anything about it.'

'You're magical.'

He nodded. 'I knew that. I realized that was why I had been taken – by the Maladons. What is your plan?'

'To beat them.'

He smiled. 'That is a very good plan.'

As we left the house, I said to the others, 'That shows the Maladons are not infallible. Which is good.'

The next home was one of the largest we had yet seen. Indeed, so large was it that there were *two* people here who needed rescuing from their enslavement: Anna Dibble and Sara Bond.

Like so many of the others, we found them in the bowels of the luxurious home wearing shabby nightdresses, their hair covered with ill-fitting bonnets.

We sprinkled the dust, and they slowly came around to their stolen pasts, as had the others. But then I looked over at the doorway, only to see someone who I presumed was the owner of the opulent place. He was wearing silk pyjamas and had on an expensive-looking robe with a tassel waistband.

In one hand was a morta.

He pointed it at me and shouted, 'What the—'

He got no further because Petra said firmly, '*Paralycto*,' and he froze with the morta still pointed at me.

'Thanks, Petra.' I studied him leisurely. 'He's your master?' I asked the pair.

'Yes,' they both said.

'Wrong. He *was* your master. He no longer is.'

Sara and Anna looked at each other, and then tears slid down their faces.

'Is he the only one who lives here with you?' I asked.

'There's his wife, but you can't wake her, aye, even if you dropped every plate in the house,' said Anna.

I walked around the frozen bloke and then pointed my wand at him once more.

'*Subservio.*'

His features relaxed, and I said, '*Unparalycto.*'

He slumped to the floor, his back against the wall, his eyes staring off.

'Your name?' I asked.

'Cyril Dudgett,' he said in a lifeless tone.

'All right, Dudgett, you will remember nothing of this. When we're done, you will return to your bed as though you had never awoken, is that clear?'

He dumbly nodded, his puckered eyes puckering even more.

'You own this house?'

He nodded.

'Who are your masters?'

'I have none,' he said sharply.

I smiled at this. The Maladons had done a very complete job making this fool believe his life was his own, though he was as much under their power as he was under mine right now.

'What do you do?' I asked.

'Do?' he said.

'In the way of work?'

'I am rich. I don't have to work.'

'How very lucky you are,' I said drily. 'And the source of your wealth?'

His puckered eyes widened, as though he had never pondered such a question.

'My wealth is . . . my wealth. I have always had it. I am one of the chosen.'

'Chosen by whom?' I asked.

Again, he faltered.

'I . . . I am one of the chosen,' he said again. 'Aren't I?' he added feebly.

'Blimey,' said Sara. 'He's off his noodle.'

I turned to look at her. 'His life is an empty one, not even his own. He lives in luxury and never questions anything. The perfect puppet.'

I turned back to him. 'Dudgett, do you know anything of the Maladons?'

'I do not know that term.'

'Mr Endemen, then?'

His mouth broadened to a smile. 'A fine chap. A good man. He's always visiting us in Greater True. He always makes us feel . . . feel . . .'

'Feel good about yourselves?' I finished for him.

'Exactly. So very good about ourselves.'

'Because you're the chosen ones?' I thought of something and added, 'Because you've earned the right to be . . . chosen?'

'Precisely. You've put your finger right on it. Yes. We've *earned* it.'

'And how did you earn it?'

His smile collapsed along with his features. His mouth opened and closed but nothing came out.

'All right, Dudgett, we'll leave it at that. Before you go back to bed, I want you to tell Anna and Sara that you're sorry for what you've done.'

Dudgett turned to them and said, 'I'm sorry.'

I looked at Anna and Sara. 'I don't care if he didn't mean it. I thought you just might want to hear it.'

I ordered him back upstairs and he dutifully went off.

I put Sara and Anna back to sleep and we set off for another house under cover of the invisibility ring.

'Those blokes don't know how good they have it,' said Petra.

I said, 'They've been fed a pack of lies and given stuff so they'll be nice little pets for the Maladons. Their minds have been taken over. Their lives are not their own. They're really slaves like the others, only they don't know it either.

I wouldn't call that having it good. Would you?'

'I guess not. But they have food and a roof over their heads and nice clothes and servants. Plenty of money. They don't have to work.'

'Right, plenty of *stuff*,' I replied. 'The only thing missing from their lives . . . is a life.'

'But what's the point to it all?' asked Petra. 'Why bother choosing blokes and making them better off than anyone else?'

Delph said, 'Well, it's sort of what we was talking about, isn't it? They play one off against the other, like. Like Virgil said. Create a pretend enemy so they have something to hate. It's a way to show those from True, and through them, all others living about in the country, that people *can* live better. That things can improve for folks. Those in True, brainwashed though they might be, can look at the rich from here and say, "See, that could be me if I work hard and keep on the dutiful path. I can reach the promised land," so to speak. It makes life seem fair somehow.'

'I think you're exactly right, Delph,' I said. 'When my grandfather said the most bitterly awful place of all was one that Wugs didn't know was as wrong as wrong could be, he could have also been talking about this place.'

We ventured to the next name on our list and did that one plus nine more.

The following night we did ten more. And the next night the same.

We had just returned to our hiding place in the bowels of the train station when we saw that the room we'd been using looked like it had been searched. We had left nothing here that was important, but it was still unnerving that someone had located this spot and gone through it.

'We'll have to move, I reckon,' I said dully, for it was quite late and I was knackered, as we all were.

We packed up our few belongings and set off to find a new hiding place down there.

It was eerily quiet and so very dark that I was tempted to use my wand to provide illumination.

The second I did, a spell shot over our heads, barely missing us. It hit the wall instead and left a good-size, smoky hole.

I cried out and instinctively ducked.

The others tethered to me did the same.

Another spell shot out, lower this time. Had we remained standing, we would have been goners.

Flattened to the floor, I looked around to see where the spells were coming from. All I could see was darkness.

I lifted my wand and was about to utter an incantation when Delph gripped my hand and shook his head.

'Let me,' he whispered.

He drew from his pocket a small ball. I recognized it at once as the same one that Astrea Prine had used to help train me on the *Rejoinda* spell. I'd had no idea that Delph had kept it.

I watched as Delph put the ball on the floor. He whispered, 'Keep your eyes peeled and get ready.'

He gave the ball a little push and it rolled off. Once it was past the shield of invisibility, it hadn't gone more than a few inches when a bolt of light hit it, destroying it.

Petra and I pointed our wands at the source of the light

and uttered our *Impacto* spells.

We heard a gasp and a crash.

We all leaped up and charged towards the sound.

A Bowler Hat was lying under a pile of rubble. I supposed our spells had hit the wall, and the collapse of the stone had buried him under it.

I had also supposed that he was unconscious or even dead.

As it turned out, he was neither. What he was, was dangerous still.

He exploded out of the rubble with a slash of his wand and a wordless incantation. Then he pointed his wand towards us and a light shot out. I knew he couldn't see us because of the invisibility shield, but the path of the spell was so broad that it caught us up in a whirlwind of sheer force and hurled us off our feet.

The impact with the wall I hit was so hard that I was momentarily stunned.

When I rose, the bloke was staring right at me. He was *seeing* me!

What the Hel.

I looked to my left and right and saw Petra, Delph and Harry Two slowly regain their feet. The impact must have broken the magical tethers. I looked down at my ring. It had moved round my finger. Before I could move it back the Bowler Hat roared, 'I've got you now!'

He cast another spell that I barely evaded.

Petra shot a spell at him but he effortlessly blocked it.

Delph pulled out his axe and hurled it.

The Bowler Hat laughed and said, 'Oh, why that's a stunner.'

He shot a spell right at Delph, and had I not blocked it, Delph would have been crushed. As it was, he was thrown head over heels against the wall and slumped down, barely conscious.

Petra and I kept shooting spells and the Bowler Hat kept blocking them. He shot spells at us, and between the two of us we barely stayed alive. It was clear that he was by far the superior fighter, and had it been one on one, we would be dead.

He had backed us up against a wall. I felt the cold stone behind me with one hand while my other gripped my wand. I was frantically trying to think what to do. I had cast so many spells and blocked so many of his that I was completely exhausted, while the Bowler Hat looked perfectly fresh and ready to battle on. They truly were elite fighters, as my grandfather had said.

He sneered at us. 'Well, luv, lucky for you that you're wanted alive, or I would have already killed you and your mates.'

When I was battling creatures in the Quag, it had not been nearly this tiring, but then most times a single spell had been sufficient for victory. Looking into the vile face of our opponent right now, I could see why my kind had lost the war against his kind.

My wand was so heavy it felt like it weighed a thousand pounds. I glanced at Petra. Her chest was heaving and sweat poured down her face, as it did mine. Her wand hand was twitching uncontrollably.

Our foe, sensing our weakness, smiled and moved from side to side, seeming to build both power and momentum in his mind. He raised his wand and I knew that we could fight him off no more.

So, I thought, *this is it. This is the end.*

What I had not counted on was Harry Two.

He charged straight at the bloke, an easy target.

I screamed, 'No, Harry Two!'

The Bowler Hat smiled nastily and leisurely took aim.

I raised my wand, but the spell shot out of his wand so fast I had no time to block it.

'No!' I screamed again.

The spell hit.

But Harry Two wasn't there.

The spell rebounded off the stone and blasted a hole in the ceiling.

I looked wildly around for my dog.

The fellow was looking madly around for him too.

Until Harry Two leaped out of the darkness and sank his fangs into the bloke's neck. *Then* he knew right where my special beast was.

Green shot out of the neck wound, and the Maladon screamed in agony.

He twisted sideways and managed to knock Harry Two off with a glancing blow from a spell.

Harry Two hit the stone floor and rolled away.

I could see the venomous look in the Maladon's eyes as he located Harry Two and pointed his wand.

'Rigamorte.'

I said the spell, not him. The killing incantation shot from my wand and hit the Maladon right in the chest.

He staggered back, looked at me with a disbelieving

expression and slowly sank to the floor.

Dead.

I looked down at my shaky wand and then over at the dead man.

I didn't know how I had found the strength to do that. But I had. I could not allow Harry Two to die. There was nothing I wouldn't do to prevent that.

I felt something nudge my arm.

It was my dog. He looked perfectly fine.

I wondered if he had done what he did to give me the motivation to finish off the Maladon. Putting himself in jeopardy, to give me the emotional strength.

But *how*? He had vanished and reappeared behind the Maladon. I really wanted to know the answer, but it wasn't like I could ask him.

Yet in those bewitching mismatched eyes, I think I received all the answer I required.

He truly was more than a mere beast. In some ways he was as magical as I was. This was a thought that gave me shivers up and down my spine.

And they were *good* shivers!

I knelt down and hugged him, pushing my face into the wonderfully soft fur.

He had once more saved my life.

'Thank you,' I murmured into his one remaining ear.

'Vega Jane?'

I looked up and saw that Delph had risen on shaky legs and was staring past me.

'We . . . we need to, um . . .'

'The body,' interjected Petra. 'We need to get rid of it.'

I looked over at the dead Maladon and knew that she was right. If it was discovered, then for all I knew, every slave in Greater True would be rounded up and put to death. Our grand plan would be defeated before it had even been given a chance to succeed.

I rose and pondered the matter.

There was only one way that I could see.

While the others stayed behind, hidden in the station, I tethered the dead man to me, and, covered by the invisibility shield, I flew far out of Greater True, smack into the middle of the countryside.

I found a thicket of trees and landed in the middle of them.

It was so dark that I needed my wand to light the surroundings.

I found a patch of dirt near a mighty oak and used my wand to dig the grave. I laid the Bowler Hat in it, unable to look at his face.

He was undeniably evil and would have killed us with absolute glee in his heart, I was certain. But still, I had ended his life.

And something in me, I was sure, had died alongside him.

As my grandfather had said, that was the true difference between us and the Maladons.

I magically covered him with dirt after breaking his wand in two and then crushing it to mere splinters with an *Impacto* spell. I sprinkled the remains of the wand over the countryside as I flew back to Greater True.

The words of Astrea Prine came back to me once more.

Could we really prevail against the Maladons, who were absolutely smashing at slaughtering their enemies?

I had killed, with ample justification, but I felt sick to my stomach.

I told myself that it would become easier over time.

But as I landed near the station, I knew in my heart that it would only become more difficult.

32

A WELL-TIMED PIECE OF ADVICE

Empyrean.

The only place I had ever truly felt safe since leaving Wormwood.

But right now all I felt was frustrated.

We had freed all the slaves and then I had placed them back into a trance.

That had been the most difficult part of my plan. How do you free someone and then tell him they have to go on being a slave for a bit longer? I knew if it had been me I would have rebelled. I also knew it was the only way to make this work. Otherwise, all would be lost. Still, I had felt sick having to do it.

Now they were unconsciously waiting for the signal from me.

I was desperately trying to make sure that signal could actually be sent.

I was sitting in the old chambers of my ancestor Jasper Jane, with virtually every book I could find in the place.

They were stacked haphazardly, some in towering piles.

I had read them all, trying to make the idea in my head a reality. The problem was, I had found nothing that could absolutely do what needed doing. And there was no room for error.

I had a sudden inspiration and took the parchment out of my cloak. I summoned Silenus and he dutifully appeared moments later.

I explained everything to him, what I had done and what I needed to do.

He pondered all this for such a very long time that I seriously wondered if he had become totally frozen in the parchment.

Finally, he stirred. 'The problem is you do not have the requisite knowledge to make this happen.'

'You once told me that magic was borne of necessity,' I said sharply. 'That if I needed a spell, I could create it. I was *counting* on that, Silenus.'

'What I told you was perfectly true. But from what you've just said, you don't have in your mind the firm idea required to create the necessary spell. Are you certain that none exists currently to perform the task?'

I shook my head. 'Not that I know.'

'Then perhaps you should try to know more.'

'What do you think I've been doing?' I pointed around at the stacks of books.

'Knowledge needn't always come from books,' he noted.

Well, that was true enough, I thought. Astrea had been a font of knowledge. But she wasn't here. She was back in the Quag.

'I doubt that Pillsbury or Mrs Jolly will know how to do

263

the necessary spell work,' I said in a depressed tone. 'And there's no one else I can turn to.'

Silenus looked around. 'I sense certain *elements* here that one cannot see.'

I thought about this. There *was* Uma, but I could see her. Yet like Silenus said, she might not be the only *element* hereabouts.

'You think someone like that might be able to help me?'

Silenus said, 'Well, when one has no other options . . .'

He disappeared from the page and I put the parchment away.

Sometimes, Silenus could really be infuriating!

Immensely frustrated, I headed back to my bedroom.

Along the way I heard voices.

I stopped at the door, which I knew was Delph's room.

I put my ear to the wood.

There were two voices coming from inside, and I recognized them both.

I knew I shouldn't, but I couldn't help myself.

'*Crystilado magnifica.*'

On the other side of the wood I saw Delph and Petra sitting together, talking. They were close, their hands nearly touching.

I couldn't make out what they were saying, but I did hear my name mentioned twice.

Petra was smiling, but Delph looked unusually serious.

I released my spell and hurried down the hall to my room.

Harry Two was asleep on the bed.

My mind awhirl with dark thoughts, I lay next to him, staring at the ceiling.

I finally concluded that what I had seen was innocent enough. I had been spending a lot of my time alone searching for what I needed. I had to confess: I had been ignoring Delph lately.

I sighed. I had been through this before. I was not going down this jealousy route again. I simply didn't have time for it.

As I stared up at the ceiling, I imagined the woman's face in my mind.

Sure enough, a few moments later, Uma appeared.

'Can I ask a favour?' I said.

My words stirred Harry Two. When he saw Uma he didn't react, but simply closed his eyes and went back to sleep.

Uma nodded.

I explained my dilemma. My needing more knowledge, anything that would allow me to accomplish the task I had set out.

'Come with me,' she said.

I leaped up from the bed as she disappeared through the door.

She led me not up this time, but down.

I thought I had by now explored all facets of Empyrean, but I apparently had missed some things.

I thought we were in the very bowels of the place when suddenly a tiny door appeared that I had never noticed before. Uma passed right through it. When I reached it, however, I found it would not open.

I used every spell I could think of to open the door, but none worked.

Well, I thought. *This is a bit of a pickle.*

I wondered if Uma would come back and tell me how to get in, but she didn't.

I rubbed my hand along the old wood of the door. It reminded me of the little door back at Stacks, through which I had passed to escape a pair of murderous jabbits.

Next, I used my wand to shine a light on the door.

I gasped.

The door handle I had gripped was made of metal. And it was cast in the shape of a tiny screaming Wugmort.

Just like back at Stacks.

Then I recalled that Stacks was really the former home of Bastion Cadmus. Which meant it was the former home of Uma Cadmus too.

But this wasn't Stacks. Stacks was back in Wormwood.

I stood there feeling like an idiot.

Was Uma on the other side of the door, wondering what had become of me?

I took a step back and pondered what to do.

It began as just a trickle of sensation down my spine, the commencement of inspiration.

I looked over my shoulder. There was nothing there of course.

But there could be if I exercised one thing that I had long possessed in abundance.

Imagination.

A pair of foul jabbits had chased me all the way to the top of Stacks – or at least what I had thought was the top. That's when I had come upon a little door like this one. I never believed that such a puny thing could hold back a pair of enraged serpents. Still, I'd had no choice but to grip the tiny screaming Wug doorknob and flee inside.

In my mind, I recreated the fear, the total and complete horror that being chased by those jabbits through the darkened spaces of Stacks had instilled in me.

The awful slithers, the terrifying screams, which were their trademark cry right before they struck.

I put myself back outside that little room, so close to certain death. My lungs heaved, my heart pumped. I felt my skin tingling, my spirits plummeting and my hope near extinguished.

With all of that boiling inside of me, I reached out and gripped the screaming Wug.

The door opened and I was on the other side of it.

Uma was hovering right there. We were inches apart.

I thought I saw her smile.

'Good, Vega. Very good.'

She beckoned me onward, and I followed her down a dark corridor.

We turned a corner, and the brightest lights assaulted me from all corners. Things were swirling to and fro, bits of what looked like tiny clouds whipping around like lightning spears.

'What is this place?' I asked Uma.

She didn't answer me, but she did put a finger to her lips and point towards a distant corner.

I crept towards this spot as Uma receded a bit.

Foot by foot, I drew closer to the blackness. As I did so, I noticed the silhouette of a figure in the midst of the dark.

I edged right to the perimeter of this space and stopped.

At first the figure didn't move. I wasn't sure what it was or whether it was capable of movement.

The next moment it turned.

When I saw the face, all my breath left me.

My mind reeled back like a pitching sea to the great battlefield where I had seen her fighting valiantly, indeed saving my life, before being vanquished.

Alice Adronis was wearing the very armour in which she had perished.

My heart gave a jolt when I saw that the mortal wound to which she had succumbed remained gaping in the centre of her chest.

When I had gone into the past courtesy of Eon back in Wormwood and seen Alice for the first time, I had thought that she and Morrigone looked quite a bit alike. But now I could see quite clearly that it was Alice and I – despite our different hair colours – who looked very much alike.

Alice stared at me. We were roughly the same height; her auburn hair swirled around her broad, muscled shoulders.

There was movement in my hand, and I looked down in time to see my wand bending towards her. As it had at her grave, my wand, which formerly had been her Elemental until she had bequeathed it to me, bowed in respect towards her.

As Alice came fully out of the shadows, I saw that, like Uma, she was not truly flesh and bone. How could she be, since she was long since dead?

Her cold eyes settled upon me, but she said nothing.

Slightly unnerved, I looked at Uma.

'What is this place?'

"Tis a place of restless souls,' said Uma. 'For they need somewhere to go, and Empyrean is as good as any. We had such happy times here. And of course it was Alice's home. Naturally, she would return here.'

I turned back to Alice. She was still watching me. Then her gaze dropped to the Elemental. She flicked her fingers and the Elemental sprang out of my hand and into hers. A moment later she apparently had willed it to its original state, six feet long and the colour of lustrous gold.

She looked the Elemental up and down and I saw a wistful smile emerge on her face.

After a few moments she turned back and held it out for me to take.

I tentatively reached out for it, but before it could make contact with my hand, the Elemental shrank back to my wand and leaped into my hand, my fingers instinctively closing around it.

"Tis truly and properly yours now, Vega,' Alice said quietly.

I looked down at the wand. There was a warmth to it that hadn't been present before. I felt strangely empowered.

I said, 'Alice, I'm taking up the fight against the Maladons.'
'I know.'

'You're not by chance still alive somehow, are you?' I asked hopefully. 'We could certainly use you.'

She touched her chest at the site of the hole.

"Tis not possible, Vega.' She looked me up and down. 'You made it through the Quag.'

'I did. Astrea Prine trained me as a sorceress.'

'Astrea, ever vigilant. I'm surprised she let you pass.'

'She knows what I came here to do. She agrees with it.'

Alice slowly nodded. 'Tell me your problem.'

I explained about the slaves, and how I wanted to assemble them as an army to fight the Maladons.

Alice looked down at my wand. 'All you need to accomplish that, you now have.'

'But I don't! Not really. I just have vague ideas about how it could all work.'

'Have the courage of your convictions,' said Alice.

'Can't you just tell me how to do it?' I asked, frustrated.

She pointed to the door through which I'd entered the room. 'No one needed to tell you how to open that, did they? You figured it out all by yourself. By believing that you could do so.'

I looked at the door and realized that it had been a test. A test of my wits, maybe. But I didn't see how that was going to help me now.

When I turned back, Alice was gone. When I looked around to ask Uma where she had gone, I realized that she had disappeared as well.

And then my eyes opened and I was lying on my bed, with a snoring Harry Two right next to me.

I sat up and looked wildly around.

Had any of that happened, or had I simply dreamed it?

I looked down at my hand. My wand was in it. It did feel different. The warmth was still there. The possibilities in my head were definitely still there.

I thought about what I wanted to do. I thought about what Alice had told me. And in a tremendous flash of clarity, it all came together.

33

THE INCONCEIVABLE INCANTATION

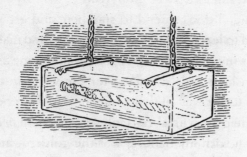

Five minutes later I was staring at it. Bastion Cadmus's golden wand in the box.

I took a breath, then reached up to lift the box off the wall. A surge of power hit me and knocked me head over heels across the room.

Groaning, I slowly rose, rubbing my head, which had hit the stone.

All right. We'll see about this.

I took out my wand, pointed it at its golden counterpart and said with a backward sweep of my hand, *'Rejoinda Bastion Cadmus's wand.'*

Absolutely nothing happened.

I tried every spell that I thought might work.

Again, absolutely nothing happened. The little box remained on the wall.

Befuddled and irritated, I looked around the room for something, anything, that might aid me. There was absolutely nothing there. I recalled the blank diary that had spoken to me when I was in the room full of battered and bloody weapons and Gunther Adronis's coffin. It said that if I did not want to pay the price, I could end my years in comfort and safety here at Empyrean.

'Oi,' I said. 'I don't intend to stay here and grow fat and old. I intend to leave and fight the Maladons and make things right. That's my decision. Now, you promised me aid if I did that. So I'm here and I'm asking for the wand in that box. May I have it? Or was all that a bunch of rubbish before?'

Before I had even finished, I felt something in my pocket. I withdrew it with my hand. It was the golden wand.

Just to be sure, I looked at the box. The wand was no longer there, because I indeed had it.

Along with it, I had a plan. And because of that, we had a chance.

I ran back towards my room.

But then I halted.

I was in front of Delph's room again. I could still hear the voices coming from inside.

Again, I shouldn't have done it. I realized that. But I did it anyway.

'Crystilado magnifica.'

Instantly in front of me appeared Delph and Petra. They were still perched on the bed. They were even closer to each other. Her hand was on his shoulder. I saw the look on her face and realized I had probably had that same expression on my face when I was feeling especially affectionate towards Delph.

I felt my features harden, and there came a coldness in my heart that I didn't think I had ever felt before. It felt strange, terrifying.

Here I was using every bit of energy I had to come up with a plan to take the battle to the Maladons, and here Delph and Petra were, supposedly my friends, being all cosy with each other. I was their leader. They had told me over and over that I was to lead them. And this was how I was paid back? Did they think it was easy doing what I was doing? Did they think I could just come up with a brilliant plan whenever it was needed? Well, we would see about that.

I released my spell, pocketed my wand and knocked on the door.

'Hello, Delph?'

I heard movement from inside.

Delph opened the door a few moments later, looking awkward.

'Delph, I have good news.'

'What's that, Vega Jane?'

'We need to tell Petra too. Let's go get her.'

'Um,' began Delph. He wouldn't meet my eye.

'I'm right here,' said Petra. She sauntered up next to Delph and gave me what I took to be a simpering smile. I felt my blood flame.

'Absolutely cracking,' I said. 'Follow me.'

I saw them glance uncertainly at each other before falling into step behind me.

We reached my room and entered.

Harry Two was on the bed, and he slowly lifted his head to peer at us.

'What's the plan, Vega Jane?' asked Delph.

I took a few minutes to tell them.

'Do you think it'll work?' asked Petra in what I, unfairly or not, interpreted as a condescending tone. Right now, nothing she said or did would be anything other than irritating.

'I don't know. Do you have a better idea?' I said sharply. She looked taken aback and shook her head.

'Now, there is another part to all of this, and you, Petra, are going to play an especially important role.'

'What?' she said curiously.

'You will go to Greater True and take up a position near the centre of town. You will be my eyes and ears, Petra. When I engage this spell, I have no real idea what's going to happen. But you can communicate with me via the wand wire incantation.'

'Vega Jane, sending her there by herself, not knowing what's going to happen . . .' said Delph. 'I don't think that's a good idea. Or fair to Petra.'

I gazed up at him with what I hoped was an expression of utter surprise.

'Delph, we're a team. We all have roles to play. Petra is part of that team. I very much trust her to do this. Don't *you* trust her? Or do you think she's not up to it?'

'O'course I trust Pet.' He hastily added, 'Petra.'

'Then I don't see the problem.'

'I could go with her.'

I shook my head. 'You need to stay here and prepare for the arrival,' I said. 'There's going to be a lot going on and we need to be ready.'

'But—'

I talked right over him. 'Petra will have the ring and her

wand. I've gone to Greater True with just those two things and come back alive. I've gone to Maladon Castle alone with just those two things and returned in one piece. If I can do it, so can *Pet*.'

I looked at Petra, slipped off my ring and handed it to her. 'So, are you ready?'

She nodded dumbly, glanced at Delph and then quickly looked away.

'You'd better get ready to leave now. The preparations will take me a bit of time, but I want you in place. Send me a wire when you get there. Aim for near the train station and then work your way to the centre when you've determined that the path is clear.'

Delph blurted out, 'Vega, if your plan causes things to go all wonky in Greater True, the Maladons might show up in full force. Petra might get trapped.'

'She has her wand. She can use the *Pass-pusay* spell to get back here if need be. It's no more dangerous than what I've done. And I don't remember you having a problem when it was *me* doing it.'

'But . . .'

'But what, Delph?' I said, staring up at him.

His voice trailed off and he looked away, beaten.

I put out my hand to Petra. 'Good luck.'

She lightly shook it, turned and hurried off.

I looked at Delph. 'You better take up your position outside by the front door,' I said.

He nodded, gave me a furtive glance and then left.

My heart was beating so fast I thought I might faint.

The flint inside my heart started to break down a bit.

275

I told myself that what I'd done wasn't really that awful. We had come and gone before from Greater True without incident. Petra was invisible. She had her wand.

But Delph was right. I couldn't predict what would happen when I performed my spell. Petra might be caught in something that she couldn't get herself out of. She might be injured, captured.

Or killed.

As soon as I thought this, my head began to pound, and then I felt something wet on my forehead. I touched it.

It was blood.

I looked down at my wand. There was blood there too. As I watched, the blood from my head was being soaked up into my wand.

Then I remembered.

The blood oath! I had sworn allegiance to Petra and she to me. By my actions I was breaking that oath. I didn't know what was going to happen to me. Was I going to oblivion?

I dropped to the floor, holding my head.. Harry Two came over to me and licked at my hand. His tongue touched some of the blood and I felt a tingling sensation all over my body.

Nothing is worth Petra being hurt by something you've planned, Vega. It's wrong. If she loves Delph and he loves her, that's just the way it is. You're acting like a Maladon. And you are not like them!

I wiped the blood off, jumped up and ran to Petra's room. She was just coming out, her cloak on.

'Stop,' I said.

'What?'

276

'I . . . I just figured out another way. You don't have to go to Greater True. You can stay here. It's OK.'

'But you said—'

'Right, I know what I said, but it's OK, you don't have to go. Like Delph said, you might get trapped there. And . . . and that would not be good.'

'If you're sure?'

'You and Delph can wait outside of Empyrean.'

She looked at me oddly and then touched my forehead. 'You're bleeding.'

'It's nothing. OK, well, I've got things to do, so . . .'

I turned and rushed off, leaving her staring after me.

In my room I sat on my haunches and laid the golden wand down directly in front of me.

I touched my forehead. The blood was gone. I looked at my wand. There was no blood there either. If that hadn't happened, would I have let Petra go? Possibly to her death? Did all the Janes actually have a bit of Maladon blood in them, as my grandfather had suggested after telling us the story of Alice's evil father?

I closed my eyes and then reopened them. I couldn't think about that now. I had to focus. There were many people counting on me.

Something that Uma had told me had given me this idea.

He was not simply my father, but the father of all of our people.

I was counting on that statement to be quite literal.

From my pocket I took the book with the names of all those enslaved by the Maladons. I set it in front of me, open to the pages listing them.

I tapped my wand against the pages and murmured, 'Accumuladis todos.'

When I looked at the pages, they had turned blank.

OK, so far, so good.

I pointed my wand at Bastion's golden one.

Drawing another deep breath, I closed my eyes and cast my mind back so that I could recall the incantation exactly as the Maladon had told it to me.

Now it got tricky. I was in totally uncharted territory. Still, I supposed every spell had to be done for the first time by somebody.

The only thing was, I was planning to use an existing spell, but in a way that it had never been used. And not just one spell. I was attempting to link three of them together and unleash them at the same time.

In my mind I formed a clear thought of what I wanted to happen. It was actually multiple things occurring at precisely the same time.

I drew one more long breath. I was totally focused. I had never concentrated like this in my life. I hadn't even known I had the capacity to do it. But somehow, I had found it.

I had three images, neatly compartmentalized in my head.

The golden wand.

The names on the list.

And Greater True.

I touched the tip of my wand to the tip of the golden one.

Then I spoke the words tightly, curtly, firmly. Never had I possessed such confidence, such sheer willpower. It was like everything I had ever done to reach this moment, every strength that had shown itself in me on this long journey, every power developed from necessity, every obstacle overcome, every loss followed by a savage desire to triumph, had all been for this very moment.

'Disassemblius projecta . . .'

I drew a breath.

'Amplifius spectrumaca . . .'

It was as though someone else was doing the talking and using me to channel the words.

I held my focus, my absolute concentration.

'Vamon recipitcus. Agante apertus.'

When I opened my eyes and looked down at the golden wand, it started to shake violently. But I kept the wands touching.

A flash of blinding light erupted from Bastion Cadmus's wand. The light covered the entire room, and I could hear Harry Two barking madly.

I kept my focus.

Those three images: the wand, the names and the place.

Next moment the golden wand shattered into tiny pieces. These splinters of gold swirled upward as though caught in an overpowering funnel of air. Up, up to the ceiling they went.

'Catapulus targerius.'

Then with a pop they vanished.

The light vanished as well.

Still, my focus never wavered.

I was only halfway done.

New images replaced the old trio.

Faces, hands, eyes.

Words slipped from my mouth.

'*Erectica. Desimminus. Plutarium.*'

I took another breath, kept the images clear in my head.

'*Emancipatico stelara.*'

Eyes flew open in my mind. Faces regained their true character. Reason returned. Real pasts supplanted magically conjured ones.

All across Greater True, hands reached out.

Still I pressed on. I had more to do.

My wand was now shaking so violently that I had to grip it with both hands.

I supposed I was at unprecedented levels of sorcery here. It didn't make me feel special. It made me afraid. If I failed, I had the terrible feeling that all these people were going to instantly die or forever remain in a limbo of my creation.

Now I had two images in mind: people and a place.

That place was not Greater True.

That place was right here.

Empyrean.

I was attempting to perform the *Pass-pusay* spell, only remotely, to move others. And not simply one. I was going to bring fifty people here, to safety.

My wand was pitching and heaving like a ship on stormy seas.

Smoke started to emanate from its core.

The poor Elemental felt like it was going to burn up in my hands.

Yet still I held on.

'*Aggretata . . . Cumuladis . . . Elevata . . .*'

My wand was nearly out of control. It gave such a violent jerk that it smacked me in the forehead. I felt blood trickle down my face.

I summoned all the energy I had left. This was the moment of truth. It was now or never, and while part of me was confident, part of me was also scared to death.

The normal spell, I knew intuitively, would not be enough. I had transported others with me using it, but not remotely and not fifty of them.

I screwed up my face, shut my eyes and—

'Pass-pusay titanticus encapsulado principium todos.'

I paused, building my energy to the level I knew was necessary.

Now, Vega, now!

'Domum nunc en pepertuum!' I cried out.

A bolt of light issued from the tip of my wand and shot straight up and through the ceiling of my room, leaving a darkened mark there.

As soon as the light vanished, I fell backwards. Then everything went dark.

I woke to Harry Two licking me on the face.

I heard a commotion downstairs and Pillsbury shouting.

I jumped up and raced out of the room and down the broad stairs, Harry Two barking at my heels.

The foyer of Empyrean was large, but it was now also crowded with figures. Pillsbury and Mrs Jolly were running around trying to restore order, although, given most of the people who had just appeared here were unfamiliar with walking and talking suits of armour and brooms, which simply generated more alarm.

I raced into the foyer and shouted, 'Everyone quiet down.' When that didn't work, I raised my wand to the ceiling, muttered an incantation and the resulting boom was so overwhelmingly loud that only quiet followed its release.

They all stood there staring back at me.

There was Cecilia Harkes, Anna Dibble, Sara Bond and Clive Pippen. Over near the door was Amicus Arnold. Next to him was the cheerful Artemis Dale. On his right was Miranda Weeks, looking confused but excited. Standing next to each other were Dennis O'Shaughnessy and Reginald Magnus, who looked so much like each other they could be brothers. Dedo Datt stared around in silent wonder.

And on and on they went.

All fifty of them. They stared at me.

I stared back at them. I saw, with immense satisfaction, that a full-size golden wand was gripped in each of their hands.

My spell had worked. I couldn't keep the enormous smile off my face.

Until I noticed something.

Or more to the point, I noticed the *absence* of something. Of two people.

I rushed over to Pillsbury.

'Where are Delph and Petra?'

'They left quite a while ago.'

The blood iced over in my veins. 'What?'

'Yes. They told me to be ready to receive what they

termed "guests" and then they left. Together.'

I couldn't process what he was telling me. Where the Hel had they gone?

At the same instant I felt my wand tingle and shake slightly.

I closed my eyes and in my head I heard:

'Vega, help us! We're in Greater True.'

It was Petra. She was communicating with me by wand wire.

I barked to Pillsbury and Mrs Jolly, 'See that our guests have all the food and drink they require and then find rooms for them to rest. I'll be back as soon as I can.'

'But—' began Pillsbury.

I shot forward and nearly collided with Alabetus Trumbull, who luckily leaped out of the way.

Charlotte Tokken and Pauline Paternas cried out after me, but I didn't really hear them. All I could hear was Petra's desperate plea.

I could not lose them. I just couldn't.

34

A CLOSE CALL

My first problem was that I could not become invisible without the ring, and Petra still had it. Thus, when I appeared on a street in Greater True, someone instantly saw me. Luckily, it was a doddering old man who continued to walk past as though someone materializing out of thin air happened all the time.

At least it was late at night, and I immediately withdrew into the shadows, attempting to regain my composure and my wits. This was hard to do because I was frantic to find Delph and Petra.

I peered around to see if anything unusual was happening in Greater True. I had just removed fifty of the servant class with one fell swoop. I had been sure that the town would be up in arms about this. But then as I thought about it, I realized that might not be the case. It was very late at night, and most if not all of their former masters would still be sound asleep and unaware of what had transpired. The first they might learn of it was when they awoke and realized no one was there to serve them their morning tea.

I wondered how my spell had manifested itself here. Had there been noise, incantation, lights? Had the former slaves been seen flying through the sky, if but for a moment? Had someone in one of the houses been up late, seen something suspicious and alerted the Maladons?

And why had Petra and Delph come here?

Suddenly in my head appeared another wand wire.

'Train station. Same room. Hurry.'

I focused on the four walls of that room where we had slept while locating those whose magic had been stolen from them. I twice tapped my wand against my leg, muttered the spell and a moment later I was standing in the little room at the train station.

I looked frantically around for Delph and Petra, but they weren't there.

However, I wasn't alone.

Four Bowler Hats encircled me, their wands pointed directly at my chest.

I was so stunned I had no time to think, which was probably a good thing.

'Embattlemento.'

Their four spells hit my shield, but my magic held. In fact, their spells rebounded off my conjured wall, causing them all to duck. I used this opportunity to tap my leg twice and say the incantation.

I was instantly on the street outside the train station.

I was frantic now. Delph and Petra had obviously been captured by the Maladons. They must have used her wand to communicate with me. I wondered if they had taken my grandfather's ring from Petra. How had they even been captured? They couldn't be seen behind its invisibility shield.

Next moment the four Maladons burst from the front of the train station and looked wildly around for me.

I scurried around a corner and then peeked back.

I performed my magnification spell and looked at them more closely.

I recognized two of them. My heart sank as four more joined them, appearing out of thin air, after no doubt having been summoned. I wondered if Endemen would make an appearance. Indeed, I was surprised that he wasn't right in the middle of all this.

Under the magnification spell, I searched the fingers of all of the Maladons for the ring. I didn't see it. I had been told that they had never learned how to make themselves invisible. They might not know the ring had such powers, or how to turn it around to engage the shield. Given time, though, they would probably discover its secret.

I looked nervously around, wondering how many more Maladons would appear to join the hunt for me. I had to find and save Petra and Delph.

Were they here? Had they already been taken to the castle? Were . . . were they already dead?

I looked down at my wand.

One wand against eight. Still, I had always been the underdog in every fight I'd ever had, including the Duelum back in Wormwood. I had won them all.

Everyone said I was special somehow. I guessed I was about to find out if that was really true.

When the Maladons had cast their spells, they had

not used the *Rigamorte* curse, which my shield would not have stopped. They obviously didn't want to kill me. They wanted to capture me alive. I was sure I knew why. They wanted to torture me to gain every bit of information they could.

That worked both ways, didn't it?

I instinctively realized that when you're outnumbered on the battlefield, you need to do one thing:

Divide and conquer.

I sent back-to-back spells sailing over their heads, each shooting off in a different direction. As soon as I'd done that, I used the *Pass-pusay* spell to disappear and then reappear behind them. Reacting to the spells, they split up, four and four. Still not good odds for me, but better than they had been.

They charged off in different directions. I followed one of the groups down the street and watched them turn a corner and hurry after the lingering lights of one of the spells I had cast.

I hurried on and caught up to them, keeping just far enough back so they couldn't see me. I aimed my wand at the Bowler Hat bringing up the rear.

My *Subservio* spell hit him in the centre of the back.

I whispered my instructions to him. He pointed his wand at the Bowler Hats in front of him and cast spells knocking them out. The fourth one turned in time to blast the one I had under control, and he crumpled in a heap.

I took aim at the remaining Bowler Hat, and my *Subservio* spell hit him full in the chest. His face went slack and his wand hand dropped.

I hurried up to him, took his wand in my gloved hand and broke it in half. I did the same with the others' wands.

I pointed my wand at the last Bowler Hat and said, 'What are you called?'

'Dullish,' he said gruffly.

I said '*Origante*,' expecting his hideous actual Maladon self to be revealed, but he looked the same. I was bewildered by this. I had thought all of the Maladons would be the same underneath.

'OK, where are my friends, Dullish?'

He looked at me quizzically. I realized I had to be more specific.

'The tall man and the young woman. Your lot used her wand to summon me here.'

He nodded. 'They are at the headquarters of the Elite Guard on the other side of Greater True.'

'They're alive?' I said sharply.

He nodded dumbly.

'Where is her wand?'

He shook his head. 'I don't know.'

'Well, then, who would know?'

He looked down at one of his fallen comrades. 'He has it.'

I performed the spell to erase any memory of this encounter from him and then knocked the bloke out.

I pointed my wand at the man he'd indicated. '*Rejoinda* Petra's wand.'

It flew from his pocket and into my hand.

I thought for a moment and added, '*Rejoinda* anything else of Petra's or Delph's or mine.'

Nothing appeared.

I put the wand away in my cloak and turned just in time to ward off the first spell.

It bounced off my shield and exploded against the side of a building, leaving a gaping hole.

The other four Bowler Hats had appeared feet from me, no doubt having heard or somehow sensed the magical fight that had just occurred here.

Then the duel began in earnest.

I thought I had no chance. I well remembered the fight Petra and I had waged against a single Maladon. It had left us breathless, barely able to lift our wand arms, while our opponent appeared fresh and full of fight. We were lucky to have vanquished him.

Yet now, for some reason I could not fathom, my wand hand started to move in ways I had never envisioned, in ways I never thought myself capable of. I danced and parried, blocked spells, and sent off my own.

The longer I fought, the stronger and more confident I became.

'Impacto. Embattlemento. Jagada. Paralycto. Embattlemento.'

I blasted one off his feet with an *Engulfiado* spell. Another fell to my *Impairio* incantation, and he started blindly firing off spells, sending his mates running and ducking.

The very air around us was boiling from all the magic cast.

I kept pounding away, saying spells and whipping my wand like it was a sword.

I charged forward, my gaze darting across the field of battle, calculating all options, tactics and strategies, my mind going full bore, my concentration total.

They fell back, and I could see the panicked looks in their eyes. They had obviously not expected me to be able to hold my own against all of them.

I wasn't done yet. If I'd learned one thing with the Maladons, it was that you had to finish the fight.

I shot a spell at the cobbles under them. An enormous hole opened up, and they fell screaming down into this abyss, their wands sailing out of their hands from the suddenness of the descent. I sent *Impacto* spells raining down into the hole, one after another. The spells thundered into their flailing forms and knocked them out.

Then I flicked my wand across the hole and it sealed up.

Not wasting another moment, I leaped into the air and sailed across the darkened sky with grim purpose.

I had never been to the Elite Guard's headquarters. But I had a very good idea of how I would find it. A minute later I saw that I was right.

The huge flag with the five-pointed star and the two burning eyes was waving in the wind atop a tall building on the western edge of the town proper. I could see several lights blazing from within. I went into a dive and landed next to the rear entrance.

Now I needed something. No, I needed *someone*. And I knew exactly how to get him.

I made the familiar motion with my wand and I said, '*Rejoinda* Dullish.'

A few moments later I could see a black blob hurtling across the sky.

Dullish landed hard at my feet. I revived him after putting

him back under the *Subservio* spell and then instructed him on what I wanted him to do.

I hid in the shadows as he approached the door.

He lifted his wand and the door opened, revealing a man in a black uniform.

He seemed surprised to see the Maladon. I used my magnification spell to see inside the doorway and to the room beyond.

It was only the one guard.

'Dullish? We've got our pair here still. Did you get the one you were after?' the guard asked.

My spell shot straight over Dullish's shoulder and hit the bloke right in the face. He fell over backwards.

I stepped inside and looked down at his prostrate form.

'No, actually he didn't, you prat.'

I pushed Dullish ahead of me as I surveyed the set of stairs that led upward.

'Where are the other guards?' I asked Dullish.

'Most are asleep in the barracks.' He pointed upward.

'And my friends?'

'In the room in the middle of the hall where the barracks are.'

'How many guards watching them?'

'A dozen.'

Wonderful.

I could imagine their mortas firing into my body until I looked like a mass of holes and not much else.

Then I had a thought. 'Dullish, where do they keep their mortas?'

'Their what?'

'Their, um, weapons?'

He pointed to the left at a doorway I hadn't noticed before.

'Their guns are in there.'

'Stay right here.'

I used the *Ingressio* spell to open the door. Along the walls were racks and racks and shelves of *guns*.

I swept my wand across the room and said, *'Interfero todos.'*

The sounds of something hardening could be heard around the room.

I closed the door behind me and once more went over to Dullish.

'Take me to my friends,' I commanded.

We stealthily went up the stairs, turned right and passed a number of wooden doors. From within, I could hear the loud snores of sleeping men.

Dullish led me over to a large metal door. There was a small, barred window in the middle of it.

I stepped past Dullish and peered cautiously inside.

With a sigh of relief, I saw Delph and Petra tied up in a corner. Delph's face was bruised and bloody and Petra was hunched over and grimacing in pain.

As Dullish had said, there were twelve uniformed men inside with them. They all carried mortas, or *guns*, rather.

But I carried something too.

My wand. And I wouldn't trade it for a thousand of their awful weapons.

I blasted open the door.

The guards all turned, as I knew they would, towards the door.

They lifted their guns to fire.

I already had my wand pointed.

'*Engulfiado.*'

The torrent of water exploding from my wand tip hit them with the force of a lightning spear.

They were lifted off their feet and blasted backwards against the wall, where they slammed into the stone and dropped to the floor, unconscious, their guns falling from their hands.

I leaped inside.

'Vega Jane!' exclaimed Delph.

'How did you find us?' asked Petra breathlessly.

'Not now,' I shot back.

I quickly untied them and led them out of the room. My spell had awoken the sleeping guards, as I knew it would.

We scrambled down the steps even as we heard doors slamming open. We reached the main floor and hurtled across its width to the door leading to the outside.

I heard someone scream, 'Get your guns and blast them to Hell!'

We were outside the building and running down the street when I heard someone yell, 'Fire!'

I turned to look back and saw forty guards with guns pointed right at us.

'Look out!' screamed Petra.

'Don't worry,' I said.

All forty guards pulled their triggers.

And all forty guns blew up in their hands, their barrels magically obstructed by yours truly.

'Wow,' exclaimed Delph.

Wow indeed, I thought, a grin emerging on my face.

I tethered us together. We shot upward, levelled out and zipped onward.

We weren't invisible, so I quickly tapped my leg twice and said the incantation.

The next moment we were staring at the front of Empyrean.

I turned on them and barked, 'Why the Hel were you in Greater True? I *told* Petra she didn't have to go. Then I find out you *both* went! You could have been killed!'

Delph wilted under my fierce gaze, but Petra stepped up and said, 'It was my fault, Vega. I thought you didn't want me to go because you thought I couldn't handle the job. I wanted to prove that I could. So I decided to go. But I told Delph.'

'And I told her unless she let me go along, I'd tell you and she wouldn't be able to go a'tall.'

I looked between them, fury and relief competing for control of my emotions. Finally, the latter won out, no doubt aided by the guilt I was still feeling for nearly sending Petra to her death.

I gave them each a hug.

I said, 'Well, thank goodness you're all right. What happened back there?'

'All Hel erupted, I guess, when you did whatever you did,' said Delph. 'I saw blokes soaring out of houses all over the place, and then they just disappeared. Good thing it was so late at night and nobody was out and about to see it 'cept us.'

'I did a mass spell for all the people on the list. They're

here at Empyrean now.'

'Eh, that's wonderful news,' said Delph.

'But how did you get caught? You were invisible.'

'*Were* being the right word for it,' said Delph. 'Your spell brought this huge wind across the town, like with the mighty Finn. Me and Pet got blown all over. Landed in a heap against a wall all dazed-like.'

Petra added, 'The ring got jostled. It never fit me proper. It spun back around and there we were, visible. Before we could move a muscle, a bunch of Maladons were on us. They . . . they took the ring.'

So my fear had been realized. The Maladons had the ring.

'That wasn't all they took,' said Delph. 'Show her, Pet.'

'No,' Petra said fiercely.

'Show me what?' I said.

'Petra, show her. She's going to see at some point.'

Slowly Petra held out her hand.

I felt sickened.

Not only was the ring gone, so was the finger on which she had worn it.

'Thanks for coming to save us, Vega,' said Petra.

I reached into my pocket, took out her wand and handed it to her.

'How did you find it?' she asked, looking delighted.

'A bit of luck,' I said dully.

'Thank you,' she said. 'You're a good friend, Vega. I know I can be quite the pain, but I also know you're always looking out for me.'

A pang of guilt hit me and I inwardly winced. Petra

wouldn't be saying that if she had known of my original plan.

'I couldn't lose you. Either of you,' I said. 'We're in this together.'

And that was truly how I felt.

'Tried to fight 'em off, but I couldn't,' said Delph.

'I saw what you did to that Maladon that took my finger,' said Petra. 'Picked him up and threw him into a wall.'

'I'm surprised they didn't kill you,' I said.

Delph said, 'They wanted to question us. They knew about you, Vega Jane. They used Petra's wand to send you a message.'

'I walked right into their trap.'

'How'd you get away?' asked Petra.

'I fought my way out. There were eight Bowler Hats, but I managed to beat them.'

'Blimey, eight of them!' said Delph, while Petra looked shocked. Delph added, 'Eh, Vega Jane, you've been hit.'

He pointed to my torn cloak and the blood soaking into it. I hadn't even noticed.

'It doesn't hurt much, Delph.' I eyed Petra's bloody stump where her finger used to be. 'In fact, it doesn't hurt at all.'

35

A MOTLEY CREW

I led the way inside Empyrean.

Pillsbury was waiting for us.

'Where is everyone?' I asked.

'They have been well fed and we have found rooms for all, Mistress Vega.'

'That's good. I wasn't sure, as big as it is, whether Empyrean could hold fifty guests.'

Pillsbury said proudly, 'Empyrean is a place that will grow to the size necessary for those who require accommodation within its walls.'

Pillsbury took his leave. I hurried upstairs to my room and came back down in a jiffy with the Adder Stone. I knew I couldn't regrow Petra's finger, but I could deal with the pain and bleeding.

I waved it over her hand and thought especially good thoughts.

The wound stopped bleeding and healed over instantly, though the finger was still missing. I did the same with my wound.

I looked at Delph. I was sure he was thinking about his father's legs, which had been crushed in an accident back in Wormwood. The Stone had dealt with the pain, but Duf Delphia now wore timber stumps. He gazed up at me with a weak smile.

'Dad,' he said, confirming my thoughts.

'That's much better, Vega, thanks,' said Petra.

Delph said, 'We should get some sleep. We'll have a lot of work to do tomorrow.'

We walked upstairs, and Delph bade us goodnight and went to his room.

I followed Petra to her door.

'So we have fifty people here who can do magic,' she said. 'Now what do we do with them?'

'We train them up,' I replied promptly. 'Just as Astrea Prine did me. As I did for you.'

'I'm not sure I'll be much good at teaching blokes,' she said worriedly.

'I taught you spells, Petra. You can do the same for them.'

'Well, they will have to be mightily well trained up to take on the Maladons. Remember the one we took on.'

I looked at her darkly. 'I don't think I'll soon forget, since I killed him.'

'That's not what I meant, Vega.'

'Well, then?' I asked.

'We had a terrible time fighting one bloke. I was exhausted and I know you were too. Whereas he seemed fresh and ready to keep fighting. If Harry Two hadn't helped, I'm not sure either of us would be here.'

'I don't disagree with that,' I said. She was speaking the

298

absolute truth. Harry Two had saved us both.

Then she looked at me, puzzled. 'But you said you fought off *eight* Maladons to rescue us.'

'That's right.'

'So what happened to you between the one bloke and the eight?'

I looked down at my wand. I knew exactly what had happened. My wand was now truly and properly mine. None of it belonged to Alice Adronis any more. It was as though her power and the entire line of my ancestors had been transferred to me. I recalled that that was exactly what Astrea had told us would occur back at her cottage.

Whatever the case, I was an infinitely more powerful sorceress. I just hoped I was powerful enough.

'I got . . . better,' I said.

Petra startled me by giving me a hug and then disappeared into her room, closing the door behind her.

I stood there for a few moments as guilt once more ate away at me. How could I have even contemplated putting Petra intentionally in danger like that?

Was I more Maladon than I had accused her of being? I shuddered at this terrible thought.

When I returned to my room, Harry Two was waiting for me.

I patted his head.

When I looked down at him, the expression on his face was inscrutable. He wasn't smiling. His eyes weren't as animated as they usually were. Perhaps he was mad at me for leaving him behind.

As soon as my head touched the pillow, I fell fast asleep.

But my sleep was troubled.

I woke in the night, feeling anxious and confused. We had accomplished much. Rescuing fifty people from a lifetime of humiliating servitude was something to be proud of. But now it seemed that the task only became harder. These people had never wielded a wand before. They had never used magic in battle. One day, they would be pitted against the most murderous band of sorcerers in all of existence.

So truly, how many of them would survive the coming war? Would Delph, Petra or Harry Two?

Hel, would I survive it?

I restlessly turned over on to my side. Harry Two was right next to me, and I instinctively reached out and rubbed his fur.

This calmed me, but only a bit.

Was it better to be enslaved and alive? Or free and dead?

The answer seemed to be obvious, only it wasn't.

It was always better to be free. That was clear enough.

But it was usually not better to be dead. That was also clear enough.

In my anxiety I sat up, climbed out of bed and started pacing.

When the sun rose I would be expected to commence shaping an army to go into battle.

Me, Vega Jane. I could feel a cold dread filling every inch of my being. Then I touched my wand and warmth flooded back into me. It was then that I realized I had accomplished a great many things I had initially thought were impossible. So why not build an army? Why the Hel not?

I got back into bed. This time I slept so soundly that I only awoke when I heard Pillsbury say into my ear, 'Would Mistress Vega like some breakfast?'

I sat straight up and noted the light streaming in through the window. I yawned and stretched.

'I would indeed,' I replied, feeling better rested and easier in my mind than I had since I'd left Wormwood.

'Very good, Mistress Vega.'

'Where are the others?' I enquired.

'Taking their breakfast in the dining room. All in good spirits and curious as to what is to come! As we all are!' he added excitedly.

I washed and changed my clothes. By the time I was done, my meal was there. I ate unhurriedly while Harry Two did the same next to me.

Finished, I picked up my wand and checked my appearance in the looking glass – giving myself a little inspirational wink.

I had a job to do, and I meant to do it.

I strode purposefully into the Great Hall.

All fifty people that we had saved were there. So were Delph and Petra. They were surrounded by the others and I'm sure were being peppered with questions.

All fell silent when they saw me walk in, and all eyes turned to me as though connected by magical tether.

I felt my face grow warm and my heart started pumping faster. Blimey! I wasn't used to all this attention. I stopped with Harry Two right next to me. My free hand went down to rub his ear while I surveyed the room as I supposed a general would their army.

They all stood there looking back at me.

My gaze fell over first Delph and then Petra.

They each gave me encouraging smiles.

Before I could speak, something totally unexpected happened. Amicus Arnold, who was in the back of the room, began to clap. Another joined him. And then another. And soon the entire hall rang with the applause.

My face turned red and tears crept to my eyes, and it was only when I raised my wand that the tumultuous sounds ended.

'I welcome all of you to Empyrean,' I said, 'the home of my ancestors and of yours. Empyrean is safe from attack, but we must maintain constant vigilance to ensure that it remains so. It is a magical place with many facets, not all of which I have discovered.' I pointed to my wand. 'You each now have a wand. This will be the source of your magical powers. The Maladons made you what they call "Ordinaries". But I know each of you to be truly extraordinary. And now, along with my friends Delph Delphia and Petra Sonnet –' I indicated both with my wand – 'without whom none of you would be standing here, we will begin the work of training each of you up so that you may realize your vast potential.'

I paused here, both for breath and a bit of clarity.

'The training will not be easy or without risk. Injuries almost undoubtedly will occur. Mistakes will be made. Frustration will be rampant at times.'

And didn't I know that better than most?

'But I promise you that if you work hard and with dedication, the sorcerer or sorceress you will become will be truly amazing.' I paused to let this sink in and watched as each of them looked around the room at the others.

'Now, once you have been trained up, the most difficult task you will ever undertake will commence.' I paused again here, because this truly was the entire crux of the matter.

'The Maladons enslaved you and have complete control of this world. They are a cruel, ruthless and evil lot. They are remarkably gifted at sorcery and employing that magic in the matter of combat. They vanquished many of our kind who were magically gifted in a long-ago war. I propose to take the fight to them once more. And this time, I intend that our side will win.' I raised my wand. 'Are you with me?'

As one, they all raised their wands.

This time I decided not to stop the cheering. I decided to let it go on as long as they so desired. For it was indeed cheering to me as well.

Perhaps to me most of all.

36

SIMPLY, A ROSE

Things were not going all that well really.

It was fine to make grand speeches and cheer. It was quite another to actually train and mould an army of magical warriors from basically nothing.

We had taken over the Great Hall and used it for our training area.

I could now well understand Pillsbury's comment that Empyrean grew to accommodate its guests, for the Great Hall, large to begin with, had seemed to inflate, and now easily held all of us and all the spells cast.

I had started the training with a short lecture on the mind, body and spirit, sounding perhaps more like Astrea Prine than I had intended. I had then moved on to simple wand motions and the most mundane of spells. I well recalled how awkward I was while being instructed by Astrea; compared to this lot, I was ten Excaliburs combined. In the back of my mind, I could imagine all of them lying dead on the battlefield after having succumbed to the Maladons in record time.

We had divided the group into two equal components. Petra had taken on the job of training one group, while I headed up the other.

Delph also had a teaching role to play, and in a separate room he explained to small groups all about our history and the journey we had taken from Wormwood to here and everything in between. We had no idea what might be important, so we had made the decision to tell them everything.

I ventured into the classroom from time to time and found that good questions were asked and lively discussions abounded.

Parchment and ink sticks had been provided by Pillsbury so that the students could write everything down and read and discuss it later.

Thirty days went by, and we finally saw some signs of improvement, but far fewer than I would have liked.

Late one night, I heard a knock on the door. When I opened it, there was Delph, looking uncertain and nervous.

'What is it?' I asked after he came in, and I sat on my bed rubbing Harry Two's ear.

'Miranda Weeks.'

I sighed. 'I know she's not very good, but—'

'She's the youngest of the lot,' he interjected.

'I know that. That's why it's going to take her longer than some of the others to get the hang of it.'

'Not what I meant,' he said.

I was growing annoyed at how cryptic he was being. 'What, then?'

'I think she's too young to be trained up to fight. I mean, I don't think it's right.'

'Delph, we need everyone we can get. The Maladons have hundreds of fully trained sorcerers.'

'Right, well, if it was your brother John, would it be OK? He's several years older than Miranda.'

I had not anticipated this line of argument, and part of me was upset that Delph would bring up my brother to make his point. Then I thought about the boys in their uniforms marching along with their terrible flag. They were older than Miranda too!

'What do we do, then? Tell her she can't be trained up as a sorceress?'

'No, she *can* be. Who knows how many years this will take? But I don't think she should be allowed to fight until she's older.'

'OK, Delph, I'll talk to her.'

He made no move to leave. 'Is there something else?' I asked.

He drew a long breath and then plunged in. 'You shouldn't go off by yourself no more without telling us, or letting us go with you,' he said.

I stood. 'What?'

'You going off to rescue Virgil or going to Greater True that time without a word. We were worried sick. 'Tain't right.'

'Did Petra put you up to this?' I shot back.

He looked truly bewildered. 'Pet? No.'

'I wonder. But in any case, I don't recall your being my keeper, Delph. I'll go where I like when I like.'

Delph's expression was not one of hurt, which I had expected. It was one of anger.

'Anything else?' I said imperiously, though I was feeling guilty at having treated him like this.

He turned and left without a word, slamming my door behind him.

I fell back on my bed and groaned.

We ate our meals in rotating groups, so as not to overwhelm poor Mrs Jolly. Delph, Petra and I made a habit of eating at separate tables so that we could get to know those we would be fighting next to.

I found most of the recruits eager, and full of both anger at what had been done to them and a thirst to strike back at their enslavers.

When the others had gone to bed, the three of us would sit up long into the night in the library to discuss matters. Delph never mentioned the confrontation in my room, but his attitude towards me was decidedly cooler. If Petra noticed, she said nothing.

One evening, six months into our training, Petra, Delph and I sat in front of the flickering fire, in the comfortable old leather chairs.

Delph was poring over parchment for his next class, while I was making flicking motions with my wand and thinking of additional spells that would be good to teach.

The silence was gratifying after a long training period with fifty people constantly barraging us with questions and seeking advice on mastering magic.

'Do you think this is going to work?' said Petra, stretch-ing out.

I stopped my wand movements, and Delph looked up from his heaps of parchment.

'What?' I asked, surprised.

Petra pulled her wand and aimed it the ceiling, where our fifty recruits were no doubt collapsed in exhausted sleep.

'Them!' she said. 'At the pace we're going, we'll be dead and buried before they're ready to take on the Maladons.'

I glanced at Delph, who continued to stare at Petra.

'We're doing the best we can,' said Delph sharply.

'I'm not disputing that,' said Petra, now sitting up on her haunches. 'But that doesn't change the fact that I'm not sure they'll *ever* be ready.'

'They'll get there,' I said hopefully. 'It just takes time.'

She glanced at me. 'Really? Artemis Dale nearly severed his own foot because he employs the *Jagada* curse like he's wielding an axe. Charlotte Tokken keeps hurling her wand across the room with the simplest of motions.'

'They're not used to any of this, Petra,' I said defensively. 'I had a great teacher in Astrea Prine, and it still took me a long time to get the hang of it. Besides that, we were forced to learn on the fly, fighting our way through the Quag, and once we left it we battled the Maladons. It was do or die. The experience made us tougher and stronger. They haven't had the benefit of that. They've been slaves without one original thought in their heads for a long, long time.'

'Maybe that's a fatal flaw in this whole thing,' said Petra.

I sat up. 'What do you mean by that?' I demanded.

Petra fixed her gaze on me. 'I mean that what if their magic being taken from them once means they can never be all that good at spells and such, even when their magic dust is returned to them? You have to admit, Vega, they are an incredibly clumsy bunch. We've been at this for a long time, and not one of them can even consistently perform a *Rejoinda* spell. How long do you think it will take them to master the *Pass-pusay*, *Paralycto*, *Incarcerata* and *Embattlemento* incantations? And do you really see any of them ever being able to perform the *Rigamorte* curse?'

I sat there looking at her as awful, terrible thoughts flashed through my mind. The one I'd had before, of all of them lying dead on the battlefield while the victorious Maladons danced over their shattered bodies, made me shiver.

I composed myself and said, 'I don't see what choice we have. We freed them. They're here. They're trying to learn. And we can't do this alone. We can't take on the Maladon empire by ourselves. We need help!' Then, full of anger and spite, I added, 'Do you have a better idea?'

Petra sighed and lay back in the front of the fire once more. 'No, I ruddy well don't.'

'Maybe I do.'

We both looked at Delph.

He put down the parchment and said, 'You mentioned it yourself, Vega. *Learning on the fly*. Having to fight our way through the Quag. That made a difference. You can't learn everything in the classroom. You know that.'

'What are you suggesting?' I snapped. 'That we take them on a field trip into the Quag?' My response was more heated than was called for, I had to admit, but I was still cross with Delph.

'No, not that.'

'What, then?' barked Petra.

'I'm suggesting that we take one or two of them with us on occasion to True or Greater True. They can get a feel for what it's like out in the real world, exercising magic. If Maladons show up, well, then, they'll have to fight.'

'Fight and *perish*,' commented Petra.

I thought Delph might have something there though. 'No, we could start off small like Delph suggested. Go into True with one or two of them and just look around. Let them see things. We'll do our best not to encounter Maladons, not until they're ready. But I think they need a lot more training up before we even think of doing such a thing.'

Petra held up her hand with the missing finger. 'Vega, you're forgetting that we no longer have the ring. If we go to those places, we go fully visible. The Maladons know what we and their former slaves look like. They'll pounce immediately.'

My spirits plummeted. I had forgotten that. I was just so used to having the ring and the cover it provided.

However, I noted Delph's anxious face, regrouped and said, 'Then we'll just have to disguise ourselves.'

Petra did not look remotely convinced by this, but Delph said, 'I bet this place has lots of clothes and stuff that we can use.'

'I think it's a good idea,' I said.

'Well, just for the record, I don't,' said Petra.

'Let's talk about this tomorrow. I'm going to bed,' I said. I rose and left.

I did not sleep well.

Petra's words kept coming back to me.

If this plan didn't work, if this 'army' ended up not being able to fight, I had no alternative plan. The war would be lost before it was even fought.

Another thirty days passed. There were some improvements – Sara Bond, a lanky female of thirty-three, performed a perfectly acceptable *Embattlemento* spell that actually blocked my incantation. I praised her, a comment that brought even more redness to her already rosy cheeks.

Tobias Holmes, on the other hand, was not progressing nearly as well. Tall and broad-shouldered and, I had seen for myself, a bit overconfident in his abilities, he could not seem to grasp the concept of pointing his wand at the actual target. Instead he vaguely waved it here and there, which meant that he ended up being a danger to himself and others around him.

I worked with him until he could at least aim straight.

I had spoken with Miranda Weeks after my conversation with Delph. She took my decision without argument, yet there was something in her look that made me think she was not OK with it. But I knew that Delph was right. She was simply too young. Besides, she had not a jot of confidence in her small bones. She held her wand as though it were a serpent about to bite her. She never looked at the target of her spells. She mumbled the words with no confidence and indeed seemed relieved when no magic was produced. She wouldn't have lasted a sliver in battle.

I stood in the corner watching her, and others like her, as my own confidence, bolstered a bit by Sara Bond's enhanced performance, now trickled away. The truth was, there were far more like Miranda Weeks among the fifty.

Several, like Louise Penny and Dom Sadan, didn't seem to want to fight at all.

I glanced over at Petra's group, and I saw that the same held for her lot.

When I caught Petra's gaze, her thoughts were clear for me to see.

This was a growing disaster of enormous proportions.

I quickly looked away.

At dinner that night there was one of us unaccounted for – no one could find Miranda.

We searched high and low. Until I stepped out into the rear grounds and heard the sobs.

I made my way down the garden path until I came to a bench nearly surrounded by large rose bushes.

Miranda was seated on the bench, her head in her hands while she wept.

Two marble statues were next to her, attempting to console her without a lick of success. The magical rake had a hankie poised on its handle, but she wouldn't look at it.

I told them I would deal with it and sent them off.

I performed a wand wire to Petra telling her that I had found Miranda and everything was fine. They were to continue on with their meal.

I sat next to her and waited until she stopped sobbing.

I was loath to break the silence. Sometimes it was better to let the person in distress speak first.

But when Miranda just sniffled without looking like she

was actually going to say anything, I decided to plunge ahead.

'Things not going well?' I began.

She shook her head and then broke into more sobs.

I took out my wand and held it in front of me.

'Take out your wand, Miranda.'

'What's the use, Vega? I'm simply all sixes and sevens with this . . . this magic stuff.'

'You're just very young. Please, take it out.'

Scowling, she drew her wand and held it in front of her. But she didn't look at it.

'Where do you come from?' I asked.

I had spoken with many of the others about their pasts, but had not done so with Miranda. It was probably because of her losing her mother. She no doubt thought about it all the time, and I didn't want to unduly add to this burden.

'Why?' she said stubbornly.

'I'd just like to know.'

She rubbed her face and said slowly, 'I was born in a little village called Drews. Me mum and me lived there. I couldn't tell you where it is now, but I remember it being pretty, with crumbling stone walls, a small creek running through it with a bridge over it. I caught a fish for dinner. Me mum . . .' She stopped, and her lip trembled. 'Me mum was quite proud when I did that.'

'I'm sure she was. Did you go to Bimbleton Station?'

She nodded. 'Mum wanted to see where the train went.'

She started to cry again, and I put my arm around her and just let her sob.

When she had recovered, I pointed to the mark on her

hand. 'They took you because of that mark. It shows you're magical.'

'So why can't I do magic, then!' she exclaimed.

She looked at me with red, puffy eyes.

'Because magic is hard, and everyone comes to it in their own way. Some faster, some slower.'

'I bet you came to it fast. I bet you were doing spells when you were born.'

'I performed my first spell when I was fifteen. Before that I had never done a lick of proper magic. I was incapable of it. It took a very long time and a lot of hard work and many mistakes along the way for me to properly wield *this*.' I held up my wand.

This confession of sorts clearly got her attention.

'Really?' she said, her eyes wide in wonder.

'How old are you, Miranda?'

'Ten, least I think.'

'I'm nearly sixteen, and I can't tell you the number of times I've messed up. But I picked myself back up and kept going. I've been watching you for a while now. Very closely.'

'Why's that?' she said nervously. 'You're . . . you're not thinking of sending me back to . . . to what I was? You already told me I couldn't fight the Maladons. So I'm no use to you.'

I gripped her shoulder. 'I would never do that even if you could never properly perform a spell in your life. You are free now. You're my friend. Friends don't hurt each other like that. You will remain free regardless of anything that happens here.' I paused and said, 'I see a lot of you in me.'

314

She shook her head hard. 'Y-you're just saying that to make me feel better.'

'I don't have the luxury of doing that, Miranda. I don't have time to make you feel better simply for the sake of making you feel better. Do you understand that?'

She sat up straight and looked directly at me. 'Yes.'

'When I first used my wand, I had no confidence. Not in it, and not in me. I wielded it like the thing and I were two separate bits of stuff.'

She looked at her wand. 'Aren't we?'

'No! That wand was created from the wand of Bastion Cadmus, the father of us all. It has a bit of him embedded in it. That bit is now your wand, which means it is also embedded in you. Your wand is you, and you are your wand. You are truly inseparable. It will perform for you better and more powerfully than it will for anyone else.'

'It won't perform for me a'tall,' she said miserably.

'That's because you have no confidence in yourself, meaning you have no confidence in your wand. It senses that. It *feels* that, Miranda; that's why it won't perform. Because you, as yet, don't trust it. And so it does not trust *you*.'

She stared down at her wand again. This time, not like it was a serpent, but with a look of intrigue; with a look of one considering certain possibilities.

'You . . . you really think that's the problem?'

'Did you trust your mother?'

'What? O'course I did. She always took care of me. Always wanted the best for me.' Tears leaked from her eyes, but she held my gaze, which impressed me.

'So does your wand. When you have it in hand, you will never be alone. It wants the absolute best for you, because it wants you to *survive*.'

She looked down at her wand, her mouth open in wonder.

When she looked back up, I said, 'Shall we go into dinner now, Miranda, or . . . ?'

I let my voice trail off and studied her, awaiting her response.

She stood, holding her wand loosely, as I had originally taught her. Then Miranda turned away from me, pointed her wand at a bush, her gaze set directly ahead, and then, while making the perfect pull-back motion, said, '*Rejoinda* rose.'

The flower was nipped off the bush and flew directly into her free hand. She looked down at it for an instant before her gaze lifted to mine. Both our mouths spread into wide grins, and then she hugged me.

'I did it!' She began to sob harder than ever. She was only ten, after all.

I hugged her back, the tears creeping down my cheeks.

'Yes, you did.'

'I promise I'll make you proud of me, Vega.'

'I know you will.'

Blimey, it was like I'd just inherited a little sister.

But I had one thought firmly in mind as I hugged Miranda.

I hope you never have to cast a spell in battle. I hope this war will be over long before you're old enough to fight.

And possibly die.

37

ONE SMALL STEP

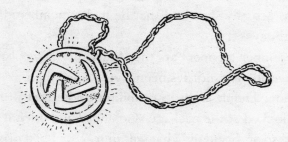

Sixteen!

I awoke with this thought. I turned sixteen sessions this morning. Or sixteen *years*. Delph, Petra and I routinely spoke this world's language now, otherwise our fifty pupils would not be able to understand us.

Delph and I had been gone from Wormwood for an entire year. It was hard to believe, but when I thought back to all that we had experienced, and survived, it felt like ten years had actually passed.

I dressed and headed down with Harry Two. When I walked into the dining room, Delph, Petra and all the others were there.

I made a plate of food and was carrying it over to a table with five of our pupils when I saw Delph waving at me to join him. Mrs Jolly and her kitchen staff swooped around, making sure that everyone was well-fed and taken care of.

When I sat next to Delph he grinned, leaned over and said, 'Happy birthday, Vega Jane.'

I looked down and saw in his hand a small, wrapped package.

'Delph, you didn't have to get me anything.'

I was actually surprised that he had remembered it was my birthday.

'Remember supper at the Starving Tove back in Wormwood?' he said. 'It's been a year since then.'

'I know, Delph. I was just thinking about that.'

He looked at the package. 'Go ahead and open it.'

I did so and held up what was in it.

It was a finely wrought chain with a tiny disc at the end.

'It's to wear around your neck,' he said.

I looked at the disc. On it was the image of the three hooks.

'Where did you get this?' I said, amazed.

'Didn't get it. I made it.'

'How?'

'There's a little smithy in the back grounds here. Gus, he's one of them marble statues – a slep, um, *horse* – showed me. Got a forge and metal and all the tools I needed.'

'Delph, it's beautiful. Truly beautiful.' I put it around my neck. 'Thank you so much.'

He turned red but smiled broadly.

I hesitated. 'Delph, about heading off without telling you?'

'It's OK.'

'No, it's not. You were right. I shouldn't have done it. And I shouldn't have spoken to you like that. So . . . so I just won't do that any more, OK?'

He smiled warmly. 'Thanks, Vega Jane.'

He gave me a hug. When he sat back, he had a funny look on his face.

'Delph? Are you OK?'

He nodded, rose and hurried off without finishing his meal, which was practically unheard of for Delph.

I sensed someone watching, and I glanced over to find Petra staring at me. She slowly looked away.

The training had been steadily improving over the last few months. Artemis Dale had mastered the *Jagada* spell, and Charlotte Tokken hadn't lost control of her wand in a while. Miranda Weeks had made enormous strides, wielding her wand with skill and confidence. All of them had worked hard and shown true grit and determination. I knew it had not been easy because it had not been easy for me either.

Training was going so well, in fact, that I had an idea. I explained it to Delph and Petra that night.

'I want to take three of them to Greater True tonight.'

They both looked startled at the abruptness of my suggestion.

'Why Greater True?' asked Delph.

'That's where we lost the invisibility ring.'

Petra looked down at her missing finger.

I said quickly, 'Petra, I don't blame you for the loss of the ring. But I think we need to try to get it back.'

'How can you?' Petra asked. 'You don't even know if it's in Greater True.'

'You said the Maladons jumped you?'

'That's right.'

'And one of the Maladons had your wand. Yet you ended up in the barracks of the Elite Guard and not in the custody of the Maladons.'

Petra looked confused.

'How did they take the ring and your finger, do you remember? By magic?'

'It . . . it . . . it happened so fast. I was half unconscious.'

I glanced at Delph. 'You managed to lift one of them up and throw them against a wall. Unlikely against a Maladon with a wand – especially as you weren't invisible that night. You said the wind knocked you around and the invisibility shield was thrown off.'

'That's . . . that's right,' said Delph, looking puzzled.

I asked, 'What were they wearing? Suits and hats? Black cloaks with red hoods?'

'Cloaks,' said Delph at the same time as Petra said, 'Coats.'

I gazed at each of them in turn. 'Well, which was it?'

They glanced sheepishly at each other.

'I don't know,' admitted Delph.

Petra shook her head in agreement. 'I was a bit wonky in the head too, from getting thrown by the wind,' she said. 'But I think it *was* a knife that cut off my finger,' she added.

'Let me see it,' I said.

She held it up and I studied the stump.

'This was not done by a spell,' I said, wishing I had examined it more closely when it had first happened. 'A spell would have been more precise, and it would have burned the skin. This is jagged and there is no burning. I think they used a knife.'

Petra said, 'They grabbed me, but I can't remember much more except that it hurt. They didn't have to cut my finger to get the ring off – it was loose anyway, that's why it got turned back round.'

'They did it to cause you pain. I think members of the Elite Guard were the ones who attacked and captured you, not the Maladons. I wondered why you were taken to the barracks and not somewhere else, like the castle. When I used one of the Maladons to get into the barracks, the guard there said, "We've got our pair here still." Then he wanted to know if Dullish had managed to trap me. When I searched the Maladons, I got your wand back but not the ring.'

'So you think one of them Elite Guards might have it?' asked Delph.

'It's possible. He might have thought it was valuable and he could sell it. Regardless of whether one of the guards or a Maladon has it, I want it back.'

'Who do you want to take?' asked Petra.

'Amicus, Sara and Dennis.'

Delph nodded. 'Yep, they're three of the best.'

'So it'll be the five of us?' said Petra.

I shook my head. 'The *four* of us. You have to stay here. If anything happens to me, you need to carry on.'

She looked at me as though the weight of the world had descended upon her shoulders.

'Me, carry on?'

'We took a blood oath, Petra. For me it was more than a way to stop our squabbling. It was also an unbreakable bond, so that if one of us falls, the other one will continue on. We can't count on both of us surviving.'

She slowly nodded, and Delph said, 'Then I'll go with you.'

'No, Petra will need your assistance, Delph.'

'Why don't I go with them, then, Vega?' offered Petra.

'You will at some point. But the first time, it has to be me, Petra. It just has to be.'

Petra studied me, and I could tell by her expression that she knew I was right. I was the superior sorceress, especially now with my wand fully and completely my own.

I rose and went to tell the others so they could prepare. They were all excited *and* scared. Exactly what I had expected.

With their magic returned and their being trained up properly, all fifty of the formerly enslaved were now fully branded with the three hooks on their hands. That meant they could be traced by the Maladons once they left the protection of Empyrean. In response to this, I had performed an intricate spell that had produced fifty copies of the glove that Alice had given me. They would wear them whenever we left Empyrean. I was pretty confident they would work, but this night we would find out for certain.

When I went back to my room to get my cloak, Petra was waiting for me.

'Delph told me it was your birthday today.'

'Yes, it is.'

She looked at the necklace around my neck.

'Delph made that for you?'

I smiled. 'He gave it to me as a present.'

'Is that what you do on birthdays?'

My smile vanished even as my heart went out to her. Of course, why would she know about presents on birthdays?

'Yes,' I said. 'When is your birthday?'

She shook her head. 'I'm not sure. I remember my mother telling me it was cold when I was born. And I know I'm seventeen because we would mark off the time when I was young. I would cut a notch in a stick I kept for each one.'

'Well, it's cold outside now, so maybe your birthday is coming up,' I said.

She shrugged, but kept staring at the necklace.

I ended the awkward silence by saying, 'I need to get ready.'

'Happy birthday, Vega. Much luck on your journey. I'll . . . I'll see you when you get back. I hope you find the ring.'

'Thanks, Petra. I hope I do too.'

She turned and left.

We silently appeared at the rear of the train station in Greater True. We were wearing long coats and hats pulled low that covered most of our faces.

Dennis, Sara and Amicus knew this place better than I did, having lived here for so long.

We had gone over the plan several times before leaving Empyrean.

When I looked at them, I could tell they were ready. Their wands were held loosely in their gloved hands; their gazes were steady and calm.

I led them through the darkness towards the barracks of the Elite Guard. Along the way I saw a paper tacked to a wooden post.

I used my wand to illuminate it so we could see what it said.

REWARD FOR ANY INFORMATION LEADING TO THE RETURN OF THE FOLLOWING INDIVIDUALS AND THE CAPTURE OF THEIR KIDNAPPERS

And there listed were fifty names.

Dennis, Sara and Amicus glanced at each other when they saw their names there. I thought they might be frightened, but I was heartened to see that each of them looked, well, proud!

I took down the paper and balled it up. 'So they turned this into a mass kidnapping instead of a mass breakout for freedom,' I said. 'No doubt they've blamed it on the awful Campions.'

As we continued on, I was hoping for something, and it turned out to happen.

'*Subservio.*'

The spell hit the uniformed bloke dead in the back.

Dennis and Amicus each grabbed an arm and dragged him into the dark recesses of an alley.

I looked at the blank-faced bloke for a moment. I didn't recognize him, which wasn't surprising. There were a lot of them, after all.

I held up the disc that Delph had made for me.

'Have you seen a ring with this mark on it?'

The man looked dully at the image and nodded.

'Where?' I demanded.

'The commander of the barracks has it. Major Nelson. He wears it on his hand. Spoils of war, he called it.'

'Did he tell anyone else that he had it? Mr Endemen or any of his blokes?'

The man shook his head. 'No. He hides it from them when they appear.'

'Because they'll take it?'

'They'll take his life.'

This comment surprised me. It showed a deeper understanding of the Maladons than I would have given this gent credit for.

'You know that they are murderous?'

'I have seen them kill.'

'Do you fear them?'

'We all fear them.'

I glanced at the others, who were staring open-mouthed at the man.

'OK, where is Major Nelson now? At the barracks?'

He shook his head. 'At home.'

'The address?'

'One Hundred Greater True Court.'

'That's right next to the general assembly building,' noted Dennis. 'Big brick building with a blue door. My mas— the ones who enslaved me lived only one avenue over.'

I nodded.

I wiped the bloke's thoughts and sent him on his way, oblivious to what had just happened. We heard him whistling as he walked down the darkened street.

I looked at Dennis. 'Lead the way.'

We hurried through the darkness. I had to keep reminding myself that we were no longer invisible. When we heard steps approaching our way, I cast a befuddlement spell in front of us.

A moment later two soldiers appeared carrying guns. They passed right by us, the incantation having done what it was designed to do.

We kept going and reached the house five minutes later.

We looked up at the place from across the street. The building was imposing and totally dark.

'OK,' I said. 'Everyone here knows that all you lot have disappeared. It's been a long time, granted, but they will still be on their guard. So if anything happens, we must act quickly and efficiently.' I tapped Amicus on the shoulder. 'You'll bring up the rear. Keep an eye out for anything that looks or sounds suspicious.'

He nodded and I turned to Dennis. 'You'll be on my left flank.' I glanced at Sara. 'And you on my right.'

She nodded.

I lifted my wand to the ready position and they all did the same.

We were all breathing fast. They had trained long and hard, but always within the safe confines of Empyrean. This was far different. This was the real thing, and there were blokes here who would want nothing more than to kill us.

Amicus looked determined, Sara keenly observant and Dennis a trifle nervous.

We entered through the back door. A simple incantation did the job.

The house was beautifully decorated and furnished but

I didn't care a whit about that. I just wanted my ring back. It was the only thing I had left of my grandfather's. Even if it couldn't turn me invisible, I would have wanted it back.

There was no one on the first three floors. That left the top floor.

I used my *Crystilado magnifica* spell to see inside the rooms until we came to the last one on the left.

The man was asleep in bed.

On his finger was my ring.

'*Ingressio.*'

The door swung open and we edged inside.

My gaze hit every corner of the room before it settled back on the bed where Major Nelson was fast asleep.

'*Rejoinda* ring.'

It flew off his finger and on to mine.

I instantly twisted it round.

When I looked at Sara, my heart sank.

She could obviously still see me.

'*Embattlemento,*' I cried out as the spell lights shot at us.

A dozen Maladons had appeared in the room and were firing spell after spell at us.

Dennis cried out as a spell ripped into his arm and blood spurted from the wound.

Using Destin, I soared above them all and fired spells downward.

'Triangulate,' I cried out.

The three of them quickly formed a three-point perimeter stance, which I had taught them.

I continued to rain spells down on the Maladons, which meant they had to lift their wands and defend against me.

That gave my lot free rein to fire away.

Sara sent a wickedly curving *Jagada* curse at a Maladon. After slashing him, it bounced off and cut through another.

Amicus was a bloke on fire, sending *Impacto* spells that blasted a half dozen Maladons across the room.

One-armed, Dennis ensnared two more Maladons and then knocked them out.

I finished off the rest with a brilliantly tricky spell that Astrea had shown me.

The first wave of the spell was a blinding wall of light. When they shot at it with their wands, they found out, too late, that the wall of light was actually a magical mirror that sent their spells hurtling right back at them.

When the last Maladon fell, I returned to the floor.

'Let's get out of here,' I said. I was just about to magically tether them and cast my *Pass-pusay* incantation when a figure appeared inches from me.

'Looking for this?' sneered Endemen.

He held up a ring – my real ring. The other had been a decoy.

'A useful *magical element*, wouldn't you say?'

There would have been a time when the mere sight of the bloke would have paralysed me. That time had long since passed.

I lowered my wand and bowed my head.

'Acknowledging my superiority, Vega of Wormwood!'

I lifted my gaze to his. Right then I could tell the bloke knew he had made a mistake. But it was too late.

I knocked the sneer off his face, not with my wand.

But with my fist.

My gloved hand, powered both by Destin and all the loathing I held for this disgusting creature, hit him so hard that he was catapulted across the room and slammed into the wall with such force that he smashed right through it and into the next room.

I stared at the crumpled mess of a Maladon for one glorious moment.

'Rejoinda my *real* ring.'

The ring shot off his hand and flew on to mine.

I tethered us together, turned the ring around, said my incantation and we vanished.

This had been my absolute best birthday ever!

38

THE END OF ME

Once we got back to Empyrean, I used the Adder Stone
to fix up Dennis's arm, a burn on Sara's face and a gash
on Amicus's leg. I praised all three of them on their
performance in battle.

At breakfast we all recounted the story of how we had
got the ring back. When Sara got to the part about me
blasting Endemen through a wall, the cheers rang out so
loudly I didn't think they would ever stop echoing through
my ears.

Having my grandfather's ring back buoyed my spirits
wonderfully, and we continued our training. I threw more
and more difficult tasks to my troops, confident that they
were up to it.

As Astrea Prine had done with me, I used the *Golem
Masquerado* spell to craft clay statues for us to use as targets.
I know it was a bit cheeky of me, but I fashioned the statues
so they all wore bowler hats!

As time passed, we moved on to ever more complex
spells. When I looked around the Great Hall, I saw lights

zipping across and smashing into the statues, either exploding them or ripping them to pieces.

I was so proud!

No doubt emboldened by having fought Maladons for real, Sara Bond had become a spell machine, whipping her wand around and incanting like she had been doing it her whole life. She had become one of the most popular among the fifty. For weeks after our adventure in Greater True, I could hear the others asking her to recount in exacting detail everything that had happened during the course of the battle.

Dennis and Amicus were inundated by these requests too. I didn't mind all the curiosity. I wanted them to explain to the others exactly what it felt like to be in a fight for your very life. I knew that would be important later on.

Now that we had the invisibility ring back, Petra and I took turns shepherding groups of twos and threes to True, Greater True and even Bimbleton Station. We had several skirmishes with soldiers and Maladons but we always survived and came back intact. The experiences were helping to mould my young army into quite the fighting machine.

I grew to take a real interest in all of them, because I knew that at some point we would depend on one another to make it through the coming war alive. So while Dennis, Amicus and Sara were well on their way to becoming fine magical warriors, I needed all fifty to be at the same level.

Cecilia Harkes was a tall, lithe girl of nineteen. She had red hair, freckled cheeks and a quick but steady wand hand. We had rescued Cecilia from an elderly Greater True couple who thought nothing of making her sleep next to the coal bin, forcing her to eat her meals from a bowl served on the floor and slapping her across the face whenever they felt like it.

I gave her some finer pointers on the *Jagada* spell, showing her how to move and turn her hips together with the wand motion. As Astrea had shown me, it added to both the speed and potency of the incantation.

I watched her do it once more, and nodded approvingly as the clay statue became riddled with innumerable cuts and slashes.

'Nice job, Cecilia. Couldn't have done it better myself.'

She swelled with pride as I moved on.

Across the hall, Petra was putting a group through the rigorous process of mastering the *Subservio* spell. I watched as Petra performed the incantation on Nicholas Bonham, a tall, sturdily built young man with handsome features, beautiful blue eyes and long blond hair. Nicholas stiffened and assumed a blank stare when the spell hit him.

Petra then made him jump and spin around, then hop on one leg.

The rest of the group laughed, but I wondered.

Did Petra fancy the strapping lad?

I could only hope.

I had James Throckmorton, a small man who had been enslaved the longest of the group, starting at age nine, perform the *Embattlemento* spell. I broke through it easily the first six times he tried, but the seventh time his shield held against my wand's blast.

His face sweaty and his chest heaving, he accepted my

congratulations with a single nod before getting back to work.

I kept moving through the group, helping Alabetus Trumbull succeed in deploying the *Engulfiado* spell, which doused poor Pauline Paternas, a pugnacious woman of twenty.

As I helped her up and dried her off with a wave of my wand, I said, 'Now it's *your* turn.'

Which she took with a flicker of malice in her eyes. Her stream of water was far stronger than Trumbull's and sent him sailing headlong into the wall.

I had to work hard to hide my smile.

Aloysius Danbury struck Tobias Holmes blind with the *Impairio* spell but forgot how to reverse it, which I quickly fixed.

Charlotte Tokken straightened out a maze I had created in one corner of the hall by employing with confidence the *Confuso, recuso* incantation.

I shuddered when I recalled how that spell had saved our lives in the Quag as we were going through the First Circle.

Anna Dibble, a tall girl around my age with brown hair cropped short by her former masters, which gave her face a severe look, trapped her sparring partner and former slave mate, Sara Bond, with the *Incarcerata* incantation. As the white lights swirled around Sara, I recalled how that same prison had held a huge jabbit in Astrea Prine's cottage. A jabbit that would have done me in, had I not been exceptionally fast with my wand!

I walked halfway up the stairs and looked back down,

surveying my little army going about its training.

Over there Dennis O'Shaughnessy used the *Rejoinda* spell to take the wand of Miranda Weeks. She promptly turned the tables on him after she got her wand back and roped him neatly with an *Ensnario* incantation. In another corner a door was opened by Reginald Magnus using the *Ingressio* incantation. Another corner was brightened by the *Illumina* spell.

People rose with the *Elevata* spell and others fell with the *Descente* incantation.

A tree I had conjured in the middle of the hall had its trunk shrunk by the *Withero* spell.

I smiled. All in all it was a good day.

I wandered into the room where Delph was holding forth.

As usual, he was dressed in a suit with a waistcoat and looked fetchingly handsome with his thick, long hair and tall, strong body. There were twenty students in the room and I noted, with a bit of apprehension, that all twelve of the young women sat there somehow managing to copiously write down every word Delph said while simultaneously gaping at him. I watched as several glanced at one another and giggled.

I closed the door to the room and walked away, shaking my head.

Females.

At dinner that night we all ate together. I usually liked to split the group up so as not to overburden the kitchen, but Mrs Jolly insisted that it was fine. The meal was particularly splendid, with chicken and ham and vegetables from the garden and soft rolls that seemed to melt in my mouth. Then followed pudding, and soon we all sat there happy and drowsy.

We said our goodnights and went our separate ways.

Petra caught up to me as I walked to my room.

'I think things are going rather well,' she said. 'Artemis Dale gets everything right after just a few attempts now. Regina Samms nearly so. Katie Watson's *Ensnario* spell is quite something. Alex Prettyman's convulsing hex is nearly unbreakable.'

'And Nicholas Bonham?' I said slyly. 'He seems awfully good too.'

Petra turned pink and looked away. 'He's all right but he also needs a lot of work.'

'I'm sure you'll give him *all* the attention he needs,' I said encouragingly.

I looked her over. Ever since coming here, it seemed to me that Petra had become even more lovely. She could now bathe regularly, wear clean clothes and wash her hair. Mrs Jolly's food had filled out her gaunt look. She was a beautiful woman, I had to admit. Nicholas Bonham would be fortunate to win her good graces.

'He tried to kiss me the other night,' she said, startling me.

'What did you do?'

'I hexed him.'

'Really?'

She smiled. 'But then I kissed him back.'

I laughed.

'Delph wants to kiss you.'

My smile faded. 'How do you know that?'

'He told me. A while back, in his room. We were talking about you. He loves you, Vega. I've always known that. I suppose I flirted with him sometimes just to annoy you. Anyway, he wanted my opinion about what he should do.'

I thought back to that night when I had almost sent Petra to her death. They had been talking about *me*?

'What did you tell him?'

'To follow his heart.'

I shot her a curious glance. 'So you're not . . . ?'

'I didn't say that, did I?' She paused, but only for a moment, before adding, 'And I plan to follow *my* heart too!'

She said goodnight, spun on her heel and went off to her room, leaving me standing there.

What else should I have expected from Petra Sonnet?

A moment later Delph came around the corner.

My face instantly felt warm and I said, innocently, 'Hey, Delph, Petra and I were just talking about you.'

'Really? What about?'

'Oh, nothing important. You've become a fine teacher.'

'Right.' He seemed distracted and I wondered why.

'What's up?' I asked.

'I'm glad you liked your present.'

I touched the necklace. 'I *love* it, Delph.'

He edged a bit closer. 'I wanted to give you *another* present on your birthday, but I wasn't . . . I wasn't sure you'd like it.'

'Delph, I'm sure I would love whatever you gave me.'

He took another step forward.

And he kissed me. I mean he really kissed me.

Before I realized it, I was kissing him back. We stood there for about five minutes. My heart felt like it might burst.

Then we heard a giggle. The sound of someone clearing their throat.

We turned to find half a dozen people standing there watching us.

The two girls watching us looked like they might melt, though Cecilia Harkes did look a bit disappointed.

The blokes, Amicus and Dennis among them, just looked embarrassed.

'Right,' I said. 'Well, goodnight, Delph.'

We uncoiled from each other and I hurried into my room and closed the door.

I don't believe my face was wide enough to accommodate my smile.

Harry Two was already there. He wasn't asleep, though he usually was by now.

He was perched on my bed looking alert. Which was strange, I thought.

I sat next to him and rubbed his fur.

'You OK, Harry Two?' I said.

Usually when I said that he would lick my face. This time he didn't. He didn't move or even look at me.

Troubled by this, I undressed, washed my face and climbed into bed.

I lay there staring at the ceiling.

I could tell that time passed, and soon it was the darkest point before the rise of the sun and still I had not closed my eyes.

I might have been thinking about Delph for part of the time. That kiss had confirmed much for me. The memory of it made my heart leap for joy. But though I really wanted to dwell on that, I was thinking principally about Harry Two. He had not moved a muscle. He was still perched in the exact same spot, his body as rigid as marble.

I would occasionally lift my head and look at him, wishing that he would finally lie down and go to sleep. But he didn't. And I knew that nothing Harry Two did was without purpose. He was my early warning signal and always had been. He sensed things long before I did.

I finally crawled over next to my faithful companion and sat with my arm around him.

I worriedly scanned his face. His eyes were pointed straight at the door. His snout was clamped shut. He looked as serious as ever I'd seen him, even when death was staring us both in the face, in the shape of a garm or jabbit or Maladon.

Finally, I got dressed and was debating whether to go downstairs and prepare for the next day's lessons when I shot a look at Harry Two. It was clear that his senses had once again been faster than mine, for he had jumped down from the bed and was intently staring at the door to my room.

I rushed over to him.

'Harry Two, what is it?' I asked.

He never once looked at me. But his remaining ear had pricked up.

Suddenly he lunged and started to scratch at the door.

I flung it open and he raced out.

'Harry Two!'

He ran down the hall and then hurtled down the stairs.

I raced after him.

He reached the first floor, turned and bolted out of sight.

I caught sight of him as he galloped down a set of stairs.

I followed in time to see him turn and go down another set of rickety stairs.

Then my heart went into my throat because I knew where he was going.

Sure enough, he reached the little door with the screaming Wug on the doorknob. When I ran up next to him he looked at me and barked, as though to say, *Hurry up, will you?*

I used my wand to open the door. Harry Two raced in and I followed.

The sound reached my ears as soon as I closed the door behind me.

It was the sound of someone sobbing.

Lights were swirling everywhere, as before, though there appeared to be more of them, and their flight more frenetic than it had been.

I gazed around looking for Uma Cadmus, or Alice Adronis, in her pierced armour and with her mortal wound. But they were not there.

So where were the sobs coming from?

Harry Two was not at a loss, though. He yipped and raced to a distant corner. I ran after him and found that the corner was actually a bend in the room that led to a much smaller room.

And in the very centre of that room was a huddled figure.

I crept forward, unsure who or what it was. I doubted

that any of the fifty people we had brought here would have found this place, or been able to access it. Was it one of the household staff? Was it another restless soul I had not met?

'Hello?' I said cautiously. 'Excuse me? Hello? Are you all right?'

When the figure turned towards me, I didn't know how I kept from fainting, or my heart from stopping.

The ethereal image of *Morrigone* was facing me.

But I had left Morrigone behind in Wormwood.

So what the Hel—

My breath caught in my throat as my lungs seized up.

Wormwood!

Harry Two and I rushed over to her and I knelt down beside her.

It was Morrigone, but it was a very changed Morrigone.

I had seen her in an image from Astrea Prine's cottage when I was in the Quag. Even then she had looked different from how I remembered. Always tall, queenly and flawless in all respects, she had looked older, withered, ill even.

The Morrigone I was looking at now was pale and frail, and the look in her eyes, even as recognition sparked there as her gaze fell full on my features, was one of abject horror undercut by a sense of complete despair.

I didn't know which terrified me more.

'Morrigone? It's me, Vega Jane.'

But she knew who I was. I had seen that clearly in her features. At first she said nothing. But her hand reached out and gripped my arm. Or rather it tried to. It simply passed right through.

'Vega,' she said in a near whisper.

'What happened?' I said. 'How did you get here?'

'I am dead,' she said in the same low voice, as though she barely had the strength to speak.

'Dead! But how?'

'They came.'

There really could only be one *they*.

'The Maladons?' I said. 'They came to Wormwood?'

She nodded.

'They killed you?'

She nodded again.

I could barely breathe. 'And . . . and the rest of Wormwood?'

She said nothing. She simply shook her head.

'It . . . it can't be,' I blurted out.

Now Morrigone's expression turned hard, cruel, loathing in every facet.

'I told you, Vega. I warned you what could happen. Well, now it *has* happened. Our deaths are upon *your* head.'

Before I could say anything in response, she faded away to nothing.

I could only stare at the spot where she had been. My mind had gone blank.

When it was filled with thoughts a few moments later, they were all terrible ones indeed.

Wormwood. My home.

They had killed Morrigone. They had killed . . . everyone?

I bent over and vomited up my dinner.

Next instant I jumped up and ran all the way to my room

341

with Harry Two right behind. I was so out of control that I bounced into walls and crashed over furniture. It was a wonder the whole house wasn't awoken, but I reached my bedroom without anyone seeing me.

I put on my cloak, slipped Destin around my waist and put the harness around my shoulders. I snapped my fingers and Harry Two jumped into the harness as he had done so many times before.

We passed by first Delph's and then Petra's rooms. But this was something *I* had to do.

Alone.

We stepped outside of Empyrean and I tapped my leg twice with the destination firmly in mind as I said the spell.

A moment later Harry Two and I arrived at the spot where we had left the Quag so long ago.

It was dark and dreary.

When I walked over to the spot I raised my wand and said, '*Exposadus.*'

There it was: the magical dome that had entombed both Wormwood and the Quag. On it was the very slightest of impressions, like an exposed seam in a garment.

We had come out here.

I looked down at my ring. I had used it to open the dome, allowing us to escape.

A useful magical element.

Those were the words that Endemen had spoken to me in Major Nelson's bedroom. Now I fully knew what he meant. I had used my ring to cut a seam in the dome to get out.

The Maladons had used my ring to get *in*.

I remembered being at the castle and seeing all the

342

pell-mell activity. That must have been when they found the spot where we came out. By making the seam, we had exposed the location of the spell wall protecting both the Quag and Wormwood. It had been pristine and thus completely invisible. They had never been able to find it before. With the seam marring the perfect surface of the dome, they at least knew what they had to break through. But they hadn't been able to get in.

Until they got hold of my ring.

My heart crumbled to bits.

I used my ring to pierce the wall. Then I tapped my wand against my leg and muttered *'Pass-pusay'* holding the image of the place of my birth singly in mind. I certainly knew it better than any other place.

The next moment my feet touched down on the high street in the town square.

I had been gone from here for what seemed like an eternity.

And it looked as though an eternity had passed.

The buildings were destroyed. The cobbles ruptured.

I walked numbly towards the Loons, where my brother, John, and I had lived after our parents had gone to the Care.

The building was a shell now, the doors and windows blown out.

I walked to the end where the majestic Council building had been located. I stared, for there was only an enormous blackened hole in the dirt where it had once stood.

I wandered the streets in a daze.

Steeples was burned, the pretty glass melted. The hospital and the Care were similarly gutted.

I flew to Duf Delphia's cottage.

Please, don't let it be. Don't let Duf be . . .

As I drew close, I noted with horror that all of the beasts that Duf typically trained lay dead in the paddocks around the cottage.

I landed and crept up to the porch of the cottage. The door was gone, the windows simply gaping holes.

With a thrill of horror, I saw it.

A pair of wooden stumps leaned against the wall.

Duf Delphia was gone.

I backed away, with Harry Two still in the harness, and pushed off the ground.

I soared above and landed in front of my old family home, where I had gone to live after Morrigone had taken in John. Surprisingly, nothing was touched there. I walked in the door and looked around in wonder that they had not demolished this place, especially this place.

Then I saw the mark of the Maladons burned into the wall.

So they *had* been here.

I raised my wand and blasted their mark away.

I ran out and lifted off into the sky, and moments later landed at Stacks.

The towers were toppled, the massive gate caved in. When I walked inside I saw that everything had been destroyed.

When I reached my old worker station where I had been a Finisher, I saw that the brass nameplate with *Vega Jane* on it had been savagely defaced.

I pointed my wand at it, and wiped the marks away so that my name and my name alone was visible.

I went to Julius Domitar's little office. The furniture had been overturned, his precious ink bottles smashed to bits.

I headed up the stairs to the second floor and from there to the door with the screaming Wug as a doorknob. None of it was there. The door and the Wug doorknob were gone. The only thing there was a blank wall.

I left Stacks and flew next to my tree house.

It was still there with the boards intact against the trunk of the tree. One of them was still blackened from when the garm had attacked me here. I leaped to the top of the planks. Again, like my home, it was undisturbed, except for one thing.

Burned into the planks was the symbol of the Maladons. I took out my wand and uttered, 'Eraisio.' The mark vanished.

I lifted off, and Harry Two and I next arrived at Morrigone's home.

The beautiful gates were torn apart. The ornate door was blasted open.

All the fine things she had possessed, the case clocks, all the wonderful books, the china, the paintings, the lovely rugs, the splendid-looking glasses – they were all gone.

And my brother?

I ran up the stairs to where I knew his bedroom was.

I opened the door, terrified of what I might find.

What I found *did* terrify me. But not for the reason I had dreaded.

The room had not been damaged at all. The horrible pictures that I had once seen on the walls were gone, but everything else was like he had just walked out of the room.

I did not know what to make of it. I simply didn't.

I had saved my next destination for last.

My feet hit the dirt at the entrance to the Hallowed Ground, where Wugs buried their dead.

With a sense of foreboding, I walked through the gates.

I found exactly what I thought I would find.

New graves were everywhere, with headstones and names etched on them.

The Loons were all lined up in a row.

Julius Domitar and Dis Fidus were buried side by side upon a little knoll.

Roman Picus, my old landlord and nemesis, rested at the end of one row, his garm-skin boots dumped on top of the pile of dirt covering his grave.

Tears spilt from my eyes when I saw Duf Delphia's plot.

To the right was Herman Helvet, who owned the confectionery shop. Next to him were Jurik Krone and Non. There was the foul Ran Digby, who Delph had beaten in the Duelum. Ted Racksport, who had shot himself in the foot. Darla Gunn, who had sold me my first set of nice clothes at Fancy Frocks.

Down near the end of another row was the grave of Ezekiel the Sermonizer, who presided at Steeples.

On and on the graves went.

Until I located the last new one.

I stared at the name engraved there.

Morrigone.

There was one more thing.

Every grave had been marked with the sign of the Maladons. Everywhere I looked, those terrible eyes stared back at me.

346

There was one grave missing.

My brother, John, was not there. I had searched everywhere for him, terrified that the next gravestone I would find would have his name etched on it.

But it was not here.

And I did not know what that meant.

I remembered Morrigone's parting words to me when I had left Wormwood. They made sense now.

She had been afraid. I had originally thought she had been afraid that I would fail and perish in the Quag.

But the opposite had been true.

She had been afraid because she thought I would *succeed* and escape the Quag.

I looked around the graveyard.

And this . . . this was why she had been afraid.

What she had feared would happen, *had* happened.

Why had I never thought to come back here before now? To rescue my fellow Wugs? Well, it was too late for that now.

I hung my head so that my tears spilt on to Harry Two's fur.

I had never felt this miserable, this lost, in my entire life.

Lost; that was the exact right word.

For I had lost everything.

I was the reason all these Wugs lay dead. My fellow Wugmorts, wiped out. No more.

I was so numb that when Harry Two licked my face, I started back and refocused.

That was when I heard it.

A sound off to my left.

My wand ready, I ran that way with Harry Two next to me.

It was coming from behind a tree.

I reached the spot, and with my wand at the ready I charged around the tree, ready to strike.

I stopped dead.

'Tha-Thansius?'

How could I have missed noticing that he had no grave here?

Our mighty Wug leader looked as I had never seen him before. His fine robes were filthy rags. His great chest and broad shoulders had fallen in. He wasn't much more than a skeleton.

He lay on the ground, a shovel next to him.

I knelt next to him and lifted his head with my hand. 'Thansius. It's me, Vega Jane. Can you hear me?'

He looked a thousand sessions old, withered and grey. When he opened his eyes I saw, with horror, that his pupils were gone. They were simply white, like the slaves back in Greater True.

'V-V-Vega?'

'Yes, it's me. What . . . what happened?'

'D-dead. All d-dead. E-except for me.'

'But how did you survive?'

Even as I said it I thought I knew the truth. I looked at the shovel lying next to him.

He touched his sunken, bony chest as though in great pain.

I unbuttoned his torn and stained garment.

Underneath, burned into his skin, was the mark of the Maladons.

When my gaze fell upon it, my eyes filled with tears.

'Thansius, I am so sorry. I'm so very sorry.'

Thansius had been so strong, so indomitable and so . . . noble, we all had looked up to him. That was the only reason the Maladons had done this. To humiliate him. To show him as weak, inconsequential.

Leaving him to dig the graves of his fellow Wugs.

'Thansius, do you have any idea what they did with my brother?'

'T-took him.'

'Took him where?'

He gasped for breath. I looked around and pointed my wand at a tree and mouthed the spell to draw water from it. I conjured a flask to catch it and then held it to Thansius's mouth.

'Here, drink this. I can help you. I'll take you with me. I'll nurse you back to health myself and everything will be just . . .'

I drew the flask back, for he had stiffened. And like Lackland Cyphers, he drew one last breath and then fell limp in my arms.

Thansius, mighty Thansius, who had stood for all that was good about Wormwood and Wugs in general, was dead.

I let go of him and rose.

With my wand I dug him a grave under a large, beautiful oak. I magically lay his body in it and covered it over with both dirt and a shield spell. I crafted the tombstone and placed it at the head of the mound of dirt.

On it I wand-wrote, HERE LIES THANSIUS, THE

BEST AND MIGHTIEST WUG OF ALL.

Then I went to each of the tombstones and removed the mark of the Maladons. Finished, I kicked off and rose into the air. I flew over a place that no longer existed.

Except in my mind.

As I soared along, I cried. I sobbed. I called out to the sky the names of Wugs I had known all my life. I cursed the Maladons. Poor Harry Two howled in misery. I drew my wand, took aim and blasted a large rock to smithereens.

When I reached the Quag, I had no idea if a great storm would blow up to prevent my flying over. Part of me wanted that to happen.

Because I deserved to die too. For what I had done.

But nothing happened. It seemed that the magical force of the place had been extinguished.

Should I try to find Astrea and her son, Archie? Had the Maladons found them already? I couldn't bear to find out.

I flew through the opening in the dome.

When my boots hit the dirt, I knew that I would never cry again, no matter what else happened.

I pointed my wand and a beam of black light heated the seam. Soon there was no longer a seam. Yet I kept my wand pointed and the light going for so long that I thought I might ignite the entire wall around the Quag.

I wanted to use my magic to accomplish something.

Something permanent.

I moved the wand around, spelling out the words.

When I lowered my wand, my chest was heaving; my lungs felt scorched.

I looked down at Harry Two. He was looking at me in a way he never had.

He was looking at me in a way that told me my dog was seeing me differently than he ever had before.

Harry Two's senses were spot on.

Because I *was* different. My trip back to Wormwood had been unlike anything I had ever imagined, even in the worst of my nightmares.

It had changed me.

I was not the Vega Jane of barely sixty slivers ago.

I turned away from the wall and kicked off.

We were sent soaring into the air.

I looked down. The words I had seared into the wall were plainly visible from here.

THIS TIME WE WILL TRIUMPH

I could feel every muscle in my body begin to harden as I turned and headed back to Empyrean.

It was not just my sinew growing in resolve.

It was also my heart that had turned to stone.

I was changed forever. I was the leader. And leaders could become close to no one.

I gripped my wand loosely as we flew along. I wanted to run into a Maladon. I wanted to run into an army of them. I wanted to kill them all.

As I flew back to the safe embrace of Empyrean, I swore to myself that I, Vega Jane, *would* destroy them all, even if it cost me my life.

A WUGMORT'S GUIDE TO
WORMWOOD AND BEYOND

adar

A beast of Wormwood often used as a messenger and trained to perform tasks by air. Although they appear clumsy on the ground, adars are creatures of grace and beauty in the sky, owing to their magnificent height and wingspan. Most remarkably, adars can understand Wugmorts and can even be taught to speak.

Adder Stone

A stone known to possess healing powers, capable of erasing all traces of a wound when held over the injury.

alecto

A lethal creature in the Quag characterized by serpents for hair and blood-dripping eyes. The hypnotizing sway of the serpents atop the alecto's head can drive its prey to its death.

amaroc

A fierce and terrifying beast of the Quag, known to possess the ability to kill in many ways. Amarocs have upper fangs as long as a Wug arm and are rumoured to shoot poison from their eyes. When captured, their hides are used in the production of clothing and boots in Wormwood.

attercop

A type of venomous spider indigenous to the Quag.

Bimbleton Station

A ramshackle station where people wait to take a train to what they think will be a better life.

Bowler Hats

The most elite fighters the Maladons have. They wear three-piece pinstripe suits and bowler hats, hence the name.

Breath of a Dominici

A long-stemmed flower with a fist-size blood-red bloom that gives off the odour of slep dung. The Breath of a Dominici grows only in viper nests.

Campions

The insurrection focused on causing as much strife as possible for the Maladons.

Care, the

A place where Wugs who are unwell and for whom the Mendens at hospital can do no more are sent to live.

chontoo

A flying beast in the Quag comprised only of a head, the chontoo is said to wildly attack its prey in the hopes of using its body parts for itself. Spawned over the centuries by the intermingling of different species, the chontoo is characterized by a foul face with demonic eyes and jagged fangs, and flames for hair. The chontoo is primarily found in the Mycanmoor.

colossal

An ancient race of formidable warriors, of an origin largely unknown to the average Wugmort. The average colossal stands about sixty-five feet tall and weighs nearly seven thousand pounds.

Council

The governing body of Wormwood. Council passes laws, regulations and edicts that all Wugmorts must obey.

creta

An exceptionally large creature used in Wormwood to pull the plough of Tillers and transport sacks of flour at the Mill. The creta weighs well over one thousand pounds and is characterized by horns that cross over its face and hooves the size of plates.

cucos

Small birdlike creatures that inhabit the Third Circle of the Quag. Brilliantly coloured as if small bits of the rainbow are embedded in their feathers, the cucos are best known for glowing wings that can illuminate their surroundings.

Dactyl

A Stacks worker whose job entails shaping metal with hammer and tongs.

dopplegang

A dangerous creature in the Quag, marked by hideous rows of blackened, sharp teeth, that morphs into whatever it sees.

The power of the dopplegang lies in its ability to trick its unsuspecting victim into injuring or even killing itself, since striking the beast in its altered form is tantamount to striking oneself.

dread

A black flying creature in the Fifth Circle created by Jasper Jane. About the size of a canine, dreads are characterized by their screeching cries and clawed wings that they use to cut their prey to pieces.

Duelum

A twice-a-session competition occurring outside of Wormwood proper that pits strong males between the ages of fifteen and twenty-four in matches against one another. Viewed by many Wugs as a rite of passage, Duelums can often be brutal.

ekos

A small creature in the Quag, exceptional for the mats of grass that grow on its arms, neck and face, and sprout from its head. The ekos have small, wrinkled faces and bulging red eyes.

Empyrean

The ancestral home of Vega Jane. Once the residence of Alice Adronis, it has remained safely under a spell that has rendered the grounds undetectable by Maladons over the years.

Event

A mysterious occurrence in Wormwood that has no witnesses. Wugmorts presumed to suffer from an Event disappear entirely, body and clothing, from the village.

Excalibur

A rare type of sorcerer born with extraordinary magical powers already intact and a profound knowledge of Wug history embedded in their mind. It may take years for an Excalibur to become aware of their innate abilities.

Finisher

A worker tasked with 'finishing' all objects created at Stacks. Finishers must show creative ability at Learning, as the requirements for the job range from painting to kiln-firing items intended for the wealthiest Wugs of Wormwood.

Finn, the

A magical element consisting of twine knotted in three places and looped around a tiny wooden peg. The untying of one knot brings a force of wind powerful enough to lift objects off the ground. Untying the second knot produces gale-force winds. Untying the third brings a wind of unimaginable strength, with the ability to level everything in its path.

firebird

A huge flying creature in the Quag known for its colourful plumage and sharp beak and claws. It's said that the firebird's feathers are so brilliant they can be used to provide light and warmth. A firebird can be a harbinger of tragedy.

frek
A huge, fierce beast of the Quag characterized by an extensive snout and fangs inches longer than a Wug finger. The bite of a frek has been known to drive its victims mad.

Furina
A Wug-like race indigenous to the Quag, made nearly extinct because of continuous attacks from beasts. The Furinas are descendants of a group of Wugs and Maladons who became trapped in the Quag while migrating from the great battlefields to the village of Wormwood.

garm
A large beast of the Quag, thirteen feet in length and nearly one thousand pounds in weight. The garm is a hideous creature, its chest permanently bloodied, its smell odious and its belly full of fire that can cremate its victim from several feet away. Wormwood lore maintains that the garm hunts the souls of the dead or guards the gates of Hel.

gnome
A creature of the Quag known for long, sharp claws that allow it to mine through hard rock. The gnomes are characterized by deathly pale and prunish faces and yellowish-black teeth.

Greater True
The land of the elites. Many of the people living here have

358

slaves to serve them. The Maladons regularly patrol here as well.

grubb
A peaceful creature that lives primarily in tunnels beneath the Quag and can eat through rock faster than most any other species. Twice the size of a creta, the grubb is known for its strong, expandable hide; long slithery tongue; enormous, jagged teeth; soft, slippery body; and eye colour that differentiates males (blue) from females (yellow).

high street, the
A cobblestone street in Wormwood proper lined with shops that sell things Wugmorts need, such as foodstuffs, clothing and healing herbs.

hob
A creature in the Quag about half the height of an average Wug, characterized by its thick frame, small but powerful jaw, stout nose, long, peaked ears, spindly fingers and large hairy feet. Hobs are typically amicable creatures that speak Wugish and make themselves of assistance in exchange for small gifts.

hyperbore
A blue-skinned flying beast indigenous to the Quag characterized by a lean, muscled torso and lightly feathered head. More closely related to Wugs than any other creature, the hyperbore may serve as an ally or enemy and responds favourably to respect and kindness. Hyperbores set on

their prey quickly, using their compact wings and sharp claws. The hyperbores live in nests high in trees.

inficio
A large fiendish beast indigenous to the Quag that can expel poisonous smoke potent enough to kill any creature that breathes it. The inficio has two massive legs with clawed feet; a long, scaly torso with powerful webbed wings; a serpent-like neck and a small head with venomous eyes and razor-sharp fangs.

jabbit
A massive serpent with over two hundred and fifty heads growing out of the full length of its body. Although jabbits rarely leave the Quag, little can halt their attack once they are on the blood scent. Jabbits can easily overtake Wugs and have fangs in each head full of enough poison to drop a creta.

Learning
The institution youngs attend until the age of twelve sessions. It is at Learning that youngs gain skills necessary for work in Wormwood.

light
The time of sunlight between one night and the next. What we would call a day.

Loons, the
A boarding house on the high street.

lycan

A beast of the Quag covered in long, straight hair, whose bite turns its victims into its own kind. The tall, powerfully built lycan walks on two legs and wields its sharp fangs and claws to attack its prey.

Maladon

From the Wugish word for 'terrible death', an ancient race whose highest calling is to inflict terrible death on others. A sessions-long war between the Maladons and Wugmorts forced the Wugs to found the village of Wormwood, around which they conjured the Quag for protection.

Maladon Castle

The headquarters of the Maladon race. It is here that Necro dwells, and also where the Maladons torture and enslave their enemies.

maniack

An evil spirit that can attach to a body and mind, driving a Wug irreversibly mad with every fear they have ever had.

manticore

A swift, treacherous beast indigenous to the Quag with the head of a lion, the tail of a serpent and the body of a goat. Over twice the height of an average Wug and three times the width, the manticore's most formidable features are its abilities to read minds and breathe fire.

Mill, the
A place of work in Wormwood where flour and other grains are refined.

morta
A long- or short-barrelled metal projectile weapon. What we would call a gun.

Noc
The large, round, milky-white object in the heavens that shines at night. What we would call the moon.

Ordinaries
Those who do not possess magical abilities.

Outlier
A threatening two-legged creature that lives in the Quag and can pass as a Wugmort. Outliers are believed to be able to control the minds of Wugs and make them do their bidding.

Quag, the
A forest that encircles Wormwood and is home to all manner of fierce creatures and Outliers. It is widely believed among Wugmorts that nothing exists beyond the Quag.

remnant
A collection of memories from an assortment of Wugs, an embodied record of their remembrances.

Saint Necro's
The church in True where the people come to worship.
It is named after Necro, the leader of the Maladons, who
insists on being worshipped by all.

Seer-See
A prophetical instrument used by sorcerers to view other
places. The Seer-See consists of sand thrown into a pewter
cup of flaming liquid, the contents of which are then
poured on to a table to display a moving picture of a distant
location.

session
A unit of time equal to three hundred and sixty-five lights.
What we would call a year.

slep
A magnificent Wormwood creature characterized by
its noble head, long tail, six legs and beautiful coat. It is
said that sleps were once able to fly, and that the slight
indentations noticeable on their withers now mark the spot
from which their wings grew. What we would call a horse.

sliver
A small unit or brief period of time, a bit like a minute.

Stacks
A large brick building in Wormwood where items for trade
and consumption are produced.

Steeples

A place the majority of Wugmorts go every seventh light to listen to a sermonizer.

True

The first town that Vega and her friends encounter. It is seemingly filled with happy people, but has sinister secrets.

unicorn

A noble and gentle beast characterized by a brilliantly white coat and mane of gold, with shiny black eyes and a regal horn the colour of silver. The soft horn of the unicorn is known to defeat all poisons, but can only be obtained by convincing the unicorn to surrender it freely or by killing the beast outright.

Valhall

The prison of Wormwood, set in public in the centre of the village.

Victus

The name given by the Maladons to those they enslave.

wendigo

A malevolent spirit that can possess whatever it devours. This ghastly, quasi-transparent creature lives throughout the Quag but is predominant in the Mycanmoor. Signs that a wendigo is nearby are a vague feeling of terror and a sense that the facts stored in your head are being replaced by residual memories of the prey the wendigo has devoured.

whist
A large, domesticated hound of Wormwood known for its impressive speed.

Wugmort (*Wug* for short)
A citizen of Wormwood.

ACKNOWLEDGEMENTS

In writing the third instalment of the Vega Jane saga, I had a tremendous amount of support that made the story far better. To the folks listed on this page, Vega and I thank you!

To Rachel Griffiths, David Levithan, Mallory Kass, Julie Amitie, Charisse Meloto, Dick Robinson, Ellie Berger, Lori Benton, Dave Ascher, Elizabeth Parisi, Gabe Rumbaut, Evangelos Vasilakis, Rachel Gluckstern, Sue Flynn, Nikki Mutch and the whole sales team at Scholastic, for helping me send Vega and her friends headlong into yet another world.

To Venetia Gosling, Kat McKenna, Catherine Alport, Sarah Clarke, Rachel Vale, Alyx Price, Tracey Ridgewell, Lucy Pearse, Trisha Jackson, Jeremy Trevathan, Katie James, Lee Dibble, Sarah McLean, Charlotte Williams, Stacey Hamilton, Geoff Duffield, Leanne Williams, Stuart Dwyer, Anna Bond, Jonathan Atkins, Sara Lloyd and Alex Saunders at Pan Macmillan, for always being so wonderfully enthusiastic and supportive.

To Steven Maat and the entire Bruna team, for introducing Vega and Company to Holland.

To Aaron Priest, for two decades of great advice and counsel.

To Arleen Priest, Lucy Childs Baker, Lisa Erbach Vance, Frances Jalet-Miller, John Richmond and Matt Belford for allowing me to focus on the books.

To Kristen White and Michelle Butler, for keeping Columbus Rose and me going strong.

ABOUT THE AUTHOR

David Baldacci is one of the world's bestselling and favourite thriller writers. With more than 150 million copies in print, his books are published in more than eighty territories and forty-five languages, and have been adapted for both feature-film and television. Together with his wife, Michelle, David established the Wish You Well Foundation® to promote family literacy. David and his family live in Virginia, USA.

VEGA JANE'S BATTLE WITH
THE MALADONS HAS JUST BEGUN . . .

THE FINAL THRILLING ADVENTURE
IS COMING SOON IN

VEGA JANE AND THE END OF TIME

Turn the page to read an extract.

AT LAST

I heard a knock on my door.

It was Delph.

'Pillsbury told me you were back from the Maladon attack last night, but I wanted to let you sleep.'

'How many did you get?' he asked.

I sat up, resting my back against the enormous wooden headboard. 'Five,' I replied tersely. 'Why?'

He sat on the bed and scratched Harry Two's ear.

'You never really told me about Wormwood,' he said abruptly.

This was not the first time he had said this. It might as well have been the hundredth.

'I told you all you needed to know, Delph. It's gone. They're all gone. They killed everyone, including your father. I saw their graves.'

'That's not exactly so,' he countered. 'They killed everyone *except* your brother.'

'At least there was no grave for my brother. But, in truth, I have no idea if he's alive or dead.'

These words suddenly caught at my heart, and I had to look away from Delph. I had lost many friends in the war with the Maladons and that had hardened me. Yet John was my brother. John was my family.

Delph stood. 'But why would they take John, if that is what happened?'

I rose from my bed and faced him. 'You've asked me that

before. And I've asked myself the same thing a thousand times, Delph. I keep coming up with a thousand different answers.'

Delph said, 'It *would* make sense in one way.'

'What way?' I said bluntly.

'Well, at first I thought they might be using John to hold over your head, you know. If you don't surrender, they'd hurt John. But they haven't done that, Vega Jane, though they've had ample time. So there must be another reason.'

'Such as?'

'Morrigone was teaching John back in Wormwood. She'd taken him under her wing, because he was so smart and all with books and such.'

'I told you that. But it was terrible stuff that she . . .'

My voice trailed off, and I looked in horror at Delph.

'Are you saying that they took my brother to . . . to . . .'

I couldn't say it. Not for the life of me.

'To maybe make him into a Maladon?' said Delph. 'A right powerful one. Judging by what a sorceress you are, I 'spect that John might make an equally powerful sorcerer.'

'But why just John? Why not take all in Wormwood?'

'John was so smart, Vega Jane. And . . . he seemed to like . . . you know . . .'

'You mean he liked all those horrible things that Morrigone was teaching him?' I said stiffly.

'Well, you told me that yourself.'

'But, Delph, he was just a little boy. He didn't know any better. He liked to fill his head up with . . . stuff,' I finished quite lamely. In my mind's eye, all I could see was a little boy with feet too large for him

2

shuffling along while holding my hand.

Delph interrupted my thoughts. 'Well, he's not a little boy now. He's very nearly fifteen. The same age you were when you ran away from Wormwood with me.'

This was absolutely correct. John was far closer to being a man now than he was to being a boy.

If they'd captured him from Wormwood, my brother would have been with the Maladons for quite some time.

'You're right, Delph,' I said contritely. 'He is almost a man. I just don't know what sort of man he is becoming.' I began to tremble and turned away from him.

'It's okay, Vega Jane,' Delph whispered. 'We're going to find him. And . . . and regardless of what sort of shape he's in, we're going to bring him back to what he was.'

'You . . . can't know that,' I said haltingly.

'But I can promise to do all I can to make it happen.'

I turned and looked at him. 'You're my best friend, Delph. You always have been.'

He smiled. 'You were the *only* friend I had, Vega Jane. And a great one.'

I could smell food downstairs. 'You had better go,' I said, smiling. 'You must be hungry.'

'I am, Vega Jane,' he said.

Later, I had just finished my breakfast down in the kitchen when Petra walked in. The shirt she wore had no sleeves and I could see marks and scars up and down both arms.

'I heard that you had returned from the raid.'

She nodded. 'The Elite Guard lost their muskets. They'll make others. But it will take time. However, they are

3

far from our biggest problem.'

'I know that,' I said. For whatever reason, I was constantly on my guard with Petra, though I knew she would die in order to save me.

'I heard your journey was also a successful one,' she said, sitting down across from me.

'If five dead Maladons are any measure, then yes, it was.'

'That makes four hundred of them dead, then,' said Petra, eyeing me.

'I can do the mathematics,' I replied coolly.

'But you know we've discovered that there are thirty times more Maladons than there are of us. That only leads to one outcome, Vega. We can't win this way.'

'We're still trying to find magicals among the countryside,' I said.

'We've found none in all this time. None since we rescued that lot from Greater True.'

We were at war with the Maladons, but there had been no great battles on broad fields. No titanic clashes of sorcery. We simply hadn't the numbers for such a style of combat. So, our war was a series of small skirmishes. Ambushes, tactical missions, two-on-two, four-on-four. Small encounters, almost all of which we had won, but as Petra had pointed out, the eventual outcome with such a strategy was inevitable. A war of attrition was always won by those with superior numbers.

'We can't attack them outright,' I said. 'We can't try and invade Maladon Castle. We would be slaughtered.'

'I know that.'

'Then what do you suggest?'

'I'm not sure I have anything to suggest. But I would say that until we work out our eventual goals, we need to do everything we can to keep what army we do have left safe and intact. If we lose even a few more, it won't matter what we do in the future. We'll still have lost.'

What she said was undoubtedly true. And yet if we stopped fighting?

'I'll think about it, Petra,' I said.

She started to say something, a sharp retort I could tell from the look on her face. But she bit back tthe words, simply nodded, rose and left.

A minute passed while I closed my eyes and tried to push the fatigue from my bones.

'Vega! Vega!'

I opened my eyes. Miranda Weeks was rushing towards me. She and her group must have returned from their scouting expedition.

Miranda was the youngest of us, but she had grown taller and stronger with the passage of time, and now she was one of the best warriors we had.

'Yes, Miranda?'

'You must come.'

'Come? Come where?'

'To the village where we just were.'

I half rose from my chair. 'Why? What happened?' 'The villagers saw her.'

'Who did they see?'

'Your mother.'

5